Barefoot in Hyde Park

The Hellion Club, Book Two

by Chasity Bowlin

DRAGONBLADE
PUBLISHING, INC.

Dragonblade Publishing, Inc. is an imprint of Kathryn Le Veque Novels, Inc.
P.O. Box 7968
La Verne CA 91750
ceo@dragonbladepublishing.com

Produced in the United States of America

First Edition January 2020
Print Edition

ARE YOU SIGNED UP FOR DRAGONBLADE'S BLOG?

You'll get the latest news and information on exclusive giveaways, exclusive excerpts, coming releases, sales, free books, cover reveals and more.

Check out our complete list of authors, too!

No spam, no junk. That's a promise!

Sign Up Here

www.dragonbladepublishing.com

Dearest Reader;

Thank you for your support of a small press. At Dragonblade Publishing, we strive to bring you the highest quality Historical Romance from the some of the best authors in the business. Without your support, there is no 'us', so we sincerely hope you adore these stories and find some new favorite authors along the way.

Happy Reading!

CEO, Dragonblade Publishing

Additional Dragonblade books by Author Chasity Bowlin

The Hellion Club Series
A Rogue to Remember
Barefoot in Hyde Park
What Happens in Piccadilly
Sleepless in Southhampton
When an Earl Loves a Governess
The Duke's Magnificent Obsession
The Governess Diaries

The Lost Lords Series
The Lost Lord of Castle Black
The Vanishing of Lord Vale
The Missing Marquess of Althorn
The Resurrection of Lady Ramsleigh
The Mystery of Miss Mason
The Awakening of Lord Ambrose
A Midnight Clear (A Novella)

*** Please visit Dragonblade's website for a full list of books and authors. Sign up for Dragonblade's blog for sneak peeks, interviews, and more: ***
www.dragonbladepublishing.com

Dedication

One day, my husband will get tired of having books dedicated to him. But not yet. So to my dear husband, I say thank you. Thank you for all that you do to support me on this crazy journey. And thank you for showing me that the kind of love I write about isn't just fiction.

"Pandora's box has been opened. Every time I touch you, you will want more…"

"Do you think perhaps you could ravish me just a little bit?"

"I hate telling you that you're beautiful," he whispered. "It seems like such a weak description of all that you are."

"Your grandmother may shun such extravagance, but I see nothing wrong with showing one's appreciation with jewelry."

"I'm not holding you to keep you from leaving. I'm holding you because it's a way of showing you how precious you are to me."

About the Book

Lillian Burkhart could not be more different from her half-sister, Wilhelmina. Suspecting that she is more like their wastrel father, she struggles against the wildness inside her, trying desperately to be the proper young woman that Miss Euphemia Darrow has reared her to be. But when she's discovered walking barefoot in Hyde Park by none other than the grandson of the elderly dowager duchess who employs her as a companion, her failure is complete.

Lord Valentine Somers, Viscount Seaburn, has been playing a part for so long that he no longer recognizes himself. As a soldier, he'd risked life and limb. Now, as a spy for Whitehall, he's risking his very soul by using his skill with cards to gain entree to circles he wants no part of. Feigning the ennui of a debauched dilettante who treats women and money as if they were both in unending supply, he's immediately struck by the beauty, vivacity and innocence of a lovely barefoot nymph... who happens to be his grandmother's companion.

Given an ultimatum by his grandmother, marry or be disinherited, Val offers for Lillian on a whim. And she accepts in order to claim her own familial bequest. But theirs isn't a normal engagement... not when someone keeps trying to murder his betrothed. Uncertain if it has to do with Lillian's inheritance, his own inheritance or the enemies he's made over the years, Val knows he will do whatever it takes to protect her... but he didn't expect to fall in love with her.

Chapter One

THE GRASS WAS cool beneath her bare feet and there was a hint of spring in the air about her, but that was only wishful thinking. Spring was still months away despite the unseasonable warmth of the day. But her mind wasn't on the hedonistic pleasures of traipsing barefoot in the park, with the sun bright overhead, though that was precisely what she was doing in that moment. It wasn't even on the fact that if she was caught behaving so recklessly, in a manner that was such an utter breech of decorum, she would no doubt be sacked from her very good position with her grace, the Dowager Duchess of Templeton. No, her mind was ensconced rather firmly on the conversations that had just taken place in the somewhat dingy and definitely very dirty office of a legal firm that appeared to have more dust than clients.

"Miss Burkhart, this is a sizable bequest," the solicitor's nasal drone replayed in her mind. One could accuse the poor man of being many things, but no one could ever accuse Robert Littleton, Esq. of being lively. The tiny little man, with his balding pate and frayed cuffs, had not appeared to be a very successful solicitor. But he had been rather kind to her, even in their short acquaintance.

"But only if I marry?" Her reply had been skeptical. It all sounded utterly impossible to her. But the solicitor had been rather insistent. Her mother's aunt, a woman she'd never even heard of much less

met—though given that her own mother had died when she was very, very young and she'd spent all of her life in one school or another where her father would not have to be bothered with her—had left her a fortune. But that fortune could only be claimed on the condition that she marry and not follow in her mother's disgraceful footsteps. Of course, it seemed reasonable that if her great-aunt had been aware of her mother's headlong and ill-fated journey on the path of ruin that she might have intervened for her niece rather than just for the illegitimate child that was the direct result of said fall from grace.

Lillian had said as much to the solicitor who had then informed her that her great-aunt had been unable to locate her mother prior to her mother's passing. It wasn't until the marriage of Lillian's half-sister, Wilhelmina, being announced in the papers, with all the scandal and kerfuffle that had accompanied it, that the frail and failing woman had any inkling of where to find her long-lost grandniece. Of course, he hadn't actually said she was frail and failing, but it had been strongly implied with the sense of urgency he had pressed upon her regarding her decision.

So there she was, employed as a companion to a dowager duchess who had the personality and temperament of a rabid bulldog, while her sister was off to the countryside with her handsome new husband whom she was completely enamored with. Effie was busy with new students who appeared to be as trying as Lillian herself had been. And she was *alone*. There was no one to whom she could go to for advice about her rather unusual situation. It wasn't simply that she was alone, though. It was something much, much worse.

Lillian was lonely. She'd always been alone—apart from everyone else somehow, including Willa. But it had never bothered her before. This was something different. Was it jealousy over her half-sister's marriage? She certainly didn't begrudge her half-sister's happiness, but was it so terribly wrong to want some for herself? Would marriage bring her happiness? She'd never thought so, but now it could bring her financial security, something she'd never truly known.

"Probably not," Lillian muttered aloud. "I've never been very good with rules." Marriage, it seemed, invariably came with a great number of them. That bit in the vows about "obeying" set her teeth on edge.

Even as a girl, Lillian had struggled with following along with what was expected of her. She liked and respected Euphemia Darrow, headmistress of her former school and now a dear friend. Even then, she'd found it nearly impossible to obey her. There was a recklessness in Lilly that had always left her straining at the bit of anything or anyone who tried to control her. She didn't understand it herself, but there it was. She yearned for freedom. The funds her great-aunt wished to bestow on her as a marriage settlement could afford her that freedom, but only if she gave up all of her personal liberty first. Unless she could find someone who would offer her a marriage of convenience, a marriage where they would, after a suitable amount of time, live their own separate lives.

At least, she thought, as a spinster companion earning a wage, she was entitled to make her own decisions about things. A husband would surely ruin all of that, unless she found someone who suited her needs.

"What a terrible muddle it all is," she mused aloud. She sounded like a forlorn child, but as she rather felt like one, there was little point in castigating herself for it.

LORD VALENTINE SOMERS, Viscount Seaburn, had taken a path through the park, not because it was shorter, but because it would delay the inevitable. He was not at all looking forward to calling on his grandmother. She would pester him about getting himself a wife. Then she'd threaten to cut him off as she always did. Then she'd point out his cousin, Elsworth, who would become the heir to the dukedom if he failed to produce a male child from whatever ill-fated union he entered into with whichever poor, unsuspecting woman was foolish enough to fall for the notorious Somers' charm.

Normally, he could easily withstand her scheming, manipulation, browbeating and whatever terrible maladies threatened her health as a direct result of his bad behavior. But there were things his grandmother did not know. Things that he feared might actually see an end to the old bird if they were to come out. Despite the manner in which they plucked at one another, he loved her terribly. And what was about to take their family by storm was not something any of them were fully prepared to deal with, certainly not some poor unsuspecting society miss who had the great misfortune to set her cap for him.

The events looming ahead were certainly things that would make his taking a wife very complicated, indeed. The exalted Somers clan now hovered on the brink of social ruin, and only he could see the precipice on which they teetered. Even his worthless cousin who'd put them there was utterly clueless. Damn Elsworth, he thought. Damn him to hell. It would serve the addlepated sod right if Val were to let it all come crashing down around his head.

Val rounded a bend in the path and stopped in his tracks. It was an entrancing sight, a barefoot goddess in a plain dress, muttering to herself and appearing as forlorn as he felt. Of course, he was also very willing to be distracted from the task that lay ahead of him. So he watched her, taking in every last and ridiculously fetching detail, including her slightly exaggerated and pouty frown. Oddly enough, he didn't find her pretty *in spite* of that frown so much as *because* of it. Her face was delightfully expressive, her dark hair swept back into a simple chignon that highlighted the length of her neck and the gentle curve of her cheek. Her full lips were pursed and her brows were drawn together in what he could only categorize as consternation as a bonnet, the ugliest creation in the history of millinery, dangled from her fingertips. Another glance at the bonnet and he was hard pressed to call it anything other than a crime, no less than an assault on the senses.

As if he'd summoned the creature with his own disparaging thoughts regarding her choice of chapeau, a bird swooped in and attacked the bonnet. The bird tugged at the ribbons looped so haphazardly about her delicate fingers until it could make off with its prize.

"Oh, you rotten beast!" she cried out.

And as Val watched, she proceeded to hoist up her skirts and attempt to climb the very tree where the offending bird had taken refuge. Perhaps it was that he was distracted by the shapely curves of her calves, or perhaps it was that he was rather taken aback by her clear mastery of the art of tree climbing, but by the time it occurred to him to offer assistance, she was halfway up the magnificent oak. She'd set her sights on her target and would not be dissuaded. The bird, as if sensing that its days were numbered, flew away and left the offending bonnet tangled in the branches.

The girl shimmied over onto the branch which swayed rather alarmingly beneath her weight. Still, she was determined.

Val was torn. He wanted to call out a warning, a caution for her to be careful. At the same time, as high up as she was, he couldn't risk startling her. It was a situation he'd have not been in at all if he hadn't been distracted when he stumbled upon her. Fetching or not, it appeared the girl was practically a lunatic and clearly lacked sufficient regard for her own life.

When she'd reached the bonnet, her dilemma became apparent. There was no way for her to hold the hideous thing and climb down at the same time, nor could she put it on as the terribly floppy brim would no doubt obscure her view. As if she'd been aware of his presence all along, she looked directly at him. "Would it be possible for you to assist me, sir?"

Definitely a lunatic. Rather than state what was clearly obvious,

Val asked, "How I may be of assistance to you, Miss?"

Unceremoniously, she tossed the bonnet to him. "Guard that with your life. If that foul, wretched fowl comes back for it, shoot him or stab him if you happen to have the means to do so on your person."

And then, standing there holding a bonnet that was too ugly to have warranted nearly so much trouble, Val began to laugh in spite of it all. His life, and the things he was forced to do in it, had taken a toll on him. One he certainly hadn't recognized until it was much too late and any semblance of joy was gone from it. But this madcap girl, with her bonnet and her personal vendetta against a misbehaving crow, had prompted him to laugh as he had not in years. It was a remarkable feeling. He was still laughing as she shimmied down the tree.

His laughter died abruptly when, a few feet from where it might have actually been safe to jump, she lost her footing. Rushing forward, the bonnet dropped to the ground in his haste, he caught her before she did herself serious injury. Though he did hear her gasp of pain as her ankle struck a protruding tree root.

Setting her down at the base of the tree, he said, "Let me examine your ankle."

"Are you a physician then?" she demanded in a caustic tone.

"No, but I am familiar enough with broken bones to recognize one," he replied just as tartly.

"I will, but first you must retrieve my bonnet. If I return home without it, my employer will be... perturbed," she finished rather lamely.

"Perturbed?" he repeated as he retrieved the hideous bit of frippery. "I should be perturbed to see you wearing it. It's terribly ugly, you know?"

"That's rather the point," she replied. "My employer feels that I am too attractive for my current position and circumstances. As such, she has taken it upon herself to dress me in a manner that will not invite undesirable attentions."

He was tempted, for a moment, to ask what sort of attention she did desire. But it was obvious to him, regardless of her unorthodox behavior, that she was not the sort of woman who would understand such a double entendre. She was, despite her rather hoydenistic tendencies, an innocent. With that thought in mind, he kept his examination of her ankle as perfunctory, proper and brief as possible. "It does not appear to be broken, but I do believe you have quite a sprain. I doubt very much that you'll be able to walk back to your place of employment. Allow me to see you home in a hansom cab."

"No. That's impossible! It isn't far," she insisted. "I'm sure I'll be able to hobble along well enough."

"Then allow me to at least assist you to your destination. It is the least I can do," he replied, his tone firm and brooking no argument. The girl was trying the last of his patience, his earlier enjoyment of the situation all but forgotten. It didn't help that, for him, in his current predicament, patience was at a premium.

"My employer will be most displeased," she said.

"I daresay your employer will be more displeased if you attempt to hobble there and injure yourself further, thus limiting your usefulness for the next few days," Val pointed out.

She opened her mouth, then closed it, then opened it again, and when it closed the second time, her full lips compressed into a firm and quite obviously irritated line. He took immense satisfaction in that. He didn't know why, but he did.

"Very well, sir," she relented. "I thank you for both your wisdom and your assistance… belated as it was."

"Yes," he said, unable to keep the sarcasm from his voice. "But please, restrain yourself, Miss. You'll put me to blush with the effusiveness of your gratitude."

"You're making fun of me."

Val shrugged. "I rather thought I was making fun of us both… now tell me, do you have footwear? Or has some woodland creature

7

absconded with that, as well?"

"They're tucked under that bush over there," she said, pointing in the direction.

Val moved away from her long enough to retrieve the simple, kid walking boots and stockings. "Put them on your uninjured foot. But I would not put them on the other if I were you."

"I cannot return with one foot covered and one foot bare!"

She would argue that it was the sky which was green and the grass which was blue. "Fine. Put it on then... the process will no doubt be terribly painful. And by the time we arrive at your destination, the swelling in your ankle will have progressed to the point that the boot will likely have to be cut off. And while it may be crass of me to make presumptions, I imagine that replacing those boots would be some-what difficult for you in your current position."

"Turn around, please," she said. "I cannot don my stocking with you watching me."

Val sighed, but dutifully turned his back while she rolled on the discarded stocking and donned a single boot. After a suitable amount of time had passed, he turned back to her. "Now, what is your direction?"

"Number Ten, South Audley Street," the girl replied.

Val felt his gut clench. "And you are employed by the Dowager Duchess of Templeton, are you not?"

Her eyes widened. "How do you know that?"

"It appears we are headed in the same direction, Miss. Your em-ployer, my grandmother, has summoned me."

"Seaburn," the girl said with horror.

"Quite right. Lord Valentine Somers, Viscount Seaburn, at your service."

Chapter Two

WELL THAT WAS the end of it, Lilly thought. She'd be sacked and turned out without recommendation. Not even being a graduate of the Darrow School would get her an interview now, not having been let go from two positions without a reference. The first one was not at all her fault. But this one, well, she couldn't exactly call herself blameless in it. Running barefoot in Hyde Park like some sort of feral creature, showing her ankles and heaven knew what else to some man who turned out to be her employer's grandson? She'd be sacked for certain and it was absolutely her own fault. Perhaps she could work for her sister as a nanny? Not in a paying capacity, but trading room and board and living off the generosity of her sister's new husband like the poor relation she was. It wasn't such an ignoble existence, was it? *Yes. Yes, it was.* The very idea of being the poor relation, even if that was an accurate description, raised her hackles.

"Let's get you on your feet and see if there is any hope of you walking," he offered helpfully as he held out his hand to her.

Lilly placed her hand in his and immediately wished to withdraw it. His hand was strong and warm, his fingers lightly callused, from what she could not imagine. Men of his standing did not have callused hands. Yet he did. But it wasn't those out of character calluses which caused her to draw back. It was that frisson of something else, a jolt of something she could not name nor fathom, that arced through her rather like the electricity machine that Lady Daschel had brought in as entertainment during her house party. It wasn't necessarily unpleasant, but it did leave her feeling unsettled.

He pulled her up almost effortlessly. Standing only on her uninjured foot, she tentatively tried to bear weight on her other leg. A sharp hiss of pain escaped her and she stumbled. She likely would have fallen had he not caught her once more. Only this time, she wasn't so overcome with fear that she didn't notice how firm his chest was where it pressed against her own much softer form, nor could she ignore the strange warmth that suffused her at having his arms wrapped about her thusly. Oh, dear. It was all so very wrong. She knew what all of those things meant, of course, even if she had not experienced them personally. And until the very moment Lord Valentine Somers, Viscount Seaburn, had crossed her path, Lilly had thought herself immune to lust. But she was not. And the man she lusted for was quite possibly the one most forbidden to her in all of England. The grandson—the titled grandson, no less—of her employer.

"I'll carry you to the gate and get a cab for us," he said. "You cannot possibly walk, nor hobble, for such a distance." The last was offered with gentle amusement.

"I'm very appreciative of your assistance, my lord," Lillian replied. And she meant it. She was grateful to him, but she had the distinct impression that she might have been better off if she'd simply fallen and breathed her last beneath that blasted tree.

Lillian had thought she was prepared. But the moment when he swept her up into his arms, she realized she could not possibly have been prepared for what it would feel like. He carried her as bridegroom carried his bride, nestled in his arms, close to his chest. So close, in fact, that she could see the faint shadow of whiskers beneath his skin, though it was just after noon. His profile was perfection—forehead high and straight, a nose as sharp as the edge of a knife, and a stubborn chin that jutted forward ever so slightly with a hint of cleft in it. Only the sweep of long, dark lashes and the fullness of his lips hinted at any softness at all, and those features fascinated her far more than they should have. Certainly more than she could afford for them to given how disparate their stations were. This was not some governess becoming infatuated with a solicitor or even an under butler. He was the heir to a dukedom, after all.

"Just hang on," he said. "We'll have it all sorted out in no time."

Whether those cheery words were intended to make her feel better or if they were solely for his own benefit, as she'd essentially ruined his afternoon, she couldn't say. So, Lilly only smiled and nodded. "I'm certain we shall." Lies. They were just rolling off her tongue one after another. There was no sorting anything out. There was her packing her things and hobbling away on some crutch procured from a passing peddler when the dowager duchess tossed her out on her ear for her unbecoming conduct.

"Not to be impertinent, but if I'm going to carry you into my grandmother's house, it might help if I actually knew your name."

Of course. Now, in addition to being a hoyden, a clumsy fool, and a complete harpy, she was also addlebrained. "Miss Lillian Burkhart, my lord."

"Miss Burkhart," he said. "I can tell you that it has been a most singular pleasure to make your acquaintance."

"Hardly that. I've been a nuisance and an inconvenience from the very outset!" she said. There was no point in trying to deny any of it.

"But I haven't been bored," he replied with a wicked grin. "And that, Miss Burkhart, makes you more than worth the trouble."

"I doubt your grandmother will agree," Lilly said with a heavy sigh. "I'm already on my very last hope with her. No doubt, she'll send me packing!"

"Why? Because a hackney traveling much too fast nearly ran you down? It was a terrible shame that you were injured by the carelessness of others, Miss Burkhart! How fortuitous it was that we were both heading in the same direction and I witnessed the incident. I was very heroic when I rushed to your rescue, wasn't I?"

As he uttered that Banbury tale, his full lips, framed so perfectly by the dark shadow of his beard, curved upward in such a way that no woman looking at him could possibly resist his allure.

"You needn't lie on my account, my lord," Lilly said. "You do not appear to be especially good at it and your grandmother will not be pleased."

"I've lied for much less worthy causes, Miss Burkhart, than that of keeping you gainfully employed. But tell me, how did such a—" He broke off, clearly uncertain how to describe her without it being an insult.

"Hoyden? Hellion? Scapegrace?" she offered helpfully.

"Woman of irrepressible spirt," he corrected, "come to be employed by my always proper, often dull, and deeply boring grandmother?"

"I had been working as a governess," Lilly confessed. It was a mistake to tell the sordid tale, but she didn't seem to be able to keep it all in. She wanted to keep talking because she wanted him to continue looking at her. And also, as long as she was talking, she wouldn't do something impossibly foolish like attempting to kiss him only to startle them both and wind up in the Serpentine.

"Governess and companion are not such disparate professions," he offered.

"No, they are not. I was working for a family, not quite the first stare, but wealthy enough and well respected. They moved in society though not in the thick of it. I tended to the two youngest girls. The oldest was set to make her debut and then there was the oldest son... he'd been sent down from school for infractions I was not to know about."

He grew very still. "Go on, Miss Burkhart."

"He made some rather aggressive advances which I successfully spurned," she said. She didn't want him thinking she was some sort of weakling who couldn't defend herself. "At any rate, in the process, I blackened his eye and then his mother walked in. He told her that I'd become angry, lost my mind with temper, and struck him because I fancied myself in love with him and he didn't return my affections. Frankly, as horrid as it makes me sound, he was rather hideously ugly and only a mother would have believed any reasonably attractive woman had fancied herself in love with such a whey-faced little toad."

"So you were turned out without a reference because of a lying, whey-faced little toad?"

"Quite so," she agreed with a nod. "And my friend who helps with placements for those who have graduated from her academy suggested that being a companion, specifically to someone of an age where there were unlikely to be young men in the house, might be better suited to someone of my appea—to me,"

He eyed her speculatively. "You started to say your appearance, did you not?"

"I did," she admitted.

"But you did not. Why?"

"I didn't wish to appear vain, my lord."

He nodded at that, another smile tugging at his lips. "Are you vain, Miss Burkhart?"

There really was no point in lying, Lilly thought. They'd never see one another again, so what did it matter if he knew another of her horrid character flaws? "Terribly. And I detest this hideous bonnet as much as you do. But your grandmother insists upon it. She says I need to look as dowdy as possible to prevent men from noticing me."

His steps slowed and he looked at her with his slashing black brows arching upward in shock and amusement. "My grandmother is a dunderhead, Miss Burkhart. Trust me when I say that it would take far more than just an ugly bonnet to render you invisible to the opposite sex."

That sounded suspiciously like a compliment and Lilly found that she rather liked the notion of getting such a compliment from him, even if it was terribly unwise. "What would it take, then, my lord?" She didn't mean to sound flirtatious, not really. Nor did she mean to look up at him through her lashes in such a way that he might believe flirtation was her intent. But she did anyway.

He looked at her and then shook his head with something akin to resignation. "Quite simply, Miss Burkhart, the Lord Almighty would have to strike us all blind."

⟫⟫⟫⟨⟨⟨

AND EVEN THEN *he would be able to smell her—all sunshine, lemons and honeysuckle.*

It had not escaped Val's notice that they were flirting. Well, he was flirting. She, simply, was flirtation. With her heavy-lidded eyes, full lips and lushly-curved figure, everything about her screamed flirtation. It also screamed other things that, as a gentleman, he should not listen to at all. She could sit stone silent before him and it would still seem an invitation, primarily because—like all men—he'd want it to be one. The difference, of course, was that if she ever told him she did not wish his flirtations, he would cease. Unlike the arrogant pup of her former employers. Val made a mental note to find out who it was and exact a bit of revenge for Miss Burkhart.

"Your friend's academy helps with job placement for young women?" he queried, hoping to get them onto a different topic that didn't require him thinking of just how pretty she was.

"I'm a graduate of the Darrow School, my lord."

The words were uttered with no small amount of pride. It was something easily understood. The Darrow School had an excellent reputation. It was also an open secret that the majority of students enrolled there were the illegitimate daughters of the aristocracy. So, Miss Burkhart might have been born on the wrong side of the blanket. The question was, who was the owner of that blanket?

"The Hellion Club," he said.

She shrugged. "Some call it that. We're not hellions... well, most of us aren't. It's funny the names men call women simply because they dare to make their own way in the world rather than be dependent on the male species. And most of the women who attend or who have graduated from the Hellion Club, as you put it, have little enough reason to put their faith in a man's ability to care for them."

It was impossible to miss the bitterness in her voice. "Many men call themselves gentlemen, Miss Burkhart, and fail to behave as such. I'm sorry you've encountered so many in your short life."

Her eyes narrowed and she fixed him with a surprisingly shrewd gaze. "You're not one of them, are you? I've heard of you, you know? Haunting the gaming hells and bawdy houses to watch for the sharps that would take advantage of country mice with more money than sense. Is that why you do it? To be a gentleman?"

He did it because if a man was so lacking in honor that he'd cheat at cards, he often engaged in other nefarious activities. *Including treason.* "That's certainly one reason."

She stiffened in his arms immediately. "That's the first lie you've actually told me."

"It isn't a lie," he protested.

"But neither is it the entire truth... omission is worse than an outright lie. People lie impulsively, they fear consequences and rattle off some half-cocked story to avoid them. A lie of omission is one of calculation," she pointed out. "You lied to me and you've lied to others in the same manner and it was premeditated."

"I've told you all the truth on that score that I am permitted to," he answered. That was as honest with her as he could be on the subject. "There are people to whom I answer that limit the amount of information I can divulge."

They'd reached the main gate, and he'd been so caught up in speaking to her that he didn't even notice the curious stares of those around them until he settled her on a small bench. Luckily, it was not a fashionable hour for riding or driving in the park and most of those present appeared to be nursemaids and governesses with their charges in tow. Rising to his full height, he doffed his hat to her. "Please wait here and I will obtain transportation for us. It isn't so very far to my grandmother's home from here, but I think we've created enough of a stir."

"Hopefully not such a stir that it reaches your grandmother's ears," she said. "Else your carefully concocted story will be for naught."

That was a complication. "We'll work out the particulars on our way there."

Chapter Three

THE HANSOM CAB rolled over the cobbled street, a luxury for residents of Mayfair that much of London lacked. "Tell me, Miss Burkhart, what had you in the park today? And so deeply in thought?" Val asked.

"I had requested the morning off because I had an appointment of a personal nature. And I was alone in the park, deep in thought, because I was trying to determine what I ought to do about the information I learned during my appointment."

Val frowned. "Are you in some sort of trouble, Miss Burkhart?"

"No. Not as such, really. My mother died when I was very young and I didn't know her family. She sent me to my father, William Satterly, who promptly put me in a terrible school. A few years later, my half-sister, Wilhelmina, was also placed there. And then together, we were discovered by Miss Euphemia Darrow and it was with us as her first pupils that the Darrow School was formed."

"And this appointment had something to do with your mother's family, I take it?" he asked. He couldn't help but feel there was more to the story than she had offered, that perhaps she was glossing over the more damaging details of it. But he supposed she was entitled to her secrets.

She nodded. "It did. I have an aunt. My mother's aunt, actually. She has left a bequest for me, but I can only claim this bequest as a marriage portion. Apparently, she was greatly concerned that my mother's weakness of character and poor judgment might be inherited."

"And you've no one to marry? No special beau who might persuade you to the altar?" he asked. He was far more invested in her answer than he wished to be. He was certainly more invested in it than was wise.

"No, there isn't… but the truth is, I'm not sure I want to be married. I'm as terrible as an employee as I was at being a student. I find it very difficult to tolerate being told what to do, my lord. And as such, I'd make a terrible wife," she admitted. There was something rather forlorn in her tone that indicated she might regret that opinion.

"Then we have a great deal in common, Miss Burkhart, as I have often considered that I would be the worst of husbands… for much the same reason," he admitted, just as the carriage slowed and the horses drew to a halt.

They had arrived at Number Ten, South Audley Street. For his part, Val wished they might have circled the block a few times. He was not eager to face his grandmother, but he was less eager to see an end to his time with Miss Burkhart. Opening the door, he climbed down and then reached back in to aid her.

Helping Miss Burkhart out of the cab, he instructed footmen to see her up the stairs. It was a better option than him carrying her, not only because his grandmother would disapprove, but because holding her so closely had affected him in ways that made being in his grandmother's presence very uncomfortable.

As Miss Burkhart disappeared from view, he returned the butler's assessing gaze. "Is there something you wish to say, Netherford?"

"Only that it was remarkably good fortune that in Miss Burkhart's hour of need, who should appear but the grandson of her employer. Most fortuitous for the young lady, my lord."

He'd never liked Netherford and Netherford, for his part, had never especially liked Val. It seemed their enmity was to continue indefinitely. Pinning the man with a cold stare, Val said, "Hardly remarkable. We were both traveling to the same location, after all, making it quite likely that our paths would cross. I know you certainly didn't intend to imply that perhaps Miss Burkhart or I engineered such a meeting for some nefarious purpose. Did you, Netherford?"

The butler, a stick of a man with a shock of white hair that defied any attempt to tame it, merely regarded him coolly. "I would never dream of making such an implication, my lord. But others might."

"Then I can trust you to disabuse them of that notion. Can't I, Netherford?" Val demanded as he stepped closer to the butler, towering over him.

Relenting, Netherford ducked his head. "Certainly, my lord. The dowager duchess awaits you in the drawing room. I shall have more tea sent in as the first pot has likely grown cold."

Ignoring the implied censure, Val went in search of his grand-mother. If he was going to get a dressing down, it would come from her and not from her lackey. Entering the drawing room, he noted that his grandmother looked at the ormolu clock on the mantel, her head tilted and an expression of disapproval on her face. Her thin lips pursed as she pressed them to the tea cup in her hand and took a long sip of the still steaming liquid.

"You are late, Valentine," she said. "If this is how you treat all women, it is no wonder you are as yet unmarried."

"There was a situation involving your companion, Miss Burkhart. She was injured by a careless coachman and required my assistance," he said.

"What sort of coachman? Was that girl in a carriage with some-one? Mark me, I hate to judge a book by its cover but, from the look of her, it's impossible not to think her fast," the dowager duchess said.

"She rode in a hack with me from the park to here because her ankle was sprained when a reckless driver nearly ran her down," Val lied as he took his seat beside her and pressed a kiss to her lined cheek. "How wicked your mind is, Grandmother!"

"What on earth was she doing in the park?" his grandmother asked. "Meeting some man, I suppose. Likely a footman. They're no good, I tell you! Footmen cannot be trusted, no matter how handsome they look in livery!"

Hoping to distract her, Val stated, "You say that as if speaking from experience! No, never mind. I don't wish to know."

She gasped, and then immediately slapped her closed fan on the back of his wrist. "Naughty, wretched boy! Enough about my companion and whatever unsavory characters she chooses to spend her half-day with—you included! What I want to know, Valentine Augustus Somers, is when you mean to marry and begin producing the next generation of the Somers line! You're past your prime, you know!"

He arched his own brows at her, unaware of just how much alike they appeared in that moment. "Really? I've been assured by very well-informed sources that I'm quite firmly in my prime, Grandmama."

"Wicked boy," she hissed out. In a less scandalized tone, she continued, "Don't think to distract me with being scandalous. You must marry, Valentine, and you must do so before the year is out! I've reached the end of my patience with you and my resolve in this matter is quite firm. You shall not charm me out of it."

"It's October, Grandmama," he replied indulgently. It was a familiar refrain from her. "Late October at that. How on Earth am I supposed to secure the hand of some deb by then?"

"Well, go and ask someone," she replied, as if perhaps his faculties were in some way compromised. "It isn't as if they'd say no! You're to be a duke, for heaven's sake! Heavens, put a notice in the *Times* that you need a suitable wife and they will line up around the block!"

"Really? Impending dukedom aside, being past my prime and all, it's hard to be certain," he replied, leaning indolently against the back of the settee. It was not the first conversation they'd had about her desire to see him leg-shackled. It would likely not be the last.

She whacked him with the fan once again, more firmly this time, as if she actually meant it. "I've already seen my solicitor, Valentine. I mean it. I'm quite serious this time, whether you choose to believe me or not. Your grandfather, God rest him, was ten kinds of a fool... until it mattered. He chose, against the protests of all who knew us, to leave me in charge of my own finances after his death and those of the rest of the family. Of course, he only did it because I'd been in charge of them while he lived. Had I not, we'd have all been paupered. I've trebled the family coffers in my lifetime, as well you know. And it will take Elsworth less than five years to spend through it like sand through an hourglass. But I will leave it to him. Mark my words, I will! The new will is drawn up and I have but to sign it. Present me with your viscountess by the stroke of the New Year, or be disinherited from all that is not entailed."

Val took in the stubborn jut of his grandmother's chin and the hardness of her gaze. She meant it, he realized. His grandmother was capable of doing anything, and she did not make idle threats.

"You don't have to leave the money to me," he said. "But for heaven's sake, don't leave it to Elsworth!"

"Why not Elsworth?" she demanded. "Next to you he's the most entitled to it. He is blood after all. He's a Somers, God knows. He certainly inherited all of their foolish tendencies. Thank heavens you got your intellect from me, Boy, or the future generations—assuming there are ever to be any—would have no hope at all. So Elsworth it is, unless you can give me some reason not to proceed. Hmmm?"

Because he is a traitor. Because he's sold secrets to France to support his gambling debts. Because if you leave the money to him, it will all be seized by the Crown anyway. It was all there on the tip of his tongue, but as he looked at his grandmother, he saw something he hadn't seen before. The slight tremor in her hand which wielded her fan like a club. Her cheeks were gaunt. And while her white hair was impeccably styled, it was thinner than it had been in the past. In short, she looked frail in a way he'd never seen before, in a way that wasn't just a manipulative affectation but a true product of her age, which even her iron will could not stave off forever. His cousin's treason would kill her.

"Because he's an addlepated clod," Val muttered finally.

"Well, of course, he is! He's just like his wretched father. Your wastrel uncle was very nearly the death of me. We won't even discuss the scandalous method in which he departed this world!" She paused then, taking a deep breath that hinted at attempts to battle back her own grief. Stupid as he'd been, Betrand had been her youngest child and a more stupid man had never lived. He'd died falling from the bedroom window of his married lover. He'd lost his balance trying to hastily don his trousers before his lover's husband entered the room. The attempt to avoid scandal had instead mired the family in it for years. But she'd loved him regardless. That was his grandmother's true weakness. Behind her hard shell, she had a soft and tender heart.

When she continued after that brief pause, her voice was firm again, any hint of emotion other than disdain completely obliterated through sheer force of will and innate stoicism. "Though, I daresay your own father isn't much better. Gallivanting all around the globe while you, his only son, run wild about the city like some sort of Robin Hood of the gaming hells! Where is he now? India? Egypt? Living like some heathen in a tent—as if he hadn't been raised a proper English-man!"

"Somewhere in China, I believe," Val said. "And no doubt he's still a proper Englishman no matter where he is."

"He should be home tending to the estates instead of doing heaven knows what in heaven knows where! He's another wicked, wretched boy!"

Val didn't tell her that his father would never tend to the estates so long as she lived because he would never do so to her satisfaction. No one would. Her own supreme competence was also the root cause of her greatest disappointments. "He is, Grandmama. He is."

"And you'll move in here so I can monitor your progress in obtaining a wife," she said. "None of that living in rented rooms like some impoverished second son. You'll reside here like a proper gentleman."

It would give him the ability to watch over Elsworth more readily. *And Miss Burkhart.*

"Fine. I shall send for my valet and a few things and have everything else sent over tomorrow. In the meantime, I find I'm a bit fatigued from my late evening at the card table."

"Your late evening with that actress, you mean!" his grandmother said. "I know who you've been keeping company with."

He had been keeping company with an actress, but they had parted ways. She'd become a bit too clinging, determined to envision a future for them where none existed. She'd been angry at him, accusing him of snobbery. But it hadn't been the fact that she'd been treading the boards which caused his affections to wane. It was that he'd grown bored in her company. Oh, in bed, she'd been energetic and inventive. But conversation had been stilted and one dimensional. Even her rather remarkable figure and unmatched carnal skills could not combat that.

"Stop sending Netherford to spy on me. It's impolite and most assuredly not standard duties for a butler of his caliber," he cautioned.

"I've more spies than my butler," she snapped. "And tell him to send Miss Burkhart to me. I need to have a word with her."

"Absolutely not. She cannot be traipsing up and down the stairs on that ankle. If you wish to speak with her, you'll have to go to her instead," he replied.

The old woman's face took on an expression of shock and rage. "I do not dance attendance upon my own servants! This is not to be borne!"

"You are not going to sack her, Grandmama," he said firmly.

"And what if I am? What concern is it of yours?"

"She's a young woman alone in the world," he said. "And through no fault of her own, she was injured. Surely you could not be so cruel as to dismiss her for that?"

"Fine. She stays… but you'll steer clear of her. I'll not have anything like *that* in my household!"

"I can't imagine what you could possibly object to! Being a Good Samaritan? Offering assistance to an injured person? Tell me, Grandmother, what is so terribly scandalous about that?" Val queried as he rose and made for the door.

"Do not mince words with me, young man! I might be a wrinkled old bat now—and do not think I am ignorant of how all young people view all old people—I was not always so. I know precisely what all young men have on their minds when presented with a pretty girl. I should never have hired her, to be honest. But she is from the Darrow School and despite her rather shocking appearance, there is an element of cachet about that."

Val continued toward the door, rolling his eyes as he did so. "Certainly, Grandmother. And we all know how important cachet is. I'm in my old suite, I presume?"

"Well, of course you are," she said. "Where else would I put you?"

"Then I shall see you at dinner. It has been a long night followed by a longer morning. And despite my youthful appearance and general depravity, I do require rest," he said. "Being past my prime and all."

"Then get it… and leave my companion be," his grandmother warned. "If she finds herself sacked and on the street, Valentine, the fault will lay at your doorstep and not mine!"

LILLY WINCED AS one of the maids wrapped a rather foul-smelling poultice about her ankle. "I'll stink to high heaven for a week," she said.

"It doesn't linger, Miss," the girl assured her. "It'll take the swelling down, and then you'll be right as rain soon enough."

Another waft of the atrocious aroma reached her already offended nose and Lillian fought back the urge to retch. "I hope you're right, Mary. Thank you for helping me. I know most of the girls below stairs will not think kindly of you for it."

The maid grimaced. "Bunch of foul tempered busybodies, they are! I know you're not one of us, not with your fancy ways of talking, but I reckon you're not one of them either," she said and gestured toward the corridor which would lead to the family wing. "And if them girls don't like it, they can just lump it, now can't they? You work here same as us and you're laid up with a bad ankle. I'd take care of them just the same, I would."

"You are very good, Mary, and I am very appreciative... even if I do complain about the smell."

The maid giggled. "It is right awful. I won't say different, but it does work, so smell or no, you leave it where it is for now. All right?"

"Quite right," Lilly agreed. She vowed to do something nice for the girl. Perhaps she could find her a ribbon for her pretty red hair, something to brighten up the unrelieved black that the girl was forced to wear per her grace's instructions.

When the girl had gone, Lillian leaned back in her narrow bed and thought about the turn her morning had taken. *Lord Valentine Somers, Viscount Seaburn.* "It's a ridiculous name for a ridiculous man," she murmured under her breath and tried desperately to convince herself it was true.

He was not at all what she'd expected him to be given what the gossip rags said of him. And she knew those gossip rags inside and out because her grace insisted that Lillian read them to her every morning over breakfast. Even in the countryside, she'd said it was important to know what was happening in London lest one inadvertently put a foot wrong when they returned to the city after a long absence. It was imperative, the old woman had said, to know to whom one must give the cut direct.

Like so much about high society, it seemed impossibly silly to her. One should speak to whoever one wished to speak and that should be the end of it. But still, those gossip rags had mentioned Viscount Seaburn on numerous occasions. They called him Viscount Chance on account of his remarkable skill with cards. It was reported regularly that he'd fleeced some sharp or other, saved some worthless and wet behind the ears puppy who hadn't the sense not to play with those that could best him easily. And there had been talk of his mistresses, as well. They did certainly love to dissect his every move, but nothing they said of him seemed especially wicked. Most of it seemed rather noble even if somewhat unorthodox in method. Still, he was a titled gentleman in possession of a substantial fortune with the promise of greater fortune still to come. It was little wonder they followed his every move like a cat chasing a fly. He wasn't just eligible, but prized above all others. Dukes were not exactly thick on the ground. Young, handsome and wealthy heirs to dukedoms were worth their very weight in gold, if not more.

With her injured foot propped on pillows, Lillian struggled to get herself into a seated position on the small bed. She couldn't just lie there looking at the ceiling and mooning over a man so far beyond her reach it was laughable. Instead, she reached for the writing box that was tucked onto the small shelf beside the bed and endeavored to write her half-sister and explain the strange events of the day. Even if she couldn't talk to Willa and hear her reply, putting the words down with the intent to send them to her would at least help her to know her own mind and what she ought to do about the prospect of finding a husband so that she might claim her fortune. A suitable husband for her station and her needs. Not him, she thought. Most definitely not him. *Even if it were possible.*

Chapter Four

V AL DRESSED FOR dinner. His valet looked on disapprovingly. But then, he was used to that. He'd grown accustomed to fending for himself in most ways during his army days and, other than the occasional too fitted coat or a stubborn pair of boots, he'd continued to do so. Fenton could see to his clothes all he liked, but his person was very much off limits, especially when it came to shaving. A man in his position, with his skills and his knowledge, would be foolish to let anyone so close to his neck with a blade. Val was many things, but he was no one's fool.

As Val tied his cravat into a simple knot that likely made his servant want to gnash his teeth in frustration, he thought of Miss Burkhart and how she might fare navigating all the many stairs in the family's townhouse. It was certainly not a house designed for an invalid, even a temporary one.

"Fenton, is that walking stick still in with my things? The one I never use because it's too short?"

"Yes, my lord. I have it in your dressing chamber." *"The dressing chamber which you also never use"* was implied by the servant's wounded tone.

Poor Fenton was a servant who needed a more conventional master. He would ever be disappointed in him, Val thought. It was a sad state for them both as Fenton managed to suffer in silence more loudly than anyone he'd ever encountered.

"Excellent. My grandmother's companion injured herself earlier. Please inquire with one of the servants here to see about getting it to her for the duration," Val said. "The poor girl can't just limp about from one piece of furniture to the next."

"My lord, you do recall that it is a very specific walking stick which is capable of far more than simply aiding one to walk?" the valet asked, his face a mask of horror.

It was, in fact, a concealed rapier. But it also had a next to impossible locking mechanism on it, one of the many reasons that Val himself chose never to carry it. The last thing he needed was an unreliable and stubbornly inaccessible blade. "As neither of us can get the blasted thing open, I suspect Miss Burkhart will have no better luck. We will all be quite safe with it in her possession. Lame as she currently is, I daresay we can outrun her if necessary."

The valet sniffed his disapproval. "I will see to it, my lord, though I am certain an item so fine will be refused. To accept it would imply inappropriateness between you and the young woman in question."

"Then you will keep your mouth shut and tell no one where the girl got it from," Val hissed out between clenched teeth. "My God. The girl has sprained her ankle and is living in a house that consists almost entirely of stairs. Not to mention, we all know my grandmother will not let her rest for long. Are you really so fixated on propriety, man, that you would wish to see her injure herself rather than utilize something I possess that only serves to collect dust?"

"It is just simply not done, my lord," the valet insisted.

"Well, it will be. I'll not be dictated to by anyone, and certainly not my own servant," Val continued. "See to it, Fenton, and if you so much as sneer in disapproval at that girl or the maid you instruct to deliver the item to her, I will toss you out personally."

"Yes, my lord," the valet replied, suddenly meek.

When the man had gone, Val followed soon after. As he neared the drawing room, he could hear his cousin, Elsworth, regaling their grandmother with some tale or other that had the old woman laughing. Not chortling or cackling with actual glee, as that would have been terribly improper but which he could, on occasion, coax her to do. Instead, she was laughing behind her hand in that very dignified manner that matrons of high society had long since mastered. Like so many things about the world they lived in, it was utterly false. He knew as well as anyone that she couldn't abide Elsworth. Only Elsworth himself seemed to be ignorant of the fact.

Taking pity on her in spite of her hypocrisy, Val stepped inside. "Good evening, Grandmother. Elsworth."

His cousin smiled, a tight and pinched expression that didn't reach his eyes. "Valentine... how nice to see you've decided to grace us with your presence. It's been ages. No doubt the actresses of Drury Lane, only the lesser ones of course, are gnashing their teeth and tearing at their hair in mourning at your absence."

Val raised his eyebrows at the censorious tone. Was the arrogant pup actually trying to undermine him in front of the dowager duchess? "I really couldn't say what's happening at Drury Lane, Cousin. Most of my dealings with actresses occur at private events. As to the great length of time that has passed between our visits, well, it never seems that long until we're together again. But I've had business that has kept me in town and, as we both know, our dear grandmother prefers the country."

"Yes, yes... *your business*. And who have you fleeced this week?" Elsworth asked, all charm and fake smile.

"No one who didn't need it," Val replied. It was going to be a very long evening. Interminable, actually. "Is there anything to drink here other than that awful sherry?"

His grandmother raised her eyebrows imperiously. "Is our company so painful for you that you must drink yourself into oblivion to bear it?"

"Yours isn't," Val replied with a grin. It earned him a disapproving glare from her, but there was a sparkle in her eyes even as she pursed her lips in that manner.

"Stop it. Both of you," the dowager duchess said. "I'll not have you sniping at one another like petty, jealous children. Valentine, you may ring for the servants to bring you brandy. I would normally never permit such a strong spirit in my drawing room, but if that is what is necessary for the two of you to be civil to one another, then I suppose needs must. Miss Burkhart will be joining us for dinner."

Val paused mid-stride. "Is that wise? She is injured, your grace."

"Only her ankle. I certainly do not see how it inhibits her ability to chew or make conversation," the old woman snapped. "We cannot have an uneven number at the dinner table and while she is only my companion, her manners are impeccable. Given the way the two of you behave, her presence can only elevate the evening."

Val had just reached a chair near the fireplace when the door opened and Miss Burkhart entered. She was dressed in another truly atrocious gown. While it was of fine silk, the hideous shade of olive made her appear quite sickly. It did nothing for her complexion and nothing for her rather exotic coloring with her dark hair and blue eyes. He also knew that gown had once been his grandmother's. She'd put the poor girl in her hideous castoff that had surely been altered to hide every curve of her figure. And sadly for him, even in a color that would flatter no one, that sack of a gown could not hide her beauty. He wanted to see her in silk the color of midnight, draped in pearls that rivaled her skin in luminescence and diamonds that flashed and winked as her eyes had that morning.

What the bloody hell? He didn't wax poetic about women, not even those he could actually take to his bed. Innocent young misses employed by his grandmother should definitely not spark such thoughts.

Cursing himself for a dozen kinds of fool, Val rose to his feet once more as she hobbled in, leaning on the walking stick that had been provided for her.

"That's an interesting piece, Miss Burkhart," Elsworth noted. "Where on earth did you get it?"

"I sent it to her," the dowager duchess said abruptly, even as she glared at Val. "I knew the poor girl couldn't possibly get by without it. Really, Elsworth! Should I have had the footmen cart her into the dining room like Cleopatra to Antony?"

Val didn't challenge the lie and neither did Miss Burkhart. Perhaps she didn't know.

"Thank you, your grace," the girl said with a smile. "It was most kind of you."

"You're welcome, my dear," the dowager duchess said imperiously. "I am always kind to those in my employ."

Val hid his bark of laughter behind a cough. But Elsworth was not about to let such an opportunity pass him by.

"Is the brandy too much for you, Cousin? One would think with the regularity with which you imbibe, it would be like milk to a babe."

Val wasn't going to take the bait. It was just what Elsworth wanted, after all. "It's far better quality than I'm used to. In the back alleys and hovels where I normally imbibe, it's typically watered down or cut with a cheaper imitation. You understand cheap imitations, don't you, Elsworth?"

>>>><<<<

LILLIAN WATCHED THE exchange between the men. No blows were exchanged, no weapons were drawn, but she would hardly call it bloodless. They skewered one another with words and all but tangible dislike. The weight of tension in the room was nearly unbearable.

"Your grace, that gown is rather lovely. The embroidery on it is simply divine," Lillian said, hoping that if she could engage the dowager duchess in a bit of inane conversation, the tension in the room would subside at least a bit. Otherwise, dinner was to be a miserable affair for all of them.

"It is. I've had it for ages, but rarely wear it," the woman said. "It was gifted to me by my husband many years ago and then dyed black after he'd passed. I didn't see the need in obtaining an entirely new wardrobe afterward. It seemed wasteful and terribly extravagant, and as I never intended to marry again—it's a terrible state for women, Miss Burkhart. If you can manage to avoid it in your life, I urge you to do so. At any rate, I never expected to shed my widow's weeds so there was little point in not taking the items that I enjoyed so much and making them useful in my widowed state rather than relegating them to the rubbish pile because they were not of a somber enough hue."

"That must have been quite awful for you. I'm so terribly sorry to have brought up such a painful topic," Lillian said, feeling as if she'd once more put her foot right in it.

"Oh, no! Not painful, at all. The boys both know I held their late grandfather in no esteem at all. Why, he was a foolish, foolish man. He might as well have thrown coins like rose petals to walk upon as terrible as he was with financial matters. I did what I could to counteract that, you know? But if he hadn't died when he did, I daresay our fortunes would look very different today," the old woman replied, her lips firming into a thin, tight line as she shook her head.

It just keeps getting worse, Lillian thought. No matter what she said, the situation did not improve. Thankfully, the dinner gong sounded and she was spared from having to make any further attempts at conversation.

"Elsworth will escort me," the dowager duchess said. "It's a breach of etiquette, I know, given that you outrank him, Valentine. But I cannot abide the smell of brandy. It reminds me of your worthless grandfather. And I daresay that given Miss Burkhart's injury, she may require someone of a slightly more strapping physique to aid her than poor Elsworth."

With that, Lillian stood there, leaning heavily on a walking stick that most assuredly had not come from her employer and waited on the man who had rescued her twice already that day to step forward and lead her into a dinner that would surely be on par with one of the seven layers of hell in Milton's great work.

"Buck up, darling girl," he said, offering her his arm as he drew near. "She won't send you packing just yet."

"You're foxed," Lillian said, shocked.

He grinned, a wicked expression that showed no remorse at all and was far too appealing for her peace of mind. "Not yet. But if I have my way, I will be before the fish course is served. Come on, then. Let's not keep the old dragon waiting."

Lillian was still sputtering under her breath, uncertain whether to laugh, cry or simply beg off and go hide in her chamber as they entered the dining room. He showed her to her seat and then made his way to his own, just across from her. His cousin, the Honorable Mr. Elsworth Somers, was seated next to him. She could feel the weight of both their gazes, one admiring and curious, one speculative and disapproving. She couldn't afford for Elsworth Somers to speculate about her. *Not yet. Not until she found a way to claim her bequest.*

"Tell me, Miss Burkhart," Elsworth began, "about this school of yours that my grandmother speaks so highly of. The Darrow School, I believe?"

"Yes, that is correct, Mr. Somers," Lillian answered. At least that was a safe topic, Lillian thought. "The Darrow School is for girls only. It's operated by Miss Euphemia Darrow. She takes girls in that have difficult situations or a lack of close family and she trains them to be governesses and companions, offering instruction in all areas that young ladies and gentlemen who will enter society would require. Upon completion of one's education, she assists with finding gainful employment. She's very good at what she does."

"And how long does one stay at the Darrow School?" he asked. "I assume this course work would be more extensive for some than others, depending on aptitude and what manner of deportment and etiquette they began with."

Lilly kept smiling, but she was beginning to see that Mr. Somers' line of questions was very specific. "Some girls are there for only a few years. Others, such as my half-sister and me, are there for significantly longer. It depends on the needs of the child, as you surmised, in terms of their education, but also their living situation and their age when they come to Miss Darrow's attention."

"That's a very practiced answer... their living situation," Elsworth said. "And where does she find these children precisely?"

"Some are brought to her, others she becomes aware of through her charitable works or through family members of the child," Lilly answered.

"And you and your half-sister... how were you discovered, Miss Burkhart?" he asked, his gaze calculating and cold.

"She found my half-sister and me at another school in the north. It was... not a good place," Lillian answered, being intentionally vague.

"This half-sister of yours that you speak so freely about, where is she now?" Elsworth continued. "I assume she's serving with some other family?"

"Is this dinner conversation, Cousin, or is it an interrogation?" the viscount demanded.

"I'm only trying to ascertain the true character of a woman who spends so much time with our dear grandmother, Valentine," Elsworth said with a sneer. "Surely it behooves us to have a better understanding of her nature?"

"It behooves you to cease this immediately," the viscount snapped. "You're being impossibly rude."

Elsworth turned back to her then, ignoring his cousin altogether.

"Your half-sister, Miss Burkhart, where is she?"

"With her husband, sir," Lillian answered, her tone crisp. "She is no longer in service at all, but has married and is in the country with her husband."

"A farmer, then? How quaint," he said with an obvious sneer.

"Not exactly," Lillian said and there was a note of triumph that she could not quite mask in her voice. "She married Lord Deveril. I think he can be called many things, Mr. Somers... but farmer is not one of them."

The dowager duchess smiled at that. "Indeed. I read all about them in the papers... I didn't ask you to read those sections to me, Miss Burkhart, as I thought that might be somewhat awkward for you. Your half-sister... what was her name again?"

"Wilhelmina Marks, your grace," Lillian replied.

"I see you have different fathers," Elsworth said.

He had managed to pique her temper to the point that Lillian no longer cared if the dowager duchess fired her. If he wanted to know what scandals lay in her past, well, she'd let him. "No, Mr. Somers. In point of fact, we did have the same father, William Satterly. No doubt you know him and have socialized with him on many occasions. Sadly, he failed to prove himself in possession of any honor at all and never married either of our mothers. Do you have any further questions about my parentage or is that information sufficient?"

"Don't be impertinent, Miss Burkhart," the dowager duchess warned. "My grandson's lack of manners is no reason to forget yours."

"Why the devil shouldn't she be?" Seaburn interjected. "Elsworth certainly had no trouble being impertinent, impudent, and utterly rude. I apologize on behalf of my relatives, Miss Burkhart. Your command of etiquette and, I daresay, basic human kindness exceeds us all."

"Oh, do stop, Valentine," the dowager duchess said. "And now that we've exhausted the topic of Miss Burkhart's lineage, we need to address the pressing matter of your finding a bride!"

Lilly felt his gaze on her for a long moment, then she saw his lips quirk slightly. It wasn't a smile, but a smirk. There was a challenge in his gaze, a question, as well. No, she thought. No! He would not.

"I've already found one," he said. "Miss Burkhart, would you do me the great honor of becoming my wife?"

He did.

Chapter Five

C HAOS WAS THE only word that could be used to describe the scene. Complete and utter chaos. Mr. Elsworth Somers and the dowager duchess were all speaking at once. The footmen stationed about the room were whispering to one another frantically while the butler made every attempt to shush them. One of them had apparently run down to the kitchen the moment the news was relayed because a great clattering, as if an entire shelf of pans and crockery had been overturned, rose to clang throughout the house. And in all of it, Lord Valentine Somers, Viscount Seaburn, remained perfectly still, almost like he was carved from marble. No, she thought, not marble. It was too cold. He'd been fashioned from bronze, from heat and sweat and labor.

"You cannot possibly do this!"

"I forbid it! How on earth will I find another suitable companion?"

"It's preposterous! You're only doing it get a rise out of me... marrying someone of her standing. Really, Cousin!"

"Elsworth isn't wrong. We'll be the gossip of the town! The *ton* will turn its back on all of us because of your impetuous behavior! How could you be so cruel, Valentine?"

"Surely, Miss Burkhart," Elsworth said to her. "You will call a halt to this foolishness, certainly?"

Lillian eyed him with his cajoling tone and suddenly conspiratorial expression. As if they were on the same side, as if he hadn't been hounding her about her background only moments before and they were now allies against his cousin's impetuous nature. "Really, Mr. Somers, I feel under the circumstances that the only person to whom I owe any answers at this moment is Viscount Seaburn."

"Well, answer him then!" the dowager duchess snapped.

Lillian glanced at her employer. Well, her employer for the moment. No doubt, after the debacle of dinner, she'd find herself unemployed soon enough. Still, there was something in the old woman's expression that didn't quite ring true. It was almost as if she were enjoying the entire drama as it played out.

Finally, Lillian said, "I will do so... but in private. Perhaps, my lord, we could retreat briefly to the drawing room?"

"Oh, heavens no," he offered drolly. "Not if you want privacy. Every servant in the house will be camped outside the door! The garden? No, not with your ankle. I suppose the terrace might be the best option. It's not too cold, I think."

He spoke as if they were planning a typical outing or considering a turn about the room. The man was insufferable.

"Very well," Lillian agreed and rose to her feet. The walking stick he'd provided earlier was on the floor beside her and a footman rushed forward to pick it up for her. No doubt, he was hedging his bets on the off chance that an upstart like her would actually marry into the family. Still wearing her shawl and leaning heavily on the cane like some sort of aged aunt, she limped toward the terrace doors, Viscount Seaburn in her wake.

Once outside, she turned to him immediately. "Why did you do it?" She couldn't even effectively categorize her response to all of it. Anger, puzzlement, even mild amusement all warred within her.

He shrugged. "They aren't wrong. I need a wife. I need one who isn't overly concerned about what society might think of her."

"And because of my low upbringing, social aspiration is beyond me?" she demanded, offended by him perhaps for the first time.

His eyebrows arched upward in obvious surprise. "Not at all. You have no social aspirations, Miss Burkhart, because you see through all the artifice of it to the ridiculousness, the pettiness and ugliness that lurk beneath its surface. Your lack of social aspiration is a mark in your favor as a human being and not a black mark against your upbringing."

"And will my upbringing—daughter of a whore and a so-called gentleman who deserves the term bastard far more than any of his illegitimate children—what will that do to your social standing?" she demanded of him. Her coarse language had been a strategy. She wanted to shock him, to make him see how ridiculous such a match would be between them and precisely what it might cost him in the long term.

He shrugged, as if it mattered not at all. "My social standing, as you put it, is teetering like a house of cards already. My own actions, and there are reasons for them, Miss Burkhart, are partially to blame. But I don't play deep at the tables because I like it, because I crave it, or because I cannot stop myself. It is part of my job. Information flows freely there and there are certain areas of the government and the military who benefit greatly from what I glean in such places."

Lillian looked at him then, noting the tightness of his jaw, the muscles clenched so tightly that it was a wonder they did not snap. This was no dissipated drunkard trying to shock his family or rebel against their expectations. There was a hint of steel in him there that she had not seen to that point. "And what have you gleaned that will see your family so utterly destroyed?"

"It may not come to pass," he said. "If I marry... and if I prevent Elsworth from being written into my grandmother's will with the expectation of considerable fortune, then perhaps I can stop all of this before it begins."

"I require more explanation that that. You said the government wanted information that you gleaned at the tables and—good heavens.

You're ferreting out treasonous plots, aren't you?"

"There isn't much ferreting. Just observation," he replied.

"He's a traitor," she surmised. It was the only thing that made sense. What else could fell such a powerful and respected family? Murder and treason were the only crimes that a man of Elsworth Somers' standing need ever fear consequences for.

"Not yet, he isn't. At the moment, he's made questionable choices but done nothing he cannot be pulled back from. But if he goes deeper into business with the individuals in question... on credit with his expectations as collateral, it will be too late for all of us. In order to stop it, his expectations must be dashed and in a very public manner. So, in point of fact, Miss Burkhart, it's your duty as a citizen of the Crown to marry me."

Lillian laughed at that. "The Crown? What has it ever done for me except perpetuate a class system where I will always be seen as less because of the sins of my parents? No, my lord, if you truly wish to wed me, you will be forced to argue the case on your own merits."

"I have a fine house," he said.

"In which I already reside," she fired back with triumph.

"True," he agreed. "But not in luxury. You live in a tiny room fit only for servants. And you, Miss Burkhart, were never meant to be a servant."

She considered his response for a moment. "I'd argue that you do not understand luxury because you've never had to share a chamber with others. But I will concede the point as there are certainly chambers more fashionably appointed in the house than my own."

"How very just of you, Miss Burkhart," he said, smiling in a way that indicated he found her answers to be greatly amusing and was attempting to hide his response. "The second point in my favor is that you'd no longer have to do everything my grandmother says."

"Yes, I most certainly would. Heaven knows you do," she shot back. "That woman barks and the entire family scrambles like she's a rabid dog. And I'll thank you never to tell her I said so."

He grinned in the darkness, a flash of white teeth that sent a shiver racing through her. "True again, and you have my promise of discretion in relation to your analogy. So allow me to put a finer point on my argument. You might still have to do as she says, but you would get to choose your own clothes."

Lillian looked down at the drab green silk that not even moonlight could render flattering. "Go on. You have my attention now."

He stepped closer to her, as close as he had been that morning when he carried her through the park. She could feel the heat that emanated from the broad expanse of his chest, and even over the cloying scent of the hundreds of roses that bloomed nearby, she could smell the sandalwood of his shaving soap. It was a heady combination—moonlight and a wicked, dangerous man.

"There are other benefits to being married to me, Miss Burkhart, but I can't really tell you what those are. With your permission, I would demonstrate at least one."

"I suppose that's fair," she said, hating that her voice sounded breathless and even giddy. Sophisticated women did not get giddy at the prospect of a kiss. But then, she wasn't a sophisticated woman, was she? She was a cynical virgin with a rather unflattering impression of the male sex. It was hardly the same thing at all.

His hands settled on her shoulders and with only the lightest of pressure, prompted her to turn to face him. He stood nearly a head taller than her, so much so that he blocked out all the light from the moon above and most that filtered out from the dining room. They existed, in that moment, in a world of velvet shadow. Then he was leaning in, his head dipping low, and his lips settled over hers.

It was not at all what she had expected. Slow, languorous, soft—this was not at all like the fumbling advances of the son of her previous employer who'd shoved her against a wall and mashed his mouth against hers while trying to shove his tongue between her lips. This was something altogether different. It promised not sweetness, that was too mild a term for it. No, that kiss promised surrender. Both hers and his. His hand came up to cup her cheek, angling her head back ever so slightly, deepening the contact between them. And when his tongue played along the seam of her lips, it was an instinct as natural as breathing to open for him, to invite him inside.

There was a rhythm to the kiss, like a waltz. It was both dizzyingly exciting and terrifyingly intimate. He laid her bare with it and, all the while, he'd done nothing more than touch his lips to hers and place his hand on her cheek. It begged the very dangerous question, what else could he do?

After a moment, he stepped back from her, breaking the kiss and dropping his hand from her face, only to reach for her hand and hold it firmly in his. It was as if he, too, were reluctant to cease contact.

"I will marry you, Viscount Seaburn," she said, struggling to make her voice sound like she had not been at all affected by his kiss. "But I have conditions of my own. Though we've been out here far too long already. We will have to discuss them tomorrow."

He smiled at her. "We will marry by special license, or would you prefer to have the banns posted?"

"By special license, I think… assuming I decide to go through with it and not cry off. It's easier to explain why my side of the church would be empty then."

"Another kiss to seal the bargain?"

"No," she said. "And for the record, I'm only agreeing because I want to burn this rag I'm wearing and never again look at a piece of olive silk as long as I live."

She didn't exactly sail past him into the drawing room, given her limp and dependence on the walking stick, but she did so with as much dignity as she could muster.

VAL WATCHED HER go, and he only just managed to keep himself from dragging her back. He'd thought kissing her, seducing her into agreement would simply save them both time. But as he stood there on the terrace, his body achingly hard and utterly seduced by the sweetest and clearly most virginal kiss in history, it was obvious to him that Miss Lillian Burkhart had once more turned the tables on him. One kiss, from an untutored girl, and he was as breathless and dizzy as if he were the damned virgin.

"Bloody, blasted, everlasting hell," he said. "So much for simplifying matters."

Wincing as he adjusted himself behind the fall of his breeches, he returned to the dining room in her wake and faced down his grandmother and cousin. If ever anything could wither arousal, it would be those two.

"I am happy to inform you," Miss Burkhart said, "that I have accepted his lordship's proposal. We will be married as soon as a license can be obtained."

Both Elsworth and Val's grandmother looked at her as if she had grown two heads. "And I could not be happier," he said, falling in to stand beside her. "I know you both wish us well. Don't you?"

Miss Burkhart had a surprisingly pointy elbow for such a curvaceous woman. He could attest to it without any question as said pointy elbow had just assaulted his ribs. Trying not to wince openly lest it result in someone questioning their status as a happily betrothed couple, he simply grinned through the pain.

"Of course, Cousin. What could possibly go wrong?" Elsworth asked. "You're marrying the bastard daughter of a lord's younger son and whose mother I can only assume was a woman of ill repute. Not to mention your betrothed also happens to be in the employ of our grandmother. That will create no scandal, at all. Why, the *ton*, known as they are for their forgiving nature and the warm welcome they provide to one and all whatever the nature of their birth, will no doubt greet her with open arms... perhaps even a parade."

Val leveled a hard, cold stare at his cousin. "Speak of my future wife in such a disparaging manner again and, cousin or not, they'll be the last words you ever utter."

"You're only doing this to embarrass us! This," Elsworth sneered, waving a hand in Lillian Burkhart's direction, "is the equivalent of a childish tantrum!"

"You'd bloody well know about tantrums, wouldn't you, Elsworth?" Val challenged. "You've done nothing but moan and whine about your fate as the spare rather than the heir since we were boys! You forget yourself, Cousin!"

The dowager duchess rose and placed her hand on Val's arm. Turning slightly, she said, "Hush, Elsworth. You've said quite enough already. Both of you have. I'll not have this family, meager as it is, torn apart by the posturing of angry young men who've had too much wine and brandy." Angling her head slightly, the dowager duchess fixed her keen gaze on the woman who had been her companion. "Miss Burkhart, please allow me to welcome you to our family."

Val looked at his grandmother and, suddenly, he saw all of it. The lot of it began to fall into place. Not their meeting, of course. That, he knew, had been chance. But his summons to the family home, his grandmother's insistence on his taking a bride, and her hiring a companion who was beyond doubt one of the most beautiful women he'd ever seen and then trying to hide her beauty in hideous cast-off clothing that would only serve to draw the eyes to her instead of making her disappear. She'd done it all with one goal in mind. That vicious old bird had intended from the outset for him to wed her companion. Indeed, had they not met by accident, she would no doubt have put Lillian Burkhart in his path in some utterly ridiculous manner. All her posturing that morning about not having that kind of household and avoiding her companion at all costs had been naught but manipulation and misdirection. And he'd taken the bait. He'd fallen right in line with what had been her plan all along. It was quite laughable actually.

As their eyes met, it was obvious from her victorious expression that his grandmother knew he'd sussed her out. She raised her glass and offered him a triumphant smile. But then he caught a glimpse of Lillian Burkhart's exquisite profile. Managed or not, he couldn't be angry about it.

As he reached for his own glass, he met his grandmother's gaze. "You're rather proud of yourself, aren't you?"

She simply smiled. "I will be. Once I see you actually wed and know that you haven't managed to wriggle out of it, I'll be utterly thrilled. Socially, of course, there could be better connections. But she's intelligent, beautiful, and will not tolerate any nonsense from you. There are more important things than one's pedigree, after all. Don't you think?"

"I'm beginning to think you enjoy thumbing your nose at society more than I do," Val replied.

"I'm old enough not to have to suffer their nonsense for too much longer," she replied. "Why shouldn't I see them all set on their ears before I shuffle off this mortal coil?"

Why indeed? Val looked across the table at his betrothed. However it had happened, he wouldn't be sorry for it. At least not in the short term. The long term remained to be seen.

Chapter Six

A S A BETROTHED couple, it was perfectly acceptable for them to drive in the park together. To that end, Val had sent a note to Miss Burkhart the morning after their grand announcement and when she replied via the same scullery maid turned messenger, he'd arranged to have the phaeton brought around. As she made her way down the stairs, he noted she leaned less heavily on the walking stick.

"I see you're starting to mend. Good morning... Lillian," he said. He waited for her to take umbrage at his use of her given name, but she was a practical girl. Rather than give in to temper or spite, she simply arched one eyebrow at his taking such a liberty.

"Good morning, Valentine," she answered in a mirroring tone.

"Oh, good lord, no. Not that. Don't ever call me that. I hear it enough from my grandmother. You may call me Somers, Seaburn, Val... you may call me the very devil, but I beg you, do not call me Valentine," he said as the butler opened the door for them and they stepped out toward the waiting vehicle.

"Very well. If we're confessing our hatred of our given names, I detest Lillian. My half-sister and my friends call me Lilly," she said.

"Lilly. It suits you," he said.

"Surely you don't mean to wax poetic and compare me to what I've always found to be a rather smelly flower," she demanded, her voice ringing with disdain.

He smirked in response, amused by her forthcoming nature and her wit, not to mention her truly horrified tone at the prospect of such a ridiculous ode to her beauty. "Hardly. I comment only on the simplicity and straightforward nature of the name itself and not the flora that inspired it."

"Thank goodness for that. I'm perfectly willing to go through with this—"

"Thank you for making the prospect of marriage to me sound comparable to an unpleasant chore," he said, helping her up into the phaeton. "I can't tell you how much I appreciate your efforts to keep my vanity in check."

Her lips pursed in disapproval. "I said nothing of the sort. But you must admit, we are embarking on a rather impetuous scheme... and I intend to see it through. But I'd prefer, at least when it is only the two of us, not to pretend that this is anything more than what it is."

"And what is that precisely?" Val posed the question as he climbed up and took his seat beside her, looping the reins securely in his hand.

"You are marrying me as a means to an end and, for better or worse, I am marrying you for the same reason."

"To escape your servitude to my dragon of a grandmother?"

"No," she said, shaking her head. "Well, not entirely, at any rate. When I was coming home yesterday and had my unfortunate accident in the park—"

"You mean that bit where you recklessly climbed a tree and nearly broke your neck?" He felt it was an important distinction.

Her lips pursed again, a clear indication of her degree of annoyance with him. "Fine. Yes. That. At any rate, as I told you, I had been returning from a meeting with a solicitor. Despite how far my mother had fallen, she came from a family that had both wealth and connections. With the marriage of Willa to Lord Deveril, one of my mother's relatives—her aunt—discovered my general direction and made inquiries at the Darrow School as to where I might be found. The woman is on her deathbed. Indeed, the solicitor said that even if I were to set out now to meet her, I would likely not reach her in time. But she's arranged a bequest for me that can only be released if I marry. And I know you don't understand, having never been without wealth or family in your life, but it's very important to me that such a bequest be claimed. It's the only connection I have to family on my mother's side. In truth, it's the only evidence that they cared for her and, thusly, me at all."

That effectively set him on his heels. "I am sorry for what you have gone through. You must miss your mother terribly."

She drew back, somewhat stunned by his words of sympathy. "You are mistaken, my lord. I wasn't dishonest when I told you about my upbringing, but I may have smoothed out the rougher bits. I do not miss my mother. I'd have to remember her to miss her, I think. She left me on my father's doorstep and then walked into the Thames with enough stones in her pockets that there was no hope of rescue," she said matter of factly. "And I only know this because my father took great pleasure in telling me the tale and informing me that they'd have all been better off if she'd carried me with her."

"Christ above," he whispered. "And I thought dealing with Elsworth and my grandmother was bad! Your father needs a good—well, suffice to say, something a bit more bloodthirsty than just a talking to!"

Lilly smiled tightly at that. "I don't like talking about him. I prefer to forget that he exists, in all honesty. Back to my mother. Alas, she did not see fit to end my existence with hers. Instead, she abandoned me at my father's family residence here in London. His mother discovered my existence and despite the circumstances of my birth and her desire to have naught to do with me, she did insist that he at least provide for me. So I was sent to a farming family on one of his estates and eventually to the school where I met my half-sister and Effie Darrow discovered us both."

They'd made the turn down Park Lane and were heading toward

the park's entrance. His mind was reeling with what she had revealed, not just about her upbringing, but also about herself. She was pretty enough, and might have looked delicate and fragile. But inside, Lilly Burkhart was forged of steel. He admired her greatly for it, and also felt somewhat ill at ease in her presence because of it. Knowing her character in that way made his own failings even more apparent to him. So he focused on something else. "You speak very dispassionately about what must surely have been a painful past."

"Oh, it was quite painful... when I was younger. I do not deny that at all. But I see no point crying about it all now. I shed my tears and moved on. I refuse to be a victim either of circumstances or people, my lord... Val," she said. "And I say all this to let you know, that I will not be some quiet, meek society wife. And if that is what you expect of me, perhaps we should revisit our agreement."

The deeper they went into the park, the more slowly they had to travel. After all, a drive in the park wasn't actually about getting anywhere. It was about letting people see you. Val cast a sidelong glance at her. "And I presume you tell me all of this in order to set the stage for the conditions you wish to place on our arrangement?"

"Am I so very obvious?"

He laughed. "Like I've been beaten over the head with a club by it. Subterfuge is not your strong suit, Lilly."

"But it is yours, isn't it? I mean, essentially you did confess to me last night that you're a... well, for lack of a better word, a spy."

Val cleared his throat. "I wouldn't call it that."

"What would you call it then?"

"I would say that if in my daily endeavors, information that poses a risk to our nation is discovered, I alert the people who can deal with that information appropriately."

Her eyebrows shot upward and her lips curved in amusement. "You do know that is precisely what a spy does, don't you?"

Wanting desperately to change the subject to anything else, Val demanded, "Name your conditions, my lovely betrothed. But when you are done, I will be levying conditions of my own."

She relented. "Very well. Then the bequest from my great-aunt is mine and mine alone. Regardless of what occurs between us and even if you decided you cannot bear the sight of me after a suitable amount of time, that small sum is mine to live on for the rest of my days."

"Done," he said. Whatever became of their relationship, should they even manage to develop something akin to one, she would not be subsisting in penury. He'd certainly be able to afford to support her in the style of her choosing. "Is that all or is there more?"

She looked away for a moment. "I'm not very good with rules. You've seen the evidence of it yourself. You will undoubtedly, over time, grow quite frustrated with me for that reason. When that occurs, we will simply lead our separate lives. You may do as you please and so shall I."

A dozen emotions flitted through him. Outrage, jealousy, indignation. Those were the ones closest to the surface, however. There might have been a bit of hurt pride and wounded vanity, as well. He hadn't even taken her to bed yet and she was already mapping out a future where other men would. "I should say you are not very good at rules at all, Miss Burkhart. It's quite brazen of you sit here in this phaeton, the morning after we are betrothed, and inform me that you intend to have lovers."

"I never!" she gasped in obvious outrage. "Doing as we please does not include that!"

"Then what the bloody hell does it include?" he demanded. "When husbands and wives lead separate lives, Lilly, they don't tend to involve celibacy!"

TO SAY THAT her future husband's reaction and interpretation were shocking was to put it mildly. Even if such a thing were to enter her mind, she would not broach the subject so callously. "It means that if you wish to take... to do... to have... that is to say that if and when we part ways and you elect to have relationships outside of marriage, I certainly understand and would not expect you to... not do that." She paused then, attempting to regain her composure. To even utter such things left her terribly embarrassed and created a dull ache in the vicinity of her heart that she would not even deign to acknowledge. After all, they didn't know one another well enough for her heart to be engaged in any way that could result in significant damage. It was just that the idea of him taking a mistress, or heaven help her, for him to take *mistresses*, was humiliating. The very idea of it had her terribly flustered and strangely disappointed.

Drawing in a deep breath, she continued, "For myself, should we part ways, I intend to live a quiet life, away from society, with my books and possibly a cat or a dog to keep me company. I want to read and write and paint if I take a notion. But I just don't want to be told what to do all the time. Even when it's something I know I ought to do and normally would want to do, the moment someone tells me I must do it, I immediately want to do anything and everything else! Do you not understand what it's like to have your every thought and action dictated by others?"

He sighed heavily and eased the phaeton off the path. A boy, dressed in stained and rumpled clothing ran forward to take the reins. Lilly watched as he gave the boy a coin and promised another if the horses were still there when they returned.

"Let me help you down. We need to discuss this and I'd prefer not to do so in front of the very interested gossips," he said and reached up to help her down. "Given that you have a rather animated way of expressing yourself, it is not in our best interest to be observed."

Lilly braced herself for the familiar rush that always seemed to accompany his touch. When his hands closed about her waist, deftly lifting her from the coach and settling her in front of him, she had to fight the urge to lean against him. Even then, when he leaned past her to retrieve her walking stick, she felt the firmness of his chest and shoulders beneath his coat. Contrary to so many men of the day, his impressive physique had nothing to do with the artfully placed padding courtesy of a skilled tailor.

With her walking stick in hand and him far enough from her that she could actually breathe, Lilly felt marginally more herself as they set off down one of many graveled paths.

"Your ankle isn't paining you too terribly?"

"No," she answered. "A bit of exercise will be good for it, I think. Mary, the maid, helped me to wrap it in a bandage before we left this morning for a bit of extra comfort."

"Good," he said, and led the way down a small path that was heavily canopied by the twisting branches of trees that lined it. "I jumped to a rather disheartening conclusion back there and I must apologize for that. Society marriages and my acquaintance with them have left me somewhat jaded, I suppose. I should never have assumed you meant anything of the sort."

"Oh," she said. "Well, perhaps I could have worded things differently. I didn't realize that particular turn of phrase would have such significance. I truly only meant that if we tire of one another's company or grow to dislike one another's habits so very much that we can live apart. But I can't imagine that I would want do anything so improper as to... well, have relations outside of marriage."

He smiled at that. "That is a testament only to your lack of experience. Passion, Lilly, is a bit of Pandora's box. Once you've experienced it, it becomes a very difficult thing to live without. I'm hoping that is something that neither of us will have to think about."

Recalling the kiss they'd shared the night before, it was easy to see that he was correct on that score. Even now, just being in his presence, she'd lost count of the number of times she'd wondered idly if he would steal another kiss during their outing. Though stealing was a bit of a misnomer, since she'd go quite willingly into his arms. But kisses aside, he was speaking of something far more permanent and her trust of any man only went so far. She eyed him cautiously. "Do you really think that we, standing here as virtual strangers, can make any long-range plans for what our future together will hold?"

They strolled amicably along the path, weaving in and out of sight of others who were enjoying the fine weather and the beauty of the park. "I think we can, so long as we agree to be forthcoming with one another about our expectations."

"Very well. What is it that you expect?" Lilly asked.

"I want to address your concerns, Lilly. I don't perceive my role as a husband to be that of dictator. The blame can be laid squarely at my grandmother's door, I suppose, but I've never been permitted the conceit that so many men have of thinking women were inferior to me... not in intelligence, not in ability and not in will and determination. If such a thought had even entered my mind, my grandmother would likely have beaten it out of me. I don't expect to tell you what to do and how to do it every day of your life, henceforth. I had assumed we would have a certain degree of respect for one another that would preclude such behaviors."

"And you think my earlier assumption was disrespectful to you?" she asked. That had not at all been her intent. She didn't wish to insult him or to make him question the decision they'd made, even if it had been rash and foolish on both their parts.

"I think it's an indication that we know very little about one another. And if it were possible, perhaps we could have a long engagement and rectify that. But my grandmother has issued an ultimatum and I have no option but to meet it. So we will marry and then we will get to know one another after the fact and hope that we have both not made a terrible error in judgment," he replied. "I don't foresee that I will ever develop such a dislike of you or such a level of exasperation with you that leading separate lives would seem like the best course of action to me."

"I see," Lilly said, and tried not to smile at that. It wasn't the most flowery of compliments to be sure, but it rang with sincerity because of that. "I can be very tiresome, my lord."

"As can I. No doubt we will argue and sometimes disagree on things, but that's rather the point of being married, isn't it? To have someone in your life who challenges you, who forces you to be better than you are because the thought of disappointing them is completely abhorrent to you. There are other matters that must be addressed, but due to their delicate nature, we'll leave that for last. Why don't you tell me what your expectations are?" he prompted.

The path they'd followed went deeper into the dense growth of trees. The limbs twisted and tangled overhead, forming a sort of tunnel that shielded them from everything else. In that space, surrounded by dense foliage bedecked in flame-colored leaves that had not yet given over to the bare limbs of winter, it was as if they were all alone in a city of people numbering into the hundreds of thousands, if not more.

"They are fairly minimal," Lilly answered. "To be perfectly truthful, other than the couple I worked for prior to taking the position with your grandmother, I've never known a married couple well enough to judge their state of accord. Do not ever strike me. If our relationship sours and you do wish to take lovers, do so discreetly enough that I will not be humiliated by it, and grant me enough independence that I might not feel inclined to rebellion."

He frowned. "That is a very short list."

"It is. But to me, those are the only things I would ever deem unforgivable," she said. "Anything else, I imagine we can work out if we've a mind to try."

"So we can," he agreed.

"Well, I've presented my conditions and my expectations. But we've only covered your expectations," Lilly said. "I would think you would have conditions of your own on our arrangement, Val?"

He cast a sidelong glance in her direction, one that was rather speculative and perhaps a bit wicked. It left her tingling in its wake, as he said, "You said you wouldn't be a meek society wife. Well, I don't intend to be a boorish society husband. I also have no intention of being the polite sort who will spare you the duties of the marriage bed. And I hope very much not to be the sort of husband that would make such duties seem onerous. I need an heir, Lilly, and that requires the consummation of our union... likely more than once."

That was a much more forthright and direct answer than she'd expected on what should have been a terribly delicate matter. It left her feeling flustered but also very curious. "Oh, well... that is to say, I really have no notion how to respond to that."

He smiled. "No, I don't suppose you do. But I imagine we have a few days before we stand before whatever parson is unlucky enough to be given the duty of seeing us wed. I think perhaps we should use that time wisely and you may acquaint yourself with some of the lesser intimacies of marriage."

That sounded quite shocking and also impossibly tempting. "What did you have in mind?"

"Only that you let me kiss you again... every day. Just as I did last night," he said.

Her heart began to beat faster. "That's all? Just a kiss?" As if that were such a small and inconsequential thing! It had been one kiss from him that had robbed her of the rejection and set down she'd intended to blast him with on the previous evening. If not for that kiss, she'd still be just a companion and he'd still be hunting for a bride.

"Until you want more than a kiss." There was a wealth of promise in that statement. He looked at her as if he could see straight through to the heart of her and knew, even in that moment, just as she did, that a kiss would never be enough.

Her breath caught and she felt the heat building inside her. "You are very certain of yourself."

"I know what I felt when I kissed you, Lilly," he said, and stepped forward.

Almost against her will, Lillian backed away, but not out of fear of him. She feared herself and the response she had to him much more. He was the embodiment of temptation, of every wicked and half-formed fantasy she'd ever had. When the girls at her school had whispered in the night about kisses and passionate embraces as they poured over the more lurid passages of contraband gothic novels, the man who'd lingered in her mind then had been faceless and unknown. No more. Valentine Somers had conquered those dreams, stamping that faceless memory out and putting himself in place there forever more.

He continued, "And I know what you felt, as well. My belief is a simple one... passion can exist without love, but love cannot exist without passion. If we deny that aspect of our relationship, we deny ourselves the opportunity to have so much more than simply an arrangement."

She only stopped because her back was against a tree and there was nowhere left to go. Still, he advanced, not stopping until they stood so close that her breasts were crushed against the hard wall of his chest and she could feel his thighs against hers even through the layers of their clothing. "This is quite improper."

"You don't like rules," he reminded her.

"I don't have a problem with every rule," she hedged.

Those were the last words that escaped her before his lips descended on hers once more. Where the kiss the night before had been a thing of gentleness, even as it had overwhelmed her with sensation, this was a different thing altogether. It was hard, his lips moving over hers forcefully, demanding entrance which she granted. She was helpless to do anything else. Her own need to know where it could lead drove her. He didn't hurt her, but he gave no quarter. There was no concession to her innocence or inexperience. He kissed her as if she knew precisely where it would take them. It felt hungry, as if he would devour her right there on the spot. And heaven help her, she wanted him to.

Her arms closed about him without conscious thought, holding him close and clinging to him for purchase all at once. Surely, weak as her knees had become, she could not support her own weight. And he drew closer still, pressing her fully against the tree, mindless of the rough bark as he nipped at her lips with his teeth. Unable to do anything else, she returned every stroke of his tongue, every scrape of his teeth upon her lips. And then he was pulling himself away from her, his lips coasting along her jaw and down the column of her neck. It was as if every part of her had come roaring to life. Her heart pounded and her breath quickened, as if there simply wasn't enough air to be had. She could feel the blood rushing in her veins and she could feel him. Everywhere. The weight and press of him, the rough texture of his whiskers on her skin, the heat of his mouth, all of it simply consumed her.

A sound escaped her, half-sob and half-plea. She knew not which, nor did she care. But as abruptly as their kiss had begun, he tore himself away from her. He strode several paces away, his breathing heavy and ragged as was her own. Then she heard it. The slight snap of twigs. Someone was near. *Someone had seen them.*

He glanced back at her over his shoulder, his gaze holding an apology that she did not want. Then the tree, only inches above her head, seemed to explode. A shower of bark and wood chips rained down on her, some of them stinging her flesh.

Then she felt Val's arms around her, taking her to the ground, his body covering hers.

Touching one hand to her face, it came away wet with blood. "What happened? What was that?" she asked, staring at the red stains on her fingertips in horror.

His expression quizzical, he said, "Someone tried to shoot you. Tell me, Lillian Burkhart, how many enemies have you amassed in your short life?"

"There's no one," she said.

Suddenly grim, he said, "That's what I was afraid you would say. You might not have any enemies, but I have them by the score. And it seems I've given them a new target."

Chapter Seven

H E'D NEVER BEEN more furious in his life. Having such an intimate moment in such a public place had been undeniably foolish. It had been bad enough when he simply thought someone had spied on them. But afterward, with Lilly lying on the ground, blood streaking the porcelain perfection of her cheek, Val could admit that he'd been afraid. It was an emotion he'd experienced very infrequently in his life, and it was one that he detested. The urge to run after the person who'd tried to hurt her had warred with his need to keep her close, to be certain of her safety. In the end, that had won out.

They'd left the park quickly and returned to the townhouse where a physician had been summoned. He'd taken one look at her, proclaimed her healthy enough, advised them to keep the wounds clean and left with the promise of a hefty bill to be sent.

"You need a better physician," Val snapped at this grandmother.

"He's a perfectly capable physician, and you, Valentine, are being unreasonable," the dowager duchess replied sourly. "She's not the only woman to ever be injured. Good heavens. One would think this was a love match rather than a blatant attempt to goad your old grandmother into an early grave!"

Val halted his pacing and glared at her. "Don't pretend with me. You're as pleased as punch about all of this because you led me right into it. It's just like playing chess with you when I was a boy!"

She smiled then. "Prove it."

"I don't have to prove it. I bloody well know," he snapped.

"Do not curse in my presence. I will not have it, Valentine," she admonished.

"Someone shot at her!"

"Someone fired a shot that happened to go wild and in her general direction!" His grandmother waved her hand dismissively. "Do not seek plots where plots do not exist!"

"It missed her by mere inches," Val said. "She could easily have died." The very thought of it made his blood run cold. It also tweaked his conscience. Had he not been so distracted by his own carnal desires, no one would have gotten close enough to them to take such a shot at her.

"And we are all eternally grateful that she did not. And if—mind you that is a very great if—someone did try to harm her intentionally, there is no greater protection any woman can have than that of her husband's name and title. The sooner you are married, the safer she will be. A companion might be killed without consequence, as we all sadly know, but a viscountess carries a far steeper penalty."

Val considered it for only a moment but, ultimately, he knew she was right. "Fine. In the meantime, keep Elsworth away from her."

His grandmother rolled her eyes. "Good heavens. You are in a terrible way if you're jealous of your cousin! Why, she practically towers over him. Not so say she's a long meg. Lovely girl, but Elsworth is... well, he's Elsworth."

Val stopped. "I'm not jealous, Grandmama. But the simple fact is that you were going to leave all your wealth to Elsworth if I failed to marry. Within twenty-four hours of being betrothed to me, Miss Burkhart is nearly shot and killed in the park. I asked her who her enemies were and she said no one. But we both know that isn't true now, don't we? There is only person who will benefit from her death and he's under this very roof." With that, Valentine left. He didn't bother with his horse or a hack. His destination was only a few streets over. There was one man who could help him—Highcliff.

By the time he reached his friend and mentor's residence, his temper had cooled enough that he could at least speak civilly. When the butler answered the door and proceeded to tell him that Highcliff was indisposed, Val simply pushed past the man rather than punching him in the nose. It was proof that he was in control of his rage.

"Study or solarium?"

"Study, my lord," the butler said, with a heavy and much put upon sigh.

Val knew the way. Marching down the hall, he rapped sharply on the door and let himself in.

Highcliff was seated at his desk, dressed only in his shirt and breeches. His long hair was disheveled and there was a nearly empty bottle of brandy at his elbow.

"Is that left over from last night or are you getting an early start?"

"A late finish," Highcliff answered. "Did I miss the part where my butler announced you? No. No, I did not. I did miss the part where I told him I was willing to receive callers this morning, however."

"I need your help," Val said.

"You and everyone else," Highcliff retorted. He eyed the brandy speculatively for a moment, then without bothering with a glass, tipped it to his lips. When he lowered it to dangle from his fingertips, with a significantly decreased volume of liquid within, he added, "I'm not sharing. You're not a guest, so I don't have to."

"Then what the hell am I?" Val demanded.

"At the moment? An interloper and a bloody nuisance. What do you want?"

Val seated himself in the chair opposite the desk, ignoring his cantankerous friend's indignant expression. "I need a special license."

"For what?"

"To get married."

Highcliff set the bottle down with a thud. "Not this again. Bloody hell. You and Deveril are about to be the damned death of me. Can't you just post the banns and get married the way normal people do? All this wedding business is making my head ache."

"I would be happy to, except that someone tried to shoot my betrothed this morning... and I think it was Elsworth," Val explained. "I don't have time to wait for the banns."

That certainly got his attention. No longer bleary eyed and appearing for all the world to be a dissipated rogue, Highcliff sat up straight. "Why?"

"Grandmother's ultimatum. Marry by year's end, just over two months from now, or be written out of her will. All the wealth would go to Elsworth. I would get only the entailed properties which I'd never be able to support and would wind up a pauper."

"And he knew this was coming... he banked on your rebellious nature, didn't he?" Highcliff said. "He's never understood that you and your grandmother butt heads because you enjoy it and that it's the way the two of you show affection to one another. He thinks your little spats are legitimate."

It made as much sense as anything else. "Something like that. But I think he may be in over his head and desperate. He needs the money, more so now than he ever has."

Highcliff cocked his head to one side, drummed his fingers on the desk, and said, "Go on. I'm listening."

"He's been looking for investments for months now, talking primarily to people who will take him on credit of his expectations. So he's clearly had an inkling for some time that this ultimatum was coming," Val explained. "I suspect he's bribed my grandmother's man of affairs to give him intelligence on that score. And then I discovered, while I was at the tables, that he's been in deep with some individuals who have been supplying arms to that small fraction of Frenchmen who think to pick up where Bonaparte left off—those that are already being watched by agents of the Crown."

"And where are these shipments of arms coming from… or where were they intended to go?" Highcliff asked.

"And with one question, you have cut straight through to the heart of the matter," Val said on a heavy sigh. "All of those shipments that have been lost en route to our soldiers in India… they have been diverted by these individuals directly into the hands of our would-be enemies in France."

Highcliff let out a curse. "Does he know what they're about? I've no great admiration for Elsworth, but this seems more brazen than something he would typically do."

"I think he does now. I do not believe he went into it knowingly. Regardless, he can't just walk away from them. The only way to extricate him now is to cut off his funding… by getting married and meeting my grandmother's demands."

"Deveril's niece…" Highcliff paused as if deep in thought. "She was fathered by a man by the name of Alaric Munro… also known as Alaric West. Is there a connection?"

Val sucked in a breath. "Yes. There is. One of the munitions factories that is frequently having shipments diverted through attacks by pirates or other brigands is owned by his stepfather. As you are aware, no doubt."

"I was aware, but I did wish to confirm. Have we identified all of the players yet?"

"No. There are still a few shadowy figures, likely silent partners and perhaps even our peers who are invested in these companies or who are awarding government contracts to these companies when time and again they have failed to fulfill them," Val answered. "You know as well as I do that this goes far beyond West and far beyond Elsworth."

"I do know that. And you're right. We can't afford to let all of this blow up in our faces until we've managed to out every last one of the villains." Highcliff steepled his hands. "But there are other matters to consider in this moment. If it comes out, you'll be ruined. And despite all you've done, Whitehall will wash its hands of you. They will not tolerate an operative with ties to a traitor. You know that, don't you?"

"I'm nearly done with it all anyway. I don't know how much longer I can do what I do, Highcliff. Not if I want any shred of my soul left," Val admitted.

The other man nodded. "You've certainly done your part and then some. I do hate to lose you, though. Gambling and women are the best ways to get information out of anyone and no one plays cards like you. Fine. I'll get your license for you. And you get Elsworth in check. I don't want it to go down like this. He might be the nephew of a duke, but if it's treason, that won't keep him from Tyburn and it certainly will not keep society from turning on you like a pack of jackals."

"If another attempt on Lilly's life occurs, Tyburn will be the least of his worries."

Highcliff drummed his fingers on the desk thoughtfully. "It may not be your cousin. You, my friend, have a very divisive effect on society. Those who have been saved from disgrace by your skill versus those who have been ruined by it have very different viewpoints of you. Have you considered that your decision to take her as your bride might be putting this young woman in terrible danger from sources outside your family?"

"I have," Val admitted. "But not even the best gossips in London move that quickly. It was only announced at dinner last night."

Highcliff nodded sagely. "That does seem fast, but rumors have spread faster. Don't be so focused on Elsworth that you miss other very real threats."

"I won't. If something happens to her because of me—" Val broke off abruptly, unable to complete the thought.

"May God or the devil himself preserve me from the fate you and

Deveril have succumbed to," Highcliff replied with a dramatic roll of his bloodshot eyes.

"And what fate is that?" Val demanded.

Highcliff laughed. "If you don't know yet, I'm not going to bloody tell you. When is this wedding to take place? For your sake, I hope it's soon."

"As soon as the license can be obtained. It might take some doing. The archbishop holds a grudge."

Highcliff scrubbed his hands over his face. "Let me guess... you were the one who divested Selby of his ill-gotten gains?"

"I was," Val admitted, recalling the game with the archbishop's nephew. "I offered to let him out of the debt, but he insisted on paying. He should never have been at that table. Or should have folded several hands earlier and walked away—as I advised him to do, I might add. Can you sway the archbishop to grant me this favor?"

"It can be done, but you'll owe me a considerable amount of brandy when it's all said and done," Highcliff replied. "You'll need witnesses."

Val sighed. The last thing he needed was to invite his grandmother and have her show up with Elsworth in tow. The less his cousin knew of his plans the safer Lilly would be. "You can do it. Can't you?"

"I suppose. And the bride, whoever she may be, is there someone she would wish to be in attendance?"

Val scrubbed a hand over his face. "Her name is Lillian Burkhart."

Highcliff laughed again. "You do realize that you and Deveril will now be related by marriage? You're marrying the half-sister of his new bride."

"I'm aware," Val answered. "They are in the country, are they not?"

"Yes, and too far away to return in a timely enough fashion for your hasty nuptials, no doubt... but I imagine that your lovely bride-to-be would be pleased to have Miss Euphemia Darrow present as her witness, would she not? In lieu of the Honorable Mrs. Wilhelmina Ashton nee Marks, Lady Deveril, I doubt there is anyone else she would wish to invite."

There was something in the way Highcliff said the name of Lillian's former headmistress and friend, a reverence that made him think they were more than simply acquaintances. "You know her then? Miss Darrow?"

Highcliff shrugged, but there was something in his expression that hinted it was a sore subject. "I know everyone. It's why I'm an excellent spy... that and the entire world thinks my only interest is waistcoats that could blind a man at twenty paces and any woman with a reasonably pert bosom. I'll get the license and I'll be certain that Miss Darrow is present at the church. St. Paul's at nine o'clock day after tomorrow. I'll call in a favor. Now, for God's sake, go get the girl a ring and order her a posy. That's what women want, isn't it?"

Val noted the tension in his friend as he spoke of Miss Darrow. "Not all women. Don't fall into the trap of thinking you can predict one by the actions of another. Lilly is rather unlike any woman I've ever known. And I daresay that your Miss Darrow is, as well."

"She's not my Miss Darrow. She's not my anything. I'm not for the likes of her," Highcliff replied. "And she certainly is not for the likes of me. Go. You've interrupted my day long enough and added more tasks to an already exhaustive list."

"Thank you for your help," Val said. "You're a good friend, Highcliff. And a better ally than I have deserved." He didn't wait for a response, just showed himself out. As he left, he couldn't help but wonder what darkness it was that haunted the man he called his friend, because he'd seen a glimpse of it in there and it seemed to be eating the other man alive.

LILLY HAD BEEN moved from her small chamber to one much more in line with her current standing as the betrothed of the heir apparent. As she lay there, bored out of her mind, her hands stroked the silk and velvet counterpane absently. Above her head, cherubs danced on fat, fluffy clouds in the painted tester of the luxurious bed that was roughly the same size as the room she'd previously inhabited.

Neither her face nor her ankle was especially painful, and all she wanted was something to do, but everyone kept insisting that she had to rest. She'd been through so much, they all said. She would throw her very boring book at the next person who uttered those words. They expected, because she was suddenly thrust into the role of being a lady, that she would become some delicate and fragile thing that needed to be coddled and cared for. Well, that wasn't her, it had never been her and it would never be her! The sooner they all realized it the better off the lot of them would be.

Struggling to get out of the bed, she realized that the walking stick had been moved all the way across the room by the less than helpful doctor. When she'd tumbled to the ground that morning, or rather been tumbled to it by the quick thinking and quicker actions of her betrothed, her ankle had begun to ache again. Still, better a sore ankle than dead.

Half-limping, half-hobbling toward the walking stick, Lilly had almost reached it when the door opened. She glanced up and found the same maid who'd tended her previously.

"You're not supposed to be up, Miss!" Mary cried. "What on earth are you about?"

"I'm bored out of my mind. I thought I'd go downstairs and spend some time with her grace," Lilly replied.

"What? By choice?" the maid asked in horror. Realizing what she'd said, the girl clapped her hand over her mouth. "Oh, I didn't mean it like that. Please don't tell no one I said it. I'll be sacked for sure!"

"Mary, I'm not going to let you be sacked," Lilly said. "But in very short order, I am likely to require a lady's maid. Have you ever considered moving up into such a position?"

The girl's eyes widened. "I'd love to, Miss, but I've no talent for dressing hair. You'd be terribly disappointed with me, I'm sure."

"I can dress my own hair. I can dress myself, too. But they'll draw the line at letting me see to my own clothes," Lilly said. "I'm being perfectly honest when I say this, Mary. I think there are more things I'll not be permitted to do as a lady than when I was simply a governess or companion. I detest rules."

"And is that why you're out of bed, Miss? Cause someone said you couldn't be?" the maid asked knowingly.

Well, she'd been effectively called out on that score. No point in denying it. "More or less. It's rather that they've insisted I must be so overset by what happened that I need to be cosseted like a fretful infant," Lilly seethed. "That's not who I am. And I won't let them make me into that sort either."

"Beg pardon, Miss, but what did happen? You came back from the park with blood on your face and no one knows—I'd never speak ill of his lordship, but he is known to have a fierce temper! The way he and that cousin of his go on... they've come to blows more than once."

Realization dawned on Lillian then. She hadn't been asked to stay in her room because she needed rest but because Lord Seaburn didn't wish to tip his hand to everyone in the house that they understood the nature of her injuries. The downside to that was that no one else knew the nature of them either and now suspected that he'd assaulted her in some way. Perhaps he even intended for them to think it. She had no notion of what he was up to other than that he'd promised to get to the bottom of what had occurred one way or another. And she was about to spoil what could possibly be intentional subterfuge on his part out of nothing more than petulance. But she wouldn't let the servants or anyone else think him the villain of the piece.

"We had left the phaeton to take a walk and a tree branch fell. It was likely a dead limb or perhaps some sort of blight," Lilly lied. "It only scratched me up a bit because Lord Seaburn was there and quickly shielded me from it."

Mary appeared to be absolutely awestruck at the tall tale. "Oh, Miss! That sounds like it's straight out of one of those novels Sarah reads us at night. Some of them are terrifying and... well, a bit wicked She read us one last week by that Mrs. Radcliff and I've never heard such things."

Thinking of her own very boring book about the flora and fauna of Derbyshire, a wicked and lurid novel sounded like heaven. "I do love a good gothic novel! Do you think Sarah would mind very much if you brought me one of her books for a while? Only to borrow, of course!"

"If she hasn't taken it back to the book lender, I'm sure she won't mind."

Realizing that the servants were likely pooling their money to borrow such books, Lilly felt guilty. Even as a companion, she'd been paid far, far better. "Bring me my reticule, Mary. It's there on the chair."

The maid fetched it and Lilly dug several coins out of it. "That should get you all several books from the lender. Shouldn't it?"

Mary shook her head. "Oh, Miss, I couldn't!"

"I insist, Mary. After all, you'll have to pay for extra days while I read this delightful book, won't you? And if anyone questions you about where the coins came from you simply tell them I gave them to you to provide reading material to the staff. In fact, I'll speak to Lord Seaburn about stocking books in the library for all of you."

"Only Sarah can read, but it'd be nice if she could get us more books."

"And if you want to learn to read, I'll teach you. I was a governess, after all!"

"I'll go fetch the book, Miss," Mary said, an excited grin spreading across her face.

"Mary, what did you come up here for?"

"Oh!" the maid said. "I got so flustered, Miss, I nearly forgot. There's a lady downstairs with all these boxes. Dress boxes. She says his lordship sent her and you're to pick whatever you want. Shall I send her up?"

"Yes, Mary... and you should come up with her. We'll get the book later. If you're going to be my lady's maid, you should certainly be involved in the process of selecting gowns."

The prospect of shopping for something that didn't fit like a sack and make her look like she was at death's door had effectively eliminated her boredom. And Lilly wasn't so blind to her own faults that she couldn't recognize her vanity in wishing to turn the head of her all-too-handsome betrothed. It was a terrible thing to her mind to wonder which one of them was the more attractive person in their match.

Chapter Eight

APPROACHING THE ELEGANT facade of the Georgian manor just off Jermyn Street, Val didn't hesitate as he climbed the steps and knocked on the door. It was his second such stop of the day, asking favors from those to whom it was unwise to be beholden. But the kind of favor he needed now was not one Highcliff could help him with. The majordomo who answered looked more bruiser than butler, but then this was no typical Mayfair townhouse. "Is he in?"

"Is who in, my lord?" the servant demanded.

"You know bloody well who I mean, Stavers. It's urgent that I see him."

"Then you should find him at his club during business hours, my lord," the man replied with just a hint of the streets bubbling up through his cultured tones.

"If I had any other choice, I would. But this is urgent... and it cannot wait."

From deep within the elaborately bedecked bowels of the house, a rich baritone voice with a decided cockney flavor sounded. "Let 'im in, Stavers. I'd rather talk to 'im and be done wiv' it."

The servant stepped aside, his lips pulled into a tight, thin line. It was the most butlerly the man had ever appeared. "Silk purses and sow's ears, Stavers... you may prove us all wrong yet," Val said to the man as he walked past him.

Val followed the sound of the voice to a room laden with books. It wasn't novels or even boring nonfiction. It was ledgers. Rows and rows of them. What they contained was anyone's guess, but there'd likely be enough dirt in any of them to bury half the *ton*.

"Don't be getting any ideas," the dark-haired and rough-looking man behind the desk said. His hair was disheveled. He was bare-chested, wearing a silk banyan open over trousers rumpled from the night before. A heavy growth of whiskers covered a granite jaw and he was already sipping brandy and smoking a cheroot. "Nothing in this room is for the likes o' you. What you want, Seaburn?"

Val didn't mince words, but spoke as bluntly as he knew the man in front of him would. "I need to know if someone has been hired to kill a woman."

The man leaned back in his chair, displaying an impressive phy-sique that could only be honed from hard, physical labor. Val knew that most of it took place on the docks and the warehouses that people of his class would turn their noses up at.

"I don't do that sort o' work," the man said. "You know that."

"It's not an accusation," Val replied. "It's a request for assistance."

The man smirked. "Favors ain't free, m'lord. I do one for you, and you'll owe one back. You sure you're ready for that?"

And that was the crux of it. Being beholden in any way to the Hound of Whitehall wasn't a good place to be, but under the circum-stances, he had little choice. It was unlikely that even if Elsworth were the guilty party, that he'd dirtied his hands himself. "I'm prepared for that. The woman's name is Miss Lillian Burkhart."

"Soiled dove, lady o' the night? No, it's actresses you like, ain't it? Where does this dirty little minx tread the boards at?" the man asked with an insolent grin.

"She is none of those things, but is a companion to my grand-mother and now my betrothed," Val replied. "Respectable enough that neither of us ought to be speaking of her at all. Alas, someone nearly put a pistol ball in her brain this morning and I need to determine who ordered such an attempt on her life."

"Pretty thing, I'd guess," the man said. "Be a shame to see 'er all scarred up."

"Or dead. It would be very much a shame to see her dead," Val replied. "And I very much fear that was their mission."

The man laughed again. "You've gone soft. The biggest shark at my tables, the very one eating up all the lil' fish. And 'ere you are... sunk by a 'oity toity companion."

"She's not hoity toity. In fact, you'd be impressed to know that she is a graduate of the Darrow School. You're familiar with it, aren't you? If I'm not mistaken, you've sent a few girls there yourself." Val knew he wasn't mistaken. It was that reason alone which had prompted him to come to the Hound in the first place. The Hound would feel beholden to Miss Darrow and would not allow one of her pupils, former or current, to come to harm. Crook or no, he was reported to always pay his debts.

"Not my bastards," he said evenly. "Try not to 'ave any of those. But, aye, a few little beggars 'ose fathers couldn't be bothered to act like the 'onorable men they claim to be... they needed a bit o' 'elp and I offered it."

"And are they obligated to you as I will be?" Val asked.

"Don't work like that for them... those too young to bargain wiv' the devil are free from consequence," the man answered. "I'll find out if anyone 'as been paid to take out your pretty miss. And I'll 'andle it. Putting a price on the 'ead o' a pretty girl, specially one of Miss Darrow's, goes against the rules."

"What rules are those exactly?" Val asked.

"My rules," the Hound answered. "Only ones what matter. Now, get out. I'll send word when there's word to be 'ad."

"Thank you."

The Hound laughed then. "You'll not be thanking me when that favor is called in, my lord. You'll be wondering if she were worth it!"

"She is," Val replied. "Whatever the cost." With that, he turned on his heel and left the deceptively posh and respectable home of a man who was literally the self-crowned king of London's underworld. He very much felt as if he'd just sold his soul to the devil. And perhaps he had.

»»»«««

THE HOUND SAT up then, his indolent posture giving way to a bearing that was almost aristocratic. "You can come out now," he said, all traces of cockney gone from his voice.

A woman emerged from behind the ornate chinoiserie screen in the corner. Her brilliant auburn hair was flowing freely down her back and she wore only the thinnest of chemises. As the light from the window touched her, the fabric was rendered completely transparent. To say that the sight was erotic would have been to do her a great injustice. Annabel was, without a doubt, one of the most beautiful women in the world, even if she was also one of the most maddening.

"Why do you do that?" she asked, her full lips pursed in a ridiculously appealing pout.

"What did I do?" he asked, forcing himself to look away from the light-gilded beauty displayed before him. There were accounts to balance and debts to be collected, after all. He didn't get to where he was by shirking his duties, even with so tempting a distraction all but laid bare before him.

"Speak in that horrible cockney accent when you and I both know that your natural way of speaking is as perfectly enunciated and articulate as anyone in society. In fact, I'd daresay it's better than most!" she teased with a slight smile that gave her a very feline appearance.

Cockney was his native tongue, but he'd fought long and hard to shed himself of it. He used it when it served his purposes and set it aside when it did not. Like everything else in his life, it was expendable. "Because it does not suit my needs for Lord Valentine Somers, Viscount Seaburn, to know that I am anything more than a grubby, cockney street rat who made good."

She smiled as she perched on the edge of his desk. He could smell her perfume, a light and pretty scent that he'd gifted her. Then she leaned forward, so close that he had but to turn his head and claim one of the perfectly formed breasts displayed so prettily by the confection whisper-thin silk she wore.

"Why don't you come back to bed, my love? It's so early when we've had such late nights," she whispered suggestively. "And it's so terribly lonely there without you."

"I cannot, Annabel," he said regretfully.

"You know I have to leave soon," she said, suddenly petulant and even childlike in her temper. Agitated, she got up and began to pace the room, working herself up into one of her tantrums. "I have to go back to my wretched husband and that monstrosity of a house in the countryside! But you don't even care! You never cared. You're just like all the others!"

"It's not a house in the countryside, Annabel. It's an elegant if somewhat gothic-inspired manor on the seashore. And I do care, but I have work to do," he said, tallying numbers in his head even as he talked to her of something unrelated. Numbers didn't lie. Numbers always gave him the truth. He didn't love Annabel, but he desired her. In fact, he wanted her as he'd never wanted another woman. She was like a fire in his blood, one that gave him a fair bit of sympathy for the opium eaters and those bedeviled by the ruination of gin. But that wasn't love and it never would be. Love wasn't something that could grow and flourish in his very dark corner of the world, much less in the hardened black recesses of his miserable heart.

She grabbed the account book he'd been working on and flung it across the room. Her rage, erratic to the point that he sometimes wondered if she truly was mad, had flared again and would not be soothed. It was the way of things with her. Volatile, unpredictable, dangerous. But he was beginning to lose patience with it all. Even their passionate bed play and her loveliness could not counteract the difficulty inherent in being with her. He was a man who liked order, and she was a creature of chaos and temper.

"Do not do that again," he warned.

"Why not?" she demanded, baring her teeth at him as if she might actually take a bite.

"Because I'm not your husband," he snapped. "And I'll toss your naked arse right into the street, scandal be damned!"

She shrieked at him, a wild sound that was half-crazed. Then she came at him, hands clenched into claws as her nails raked over his chest, leaving a burning trail of blood in her wake. Abruptly, he shoved her away from him and her screeches turned to sobs as she collapsed, sprawling to the carpet. She laid there and wept like a broken child, as if she were the victim rather than the attacker. Reaching into his desk drawer, he retrieved the red leather box that had been delivered the day before and he tossed it to her where she remained, crumpled by her own grief at his imagined slights. Perhaps the diamond and emerald parure would soothe her clearly over-wrought sensibilities. "That was to be your parting gift. Take it and go. I'll have Stavers send for the carriage."

He didn't look back, but walked out of his study and retreated to his chamber. Temper was a wasted emotion, but she'd managed to stoke his. Pressing his fingertips to the deep gouge on his chest, he drew it away covered with his blood. Men had died for less, but he'd never struck a woman before in his life. Even pushing her away, he hadn't intended for her to fall, only to protect himself from further injury. He regretted that their parting would be so bitter.

Annabel was a beautiful broken doll, he thought, pretty enough sitting on the shelf at a distance. But when you got close enough, you could see the cracks in the porcelain. He'd enjoyed the unpredictability in the beginning. Living in a world where every person he encountered kowtowed to him, it had been a refreshing change. Now, that unpredictability was also the thing about her that tried his patience the most.

"And 'er 'usband is welcome to 'er," he whispered, as he reached for a shirt and pulled it on, heedless of the blood. He needed a brawl, something to get out his anger and get his mind right again. Right and free of the vicious witch whose weeping still echoed through the halls. There was only one place to find such a thing in the middle of the day—Whitechapel. The very place that had spawned him.

Chapter Nine

TEA TIME WITH the dowager duchess was not something that Lilly was especially looking forward to. It wasn't that she felt that her grace would be unfriendly or hostile toward her. In fact, she had the strangest idea that the woman was actually pleased with the rather unorthodox turn of events. Regardless, she was traversing uncharted territory. How precisely did one transition from hired help to future viscountess?

Easing her way down the stairs, she placed her foot carefully on each step lest she turn her ankle again. She was less dependent upon the walking stick but kept it with her as a precaution. Mary had insisted on another foul-smelling poultice and Lilly had submitted to it. Much as she hated to admit it, the concoction worked. Both the pain and swelling had eased tremendously. The last thing she needed was to take a tumble down the stairs or she'd be back in bed with another horribly offensive remedy slathered on her. Lilly shuddered at the thought of it.

As she reached the bottom of the stairs, Elsworth Somers appeared. He'd emerged from some hidden location, almost as if he'd been lying in wait for her. His expression was one she recognized. She'd seen it on countless people in her life. The sons of the family who had raised her until she'd been old enough to go away to school, the bullying headmaster and instructors at Millstead Abbey School—

bullies always wore it. Cold, calculating, mean, threatening. Because they were alone at that moment, he did not need to hide it.

"Miss Burkhart," he said, his tone snide and full of spite. "I see you're up and about after your morning mishap. Either you are remarkably clumsy, my dear, or you have terrible luck. Which do you think it is?"

He'd stepped closer, placing himself directly in front of her and widening his stance so that she was essentially trapped there at the bottom of the stairs. She couldn't go around him without touching him in a manner that would be more than just inappropriate. It wasn't by accident, either. He knew precisely what he was about. He wanted her to feel trapped. And he wanted to feel that he had some power over her.

Refusing to be cowed by him, Lilly lifted her chin and met his gaze directly. "I really couldn't hazard a guess, Mr. Somers. Now, if you'll excuse me, her grace is waiting for me."

"The old bird will wait a little longer," he replied, his lips twisting into a cruel mockery of a smile. "I'd like an answer, Miss Burkhart. Nay, I demand one. You are very nearly family, after all, and we must look after one another! What, precisely, happened in the park this morning?"

Did he know? Was he simply trying to get her to admit that someone had shot at her? Or was he worried that she might have seen the shooter and been able to identify them? Was he the guilty party? "I had the misfortune to be standing under a tree when a rotten branch fell. It made a terrible racket, really, but it was only a minor mishap and nothing more," she lied. "I was very lucky that Viscount Seaburn was with me. He is forever playing hero to my damsel in distress, it seems. I really must go, Mr. Somers. Please let me pass."

"He is certainly playing the hero for you, Madam, to be sure," Elsworth agreed, continuing on as if he hadn't even heard her second request to move from her path. In fact, he leaned in closer, close enough in fact that he had but to whisper to be heard. She could smell his breath which was rather unpleasant. "And yet a less noble and heroic figure I've never known. A gambler and a cheat. A man who cavorts with whores as if he has no shame. Though, I daresay, that has worked to your benefit, hasn't it, Miss Burkhart?"

"I do not have to tolerate your petty insults and crass insinuations, Mr. Somers. For the last time, let me pass!" she snapped.

He eased back from her, just a bit, a cold smile playing about his lips. "Did you know that his mother committed suicide?"

"I was not aware," she said simply. It made little matter to her one way or another except that she regretted any pain it might have caused him. She would hardly be one to throw stones on that score as her own mother had done the same. But it did prompt her to wonder if what Elsworth said was true and, if so, why had Val not disclosed it to her when she'd been offering confessions about her own family?

"Melancholy," Elsworth said. "That was what her doctors said. Personally, I think it was simply vice. She really loved her laudanum, you see. Above all other things, including her husband and her precious son. Used it all the time. Then used a bit too much of it. Poor Val found her in her bed, cold and dead as a doornail."

Lilly had had enough of him and his cruelty. That anyone could speak of such a thing with what appeared to be enjoyment made her feel nothing but disgust for him. "I won't stand here and be subjected to vicious gossip about my betrothed simply because the two of you have some long-standing rivalry between one another. What you speak of is indelicate, morbid and wrong. You should have some sympathy and some compassion, Mr. Somers. If you are incapable of such feelings, I'd prefer not to converse with you at all. But as for my part in it, this particular conversation is over and I want you to remove yourself from my path."

Elsworth's smile spread into a wide grin, a chilling expression, and he stepped back. As she attempted to move past him, he placed one booted foot in front of her, causing her to stumble.

Lilly fell into the wall, smacking her head against it rather firmly but, thankfully, didn't injure herself. Glancing back over her shoulder at him, she caught his smug and triumphant expression.

"Do be careful, Miss Burkhart. It'd be a shame if something happened to you. Poor Cousin Valentine has had to stumble upon enough dead women in his life. I'd hate to see another added to his already blackened conscience," he said, and then strolled away, whistling a tune under his breath.

Lilly shivered at the obvious threat. She'd thought him harmless. A bore and a snob, yes, but harmless. Clearly, she had been mistaken.

When he had gone, Lilly rose from where she'd been leaning against the wall and smoothed her hands nervously over her skirt. It wasn't one of the new items. They required alteration but the dressmaker had vowed to have one ready for her on the morrow. In the meantime, she was still wearing the rather hideous gowns the dowager duchess had forced on her. She wished that she had the armor of something pretty to wear, something that made her feel her position less acutely. Betrothals could be broken after all. Until they were married and she was a viscountess in the eyes of the law, she was living off the same sort of expectations that Elsworth had been.

Shrugging off that thought, she entered the drawing room and found the dowager duchess waiting for her. A tea tray had been placed on the table before her and was laden with small sandwiches and cakes. Five minutes earlier, she would have happily devoured most of it. Now, she found her appetite had fled, stolen away by the encounter with Elsworth. Did the Dowager Duchess of Templeton know that her grandson was such a vile man? Had she heard any of the exchange outside?

"Are you quite well, Miss Burkhart?" the dowager duchess asked. It wasn't necessarily concern in her voice. In fact, it sounded more like accusation. If nothing else, that made it abundantly clear that she did not know and had not heard. "You're looking rather peaked."

"I'm quite all right," Lilly said. What could she say, after all? *Your grandson, not the one I'm to marry, but the other one, uttered something potentially threatening in the hall and now I wonder if perhaps he's the very person who tried to kill me just this morning. And by the way, your other grandson, the one I am supposed to marry, thinks his cousin is guilty of treason.* If ever she wished to cast a pall on her relationship with the dowager duchess, that would be the way to do so. Such information would have to be relayed by Val. She had neither the heart nor the stomach for it.

"Are you certain? You have had a rather trying few days, I suppose. It would be only natural for it to have some effect upon you," the woman replied. "Though I had taken you for someone possessed of a heartier constitution! I suppose appearances can be deceiving."

Lilly wasn't certain whether to be offended or not. Did she possess a hearty appearance? And if so, what in the world did that mean? Deciding to simply set that aside to be digested at a later date, Lilly said emphatically, "I am quite well, Madam. Thank you."

The dowager duchess nodded stiffly. "Come and sit. Where is that Valentine? He was supposed to return. Irascible man. Let me tell you, Miss Burkhart, while you pour our tea, about this grandson of mine."

Lilly took the hint and began pouring the tea as instructed, trying to still the trembling of her hands as she did so. In truth, she was grateful for a topic that might actually prove to be distracting from the strange and frightening encounter on the stairs. "What about him, your grace?"

The dowager duchess tapped her ever-present fan on the table for emphasis. "Do not let him run roughshod over you. And he will. It's the way of men. All men. Even the tolerable ones."

"I have no plans to do so, your grace," Lilly said, passing the dowager duchess her cup of tea.

"Excellent. They mean well, you know? They think we're all weak and requiring protection and coddling. Are you in need of protection and coddling, Miss Burkhart?" It sounded suspiciously like a challenge.

"I shouldn't think so," Lilly said. It wasn't exactly a lie. Well, it was a small lie, she reasoned. She might very well need protection, after all, but she hardly needed coddling. She'd tell the viscount about the encounter. Or perhaps not. If she did, no doubt he and Elsworth would come to blows. What a muddle it all was!

"Even if you do, you must be very cautious," the older woman warned. "They will assume that protecting you means that they own you, that they get to make the decisions. They. Do. Not." Great emphasis had been placed on the last three words.

"Indeed, I should think not," Lilly replied. "And I daresay that Viscount Seaburn has a slightly more radical viewpoint on women's rights after having witnessed your own rather remarkable feats in running all of the family's estates."

The dowager duchess preened. "Indeed, he does. But he is not immune to masculine posturing, regardless of what he says, particularly if his feelings are involved. Men like to say we are ruled by our emotions, but I have always found women to be the more logical sex. It's the men who are ruled by anger and temper, after all. They are easily offended, easily riled to action and are often impulsive. No. It's best, my dear, to start as you mean to go on. Take the reins where you can, and where you can't, offer firm guidance that sounds like it's his idea."

"Rather like you did with his proposal?" Lillian asked. It wasn't difficult to see that the dowager duchess had been moving them all about like marionettes while she was the master puppeteer.

The dowager duchess surveyed her critically for a moment, then her lips spread into a rare smile. "Just so, my dear. I realize it's unorthodox and many people will question my choice for Valentine, but I know him better than he knows himself. The last thing he needs is a wife who will bore him. It would lead him down a path of disaster. I beg of you, my girl, do not make me regret it, please. I detest nothing so much as being wrong," the dowager duchess said.

>>>><<<<

VAL ENTERED THE drawing room and found his grandmother and his betrothed having tea together. Needless to say, it was cause for no small amount of concern. His grandmother could not be trusted and Lillian was simply an unknown quantity. Her thoughts and motives were a mystery to him except for the few she had shared with him. Regardless of that, both women drew trouble to them like bees to honey.

"Oh, well, look what the cat has dragged in, dear," his grandmother said to Lilly in a commiserating tone as he walked in. Her gaze, as it traveled over him, was speculative and disapproving. "Where have you been, Valentine? Doing something thoroughly disreputable, no doubt."

Since he had been doing just that, albeit for very good reasons, he elected not to answer rather than to lie. "A cup of tea sounds delightful."

"Well, you can't have one," the dowager duchess said. "The maid only brought service for two. We weren't expecting anyone else. If you'd wanted to have tea with us, you might have sent around a note to that effect. But you didn't because you're rude, insensitive and spoiled. Horribly spoiled. I blame myself for that, you know?"

Val was biting the inside of his cheek to keep from grinning as he crossed the room and pressed a kiss to his grandmother's cheek. "I am all of those things, Grandmama. And those are the very reasons that you love me. Now, don't be cross."

She rolled her eyes and shook her head. "I suppose it's true. Heaven help me. It's certainly why I fell so horribly in love with your grandfather. Though I did manage to correct that and fall promptly out of love with him the very moment I realized just what a foolish man he was. Go on and ring for the servants to bring another cup. You might as well sit. We need to discuss this havey-cavey wedding business that you've begun. I think we should have the banns read on Sunday. That will give us three weeks to put something together for a wedding and a wedding breakfast after. Who shall we invite? And none of your disreputable friends, Valentine. Only quality people of good morals are to attend."

He laughed at that. "If you want quality and good morals, Grandmama, you've effectively eliminated the entirety of the *ton*. I can't think of a soul amongst them, in town at any rate, in possession of both."

"I do not wish to have a large wedding," Lillian spoke up. It was beginning to seem that it wasn't her future husband who would run roughshod over her, but his grandmother. "I'd rather not do all of that, if possible."

Val could see the protest forming on his grandmother's lips. But then, she simply let out a heavy sigh of capitulation.

"Very well, Miss Burkhart. We shall have a small wedding, family and the closest of friends only. I suppose St. Paul's might be a bit much, but it's the only place worth getting married these days. Even with limited guests, you'll still at least get a bit of coverage in the columns," the dowager duchess added.

"Do we want coverage in the columns?" Lilly asked, her tone one of horror and dread.

"Of a certain, we do!" The dowager duchess shook her head. "My darling girl, what is the point of marrying so well if no one is to know one has done it?"

For one point, it would make their lives easier. The more people that knew she had the protection of his name and rank, the fewer people who would be willing to risk the consequences of acting against them.

Val rang for the maid and requested another cup. When she'd

gone, he turned back to his grandmother. "You make all the plans you desire, so long as Miss Burkhart is in agreement with them. I will be there at the appointed time." In truth, he wouldn't. Neither would Miss Burkhart. If he had his way, they'd already be married by then. "But, I'm having Highcliff obtain a special license regardless."

"Why can't you obtain one?" Lillian asked.

"The archbishop does not especially care for me," Val admitted reluctantly. A lecture would surely follow, he was certain.

His grandmother shook her head. "You gambled with the archbishop, didn't you? We're not only ruined now, we're all bound for eternal damnation due to your recklessness!"

"No, of course not. The archbishop doesn't gamble, as far as I know," Val said. "But I might have relieved his rather idiotic and whey-faced nephew of a good portion of his inheritance. And before you say it, I tried to dissuade him. I encouraged the stupid boy to drop out of the game numerous times and he would not. At any rate, I thought it best to let Highcliff handle things."

"Really, Valentine!" his grandmother said in abject disapproval. "One day, my boy, you will get yourself into a situation that neither your charm nor your friends will be able to get you out of. What will you do then?"

The maid returned with another tray bearing a single cup. He watched as she placed it with the others and Lillian filled it from the steaming pot. Watching her, with the innate grace of her movements, he said, "Whatever is necessary, Grandmama. Whatever is necessary."

Chapter Ten

THEY WALKED IN the garden that evening. It seemed that everyone, including the two of them, were attempting to act as if it
were a real engagement or, at the very least, a traditional one. Lilly
could feel the tension in him. Something was clearly bothering him
but she didn't know what it was. And while she was prepared to marry
him, she wasn't necessarily prepared to pry into his thoughts, especially if they were about how terribly unsuited she was to the position of
Viscountess Seaburn, and future Duchess of Templeton. It was that,
more than anything else that had occurred, which gave her pause
about their arrangement.

"Are we making a mistake?" she asked.

"What?" he asked, glancing at her in surprise. "Are you having
second thoughts?"

"I wasn't. I may be now. I suppose that rather depends on what
has you so deeply in thought," she replied. "I know you offered
impulsively. As much to irritate your relatives as for the other reasons
you and I discussed. If you wish to cry off—"

"I've no wish to cry off. I understand that this is impulsive," he
said. "And the simple truth is that I owe you an apology for offering
for you in the way that I did. It was thoughtless and careless. Insensitive and spoiled just as my grandmother accuses me of being. Had you
turned me down flat, I'd have deserved it and the ensuing humiliation
entirely."

Lilly walked on a few paces ahead. "But I didn't, did I? I said yes and now we're both facing the very real consequences of that. We don't even know one another, much less whether or not we'd actually want to be married to one another!" And hot, drugging kisses aside, they had no basis for a marriage between them.

He closed the distance between them, moving so that he stood in front of her and they were facing one another directly. "That's true enough, but my consequences are, well, inconsequential comparatively. I have to marry. That is beyond question. I can't let the fortune fall into Elsworth's hands… what he'd do with it could have far reaching consequences for all of England. Thousands of lives hang in the balance if he does. And yet, your life now hangs in the balance as well."

"Weighed against so many, it cannot be considered," she replied.

"But it can," he insisted. "It must. My impulsive decision has put you in an untenable situation. And your life is in danger because of it."

Lilly thought of the exchange with Elsworth earlier in the day. It had been a threat. Veiled, yes, and perhaps his tripping her had only been an accident or mostly harmless bullying. But she couldn't help think that was not the case. "I will not say that you are wrong about the potential threat I am facing. My own clumsiness from the morning of our meeting aside, the last two days have seen more precarious circumstances than I care to consider. The timing of the attack this morning is something that should not be ignored. It cannot be coincidence that my life is suddenly placed at risk after agreeing to your offer, especially with—" Lilly turned away, unwilling to finish the statement.

He frowned at the abrupt manner in which she'd simply halted her statement. "Did something else occur?"

She hadn't wanted to tell him but, under the circumstances, it seemed foolish not to, especially since she was not the only one at risk. "Elsworth threatened me this afternoon… just before I went into tea with your grandmother. It wasn't overt, really. He didn't say he would kill me or that I was in danger."

He grasped her arm, halting her as they walked and then turned her to face him. His jaw was clenched tight with anger. "Tell me everything."

Lilly sighed. "I was coming down the stairs and he was waiting—hiding in essence, as he didn't appear until I literally couldn't avoid him—at the bottom. He blocked my path and I asked him repeatedly to move."

"Did he hurt you? Did he touch you, at all?" Val demanded. "So help me, Lilly, if he harmed you—"

"No he didn't! And you mustn't challenge him openly. I know you're trying to protect your grandmother from the truth about him and if you allow your temper to get the better of you here it will all be for naught!"

"I won't let him bully and terrorize you!"

Lillian laughed. "What makes you think he can do either of those things? I've been taking care of myself for quite some time. My betrothal to you does not alter that! Do not let his pettiness sway you from your course. Threatening him or coming to blows with him now, regardless of what he said or did to me could hamper your ability to get the information you need. Couldn't it?"

He was quiet for the longest moment, a muscle ticking in his jaw. Finally, his breath came out in a rush. "Fine. For now. But if it happens again, I will not stay my hand where he is concerned. You'd tell me if really hurt you, wouldn't you?"

"Yes, of course, I would. He didn't strike me or shove me... but he did trip me, and I'm fairly certain he did so on purpose. And then he said that I should be careful because it would be a shame if something were to happen to me. And now I am wondering if he was responsible for the other event in the park... but you already suspected that, didn't you?"

"I did," he admitted through clenched teeth. "And it does sound like a threat, but a very vague and cowardly one. And your ankle wasn't further injured with this?"

"Only my dignity, but it's taken several blows of late," she said with a laugh. Growing serious again, she added, "He also said that you had discovered enough dead women in your life without adding myself to the list. I'm paraphrasing, of course, but it was something to that effect... and he told me about your mother."

Val's expression shifted into something unreadable. It wasn't angry or even hurt, just impassive. "I see. And what did he tell you about her?"

"That she'd been using laudanum and had ingested too much of it. And that you found her after," Lilly admitted. She wished fervently that she hadn't even broached the subject. What right did she have to pry into such things? His past was his and his alone.

"That is all sadly true. And she was melancholic and there were questions about whether or not she had done so intentionally... ultimately, and likely with great influence by my grandmother, both the church and the local magistrate deemed that it had not been suicide but an accident. We were permitted to bury her near the chapel at our country estate."

Regret coursing through her, Lilly offered, "I shouldn't have asked. I should never have mentioned it at all."

"No, you should have. I should have told you without you having to ask," he said. "You're certainly entitled to know. Heaven knows you'll be confronted with gossip about it at some point or other. But it isn't just my mother that he's referring to... there was another girl. It was before I left for the army. She was a country girl, local gentry and rather free with her favors, unfortunately. I fancied myself in love with her and even thought to offer for her. Alas, I didn't. I lost my nerve. And then two days later, I was out riding with Elsworth and some other young men from the area and I found her body in the stream. There were questions."

"But no charges?" she asked.

"No," he said. "It was determined that she'd slipped and fallen into the water during a heavy rain. With her skirts so heavy, she'd been unable to get herself up and out of the water… or so the magistrate had surmised."

"You disagreed with his assessment?" Lilly asked.

"I did. I still do. She had bruises about her throat that were not caused by drowning. It was very clear to me that someone had committed an assault against her, but whether or not that was the cause of her death, I cannot say," Val admitted to her. "And I don't know why it was hushed up and never investigated. Perhaps my grandmother thought I was guilty and did the same thing she had done after my mother's death and simply made it all go smoothly."

"Or perhaps she thought Elsworth was guilty. You are not the only grandson she must protect," Lillian suggested. "And if we are right about him now, he's clearly shown that he is capable of violence against any woman who threatens his position as your heir."

She saw the shock that flitted across his face, as if it had never occurred to him to question his cousin's involvement in the death of another young woman. But no one wished to believe ill of those closest to them. It was always easier to suspect a stranger of such terrible and heinous acts than one so near.

"My God," he said. "You could be right. For so long, I had thought perhaps she had another lover, or that she'd spurned someone's advances and been met with the terrible consequences of their temper. But it makes sense for Elsworth to at least be a suspect, does it not?"

"Did he know your intentions?" Lilly asked.

Val's expression turned grim. "He did. But he didn't know that I had changed my mind about asking her. He had every reason to expect that she would say yes given my status and my expectations. And if that is the case, that he murdered her to protect what he perceived to be his future, then our betrothal has painted a target on your back. You are in danger and it is entirely my fault."

"No, it isn't. The fault lies only with those who commit such unspeakable acts. Breaking our engagement will not make this go away," she said. "He won't stop now, because he's shown me what he really is. I know the truth of him and men like that... they don't forgive that easily nor do they forget."

"You still wish to marry me," he said. "Even knowing what you do about me and about my family? Not just Elsworth, but my mother and all of it. You think we should still go through with it?"

Lilly cocked her head to one side, meeting his worried gaze. A soft smile tugged at her lips. "Without a doubt. And I would be the worst sort of hypocrite to hold the circumstances of your mother's death against you. Heavens, look at my own. If it's even true. Perhaps she's alive and well and just wanted no part of me. I certainly heard of her desperate act from an unreliable source. So, yes, I do wish to continue with our plan, foolhardy as it may seem to others. Do you?"

He frowned at her for a moment. "Oddly enough, yes, I do. Without a doubt, as you said."

Lilly arched her eyebrows. "Really?"

He grinned, dispelling the darkness that had settled over them with their earlier conversation. It was an attempt to put them both at ease, and Lilly was glad of it.

"Perhaps a few small doubts," he admitted teasingly. "Every man is entitled to question the end of his bachelorhood, isn't he?"

"Only if every woman is entitled to question whether or not tying her fate to a feckless man is the best course of action," she shot back, in her best imitation of the Dowager Duchess of Templeton.

He laughed at that, shaking his head. "I think that's fair. And I'm beginning to see why my grandmother engineered all of this. You're a bit like her, you know? In your thinking and your view of the world. More forthright and less manipulative to be certain. That's not a complaint by the way. I'll take your forthrightness and be thankful for it."

Lilly began walking again, easing along the path in the small garden. It wound around rocks and bushes, trees and statuary to make the most of the small amount of space there. "You may rethink your stance on that as time goes by."

"Perhaps. But there are other aspects of marriage that I think will allow us to be forgiving of any foibles and flaws we might see in one another," he said.

"You're referring to our kiss this morning," she said. Recalling it left her feeling weak and breathless.

"That is exactly what I meant. Perhaps if I kiss you now, in the privacy of our own little garden, we won't be interrupted by spies or attempted murders," he suggested.

"We could be interrupted by something far worse," she answered. "A dowager duchess."

His hand snaked out, grasped her wrist and tugged her to him until she fell against his chest and their mouths were scant inches apart. "I'll brave the risk," he whispered. Then his lips were descending on hers once more.

Doubt fled. Questions and rationality were banished to the furthest reaches of her mind. Instead, she simply clung to him and the sweetness of that moment. She let the heat invade her, let it wash through her until she was breathless with it. As long as he was kissing her, anything seemed possible.

GOD ABOVE, BUT the taste of her was all that was both sinful and sweet. Every time he touched his lips to hers, he only wanted more and more. It was as heady and intoxicating as any spirit he'd ever imbibed and produced its own peculiar brand of euphoria.

She sighed, her lips parting and allowing him entrance. He savored it, committed it to memory even as he took the kiss further. Maneuvering them off the garden path and into the shadows of a tall hedge, he tipped her head back and deepened the kiss even further. When her hands came up, locking behind his neck as her fingers threaded into his hair, he was lost. Any thought of stopping, any thought of where they were and what paths of impropriety he might be leading her down simply fled. He was driven by his own desire and his need of her.

There was a small bench nestled there against the hedge and, somehow, he managed to get them to it without ever breaking the kiss. Sitting down, tugging her onto his lap so that he could hold her close and touch every damnably tempting inch of her, he hadn't forgotten where they were. He simply didn't care. Discovery and scandal be damned.

The gown she wore, one of the castoffs she'd been given, fit loosely enough that it offered little or no resistance when he tugged it down to reveal the generous swells of her breasts above her stays. As much as he enjoyed the sweetness of her lips, he longed to kiss her elsewhere, to test the porcelain texture of her skin and see if it felt as smooth beneath his lips and tongue as it appeared. Dipping his head, he pressed his mouth to her breast, laving the satin of her skin with his tongue and then nipping with his teeth until she shivered against him.

"You are wicked," she said on a ragged breath.

"So are you," he replied, his whispered words skating over her skin as he shifted one hand to cup the fullness of her breast. Even with layers of cloth between them, he could feel the hardened bud of her nipple against his palm and he wanted nothing more than to divest her of every garment right there. "Wicked and, if I am the luckiest man alive, perhaps a bit wanton."

She said nothing to that, but then she didn't have to. Instead of words, she arched toward him, offering herself to him in the sweetest way she could have imagined. Unable to resist, he grasped the laces of her stays and slipped the knot free. The fabric parted just enough that he could reach inside and touch her bare flesh. Every touch was gentle—coaxing and seductive. He could see her response, the initial shock and the pleasure that followed as well as the undeniable yearning for more.

"I warned you, Lilly... Pandora's box has been opened. Every time I touch you, you will want more, you will become bolder and more brazen. Curiosity and desire will drown out your fears," he vowed.

"I think they already have," she admitted. "But we have to go in. The dinner gong will sound any moment and I need to change."

She was right, of course. And if they didn't return promptly when it sounded, there would be hell to pay. Reluctantly, he removed his hand from the confines of her clothes and helped her do them up once more. As she rose, she looked neat and tidy as ever, albeit with a sparkle in her eyes and a flush in her cheeks that had not been there before. And her lips, swollen from his kisses and more delectable for it, tempted him once more. He kissed her gently then, aware that to do more would only result in greater frustration for them both.

"Go inside. I'll follow shortly," he said. *As soon as he could walk without his breeches doing him permanent injury.*

She walked away, pausing to look back at him over her shoulder. Beautiful, innately and unconsciously seductive, it was a pose that showed her lush curves to advantage. And in the silvery light of the evening, she was truly the most beautiful woman he'd ever seen.

The realization that what he felt for her was more than lust, more even than admiration and liking, swamped him. He was entirely infatuated with her and infatuation could lead to so much more, to something that could well destroy them both. Love led to jealousy and jealousy led to the same misery that had consumed his mother. It had been her obsession with his father's, not even fidelity but disinterest, that had led to her melancholia. She'd longed for his love. And like anyone else in his father's life, she'd been denied it.

"I am not my mother," he whispered aloud. He was stronger than her and infinitely more suited to coping with life. "I will not be like her."

Chapter Eleven

VAL WAS RUSHING to get into the drawing room just after the dinner the following evening. The gong had sounded already. He noted, as he paused in the doorway, the guarded expression on his cousin's face. His face revealed nothing, but in the other man's gaze he saw nothing but malice. As if becoming aware that he was being observed, Elsworth pasted a cool smile on his face and turned to walk away.

He'd left the house early that morning and had not seen Lilly all day. He'd been too busy trying to get the information he needed. That moment, seeing the banked animosity in his cousin, made all that he'd done that day, the hours spent ferreting out the nasty details of his cousin's less than ethical business dealings, worth it. Whatever he'd owe to Highcliff, and even to the Hound, would be a reasonable cost. He'd also bribed a pretty maid from next door to flirt with Elsworth's valet. He needed to know where his cousin was on the morning he and Lilly had been in the park.

Entering the drawing room fully, he stopped short. He'd known that Madame Renaud had delivered several gowns to the house that day. The men he'd set to guarding it had reported all comings and goings to him. Even knowing he would see her in something that would be more suited to her, he was struck dumb by the sight. What he saw robbed him of breath. It wasn't the midnight blue silk of his earlier imaginings. It was the color of smoke—dark, sultry, seductive. The neckline was edged in black lace that highlighted the alabaster tone of her skin and the cut of it showed enough of her supple flesh that he wasn't sure if he'd been permanently robbed of the ability to speak. He'd touched her there, teased her to the edge of desire and just a bit beyond. But dressed in that way, her hair styled as it was, her beauty wasn't just something to appreciate. It was a weapon.

"Good evening, my lord," she said.

The triumph in her gaze spoke only of the power of a woman who knew her own beauty. She knew what she was, and she wasn't afraid to use it for him or against him, he thought. And he admired her even more for it. "That gown is exquisite on you. But you need jewelry," he said, coming to stand beside her. "I have been remiss."

She laughed softly. "You do know precisely what to say to get my attention, don't you?"

"I do, indeed. Gowns and jewels. Furs, perhaps?" he asked with a grin. He enjoyed her delight in such things. He enjoyed that she made no pretense of hiding her pleasure in anything that she enjoyed.

She frowned then. "When you put it in those terms, it makes me sound as if I'm greedy or avaricious. I'm not. But I do love pretty things. Is that wrong?"

"Not in the least. You should be surrounded by pretty things. All the time. And I don't mind if you're greedy for that... I think I might even find it charming," he admitted. "There's also something imminently satisfying for a man in being able to provide such things for the women in his life."

"Why on earth would you find that charming?" she asked.

"Because you don't hide it, Lilly. Because when you like something, you say you like it... and when you don't, well, you say that, too. There's something refreshing about being in the presence of a person who tells the truth no matter what light it might cast them, or me, in."

"Oh, dear heavens!" the dowager duchess groused. "You'll have more than enough time for little tête-à-têtes after you're wed! For now, mingle and be delightful as young unmarried people are supposed to!"

"About that," Val said, halting her with a hand on her arm. "I have the license. Highcliff presented it to me this afternoon. And I also have an appointment set for us at St. Paul's for tomorrow morning at nine sharp. Don't tell Grandmother. I don't want anyone in the house to know our plans."

"Won't we need witnesses?" she asked in a whisper.

"It's taken care of. I assume that Madame Renaud left you another suitable costume for such an event?"

Lilly nodded. "She did, indeed. You knew that of course. The guards you posted outside are not very subtle."

He grinned. "Spotted them, did you? I don't want them to be subtle, Lilly. Their job isn't to catch whoever's trying to harm you, but to dissuade them from action. Their presence is necessary. You don't mind them?"

"No," she said. "I don't. I understand the necessity. By the way, we're going to start a lending library for the servants so they don't have to spend their wages on books. I'm also going to teach the housemaids to read."

"A lending library? There are first editions of Milton in that library!" he protested.

"Well they've no interest in Milton, I assure you," Lilly replied. "I shudder at the thought. Apparently, the housemaids and I share a fondness for gothic novels."

He blinked at that. "You want me to let the housemaids read *Udolpho*?"

She cast a beaming smile at him. "Have you read it then?"

"No. But I know what it is. You do realize those books are somewhat salacious?"

"Yes, I do. That's rather why I like them," she admitted. "What an entertaining evening I might have had reading in my chamber instead of coming down for dinner! Salacious. That's a rather delightful word, don't you think?"

He did, indeed, especially as he watched it roll off her pretty lips. "You are a wicked woman, Lillian Burkhart. Wicked and wonderful."

"Wonderful, perhaps. Wicked? Not yet. But I will be... and wanton, as well," she said and then moved away toward his grandmother who eyed them both suspiciously.

"Don't let him talk you into anything, my dear," the dowager duchess warned loudly. "Men are terrible, terrible creatures."

Lillian smiled slightly as she looked back at him, a coy quirking of her full lips that highlighted the curves of them and the perfection of her face. "Perhaps they are, but I'm beginning to see their merits all the same."

"Pish posh! Worthless. The lot of them!" the dowager duchess harrumphed loudly. "Valentine, escort your betrothed to dinner and try to behave as if you have some morals, please."

***

LILLY SMILED AS he showed her to her seat. No doubt the dinner would devolve into another round of barbed comments and thinly-veiled animosity. The rate at which Elsworth was consuming his wine was telling enough.

"I take it you're letting our grandmother have free rein in planning the wedding, Miss Burkhart?" Elsworth asked as he placed his glass back on the table and a footman appeared to promptly refill it.

"We have been discussing the plans," she said.

"Well, you really should defer to her expertise. After all, what could you possibly know about planning an event for your social betters?" he asked.

"Elsworth," Val said in a chilling tone, "if you wish to keep your tongue, you will still it. Your snide comments will not be tolerated."

Elsworth's lips quirked and he looked at the dowager duchess. "He's a savage, Grandmother. Surely you won't stand for such barbaric threats at your dinner table?"

"On the contrary, Elsworth." The dowager duchess enunciated each word with cool precision. "I happen to think such threats are a credit to Valentine. Any man who would let someone insult his bride-to-be in such a manner without taking action would be unworthy of the woman in question. I think, perhaps, you are overtired and should take a tray in your room."

Elsworth began to sputter. "But, surely... Grandmother, you cannot mean to defend his choice!"

"I can, I do, and I will," she said. "Go to your room, Elsworth. If you mean to act as a child, you shall be treated as one."

Lilly said nothing. At that point, anything she added would be superfluous. Instead, she sipped her wine and bore the full weight of Elsworth's furious gaze. He glared daggers at her as he rose from his chair.

"My own family has turned against me for the worthless daughter of a whore. I suppose you're pleased, Miss Burkhart! No doubt, that was your plan all along... divide and conquer!"

Val rose then, his chair tipping backward. "Speak another syllable and I will call you out right here. Think carefully, *Cousin.* We both know I'm the better shot."

"Enough!" the dowager duchess shouted. "Valentine, sit down. Elsworth, go now and say nothing else. If you so much as open your mouth, I'll not only disinherit you entirely but cut you off from this minute forward. I will brook no such insolence in my house. Is that clear?"

Val took his seat and Elsworth stormed off, the door slamming behind him.

"Well, I think I've lost my appetite," Lilly said.

"I think we all have," the dowager duchess replied. "But we'll eat regardless. We've given the servants enough to talk about for one night. There's a lesson to be learned in all of this, my dear... rule your house. Neither servants, nor husbands, nor relatives should have more authority in it than you do. It is the only domain granted to women in this world, after all. Hold fast to it."

"Yes, your grace," Lilly murmured in agreement. It was sound advice whatever her future husband might think of it.

"With your face and at your age, you can afford to be an iron fist in a silk glove... the older you get, the silk gets worn and faded," the dowager duchess warned. "Isn't that right, Valentine?"

Val looked up at her, his lips curled upward at one side in a half-smile. "Some women, Grandmother, will be beautiful their whole lives long. Age holds no power over them."

She guffawed. "Pretty words for your pretty betrothed."

"They do apply to her, as well," Val agreed. "But, in fact, I was speaking of you."

The old woman smiled, charmed in spite of herself. In that moment, Lilly fully appreciated the power of her husband's charm.

Chapter Twelve

WEARING ONE OF her new nightrails and a wrapper of the softest velvet, Lilly was hardly dressed for roaming the halls but she'd had no choice in the matter. Declining Mary's offer to help her change after dinner would have required explanations she did not wish to make. Clandestine activities with a sprained ankle were not all what they were cracked up to be. Lilly wasn't precisely creeping along the corridor. With a walking stick and a lingering limp, she couldn't really creep anywhere. But she was moving toward her intended destination as discreetly as possible. After the fiasco of dinner and the blatant hostility from Elsworth, she needed to talk to Val and she needed to do it privately, without the dowager duchess present.

Just as she neared his chamber, the door opened and a small man in neat livery stepped out bearing the coat Val had worn at dinner, the one that had been splashed with wine when he and Elsworth had very nearly come to blows. Lilly ducked into an alcove and prayed the little man wouldn't look in her direction.

As he passed, she gave a soft sigh of relief. It was imperative that she speak to Val, but the last thing she needed was to be caught sneaking into his rooms. Betrothed or not, some scandals could not be recovered from. And while she wished to speak with him, she was left with the distinct impression that perhaps he also needed to see her. The animosity the two men had toward one another ran deep and was apparently a long-standing situation. But beneath it, at least on Val's part, she sensed a great deal of sadness. They might be at one another's throats, but she suspected very strongly that he had once loved his cousin and that he was deeply wounded by the things that now hung between them.

Pausing outside his door, she raised her hand and knocked softly.

The door opened abruptly. "Blast it, Fenton, I told you—" His thunderous expression faded slowly only to be replaced by one of shock and then utter puzzlement. "What are you doing here?"

"Preparing to be the scandal of London if you leave me standing in your doorway any longer," she said. "Let me in before someone sees!"

He stuck his head out of the door, peered down the corridor in both directions and then stepped back to allow her entrance. "I don't think I need to tell you what a disastrous idea this is, do I?"

"What is really going on with you and your cousin?" she demanded.

He stood there, staring at her in stony silence for a long moment. "I don't want to tell you."

"Well, I don't want to be kept in the dark. I've a right to know," she insisted.

He scrubbed a hand over his face. "Fine, I will tell you and then you will go back to your room. You cannot be in here… it's unwise."

"Unwise? Are you suggesting now that your intentions toward me are dishonorable?"

"Of course not," he said, appearing mightily offended. "It isn't that. But damn it, Lilly, a man can only resist temptation for so long!"

"And I tempt you?" she asked, her reasons for coming to his room momentarily forgotten.

"More than anyone ever has. But that isn't why you're here!"

"No," she agreed. "It isn't. I couldn't help but think, at dinner… it hurts you, doesn't it? That the two of you are so at odds."

He scrubbed his hands over his face. "We weren't always. At one time, I thought we were closer than brothers. But the older we got, and the more certain our differing prospects in life became, the more he resented me. For being the only son of the eldest son, and heir to everything we held, for not being as obsessed with the rules of society and the notion of propriety. Whatever it is, he resents me because he feels he deserves it more."

"That's really it? It's just jealousy? Surely he knows that you would be generous with him!" Lilly moved deeper into the room, settling herself onto one of the chairs before the fireplace. Her ankle did not pain her overly much, but she had no intention of leaving any time soon.

"That isn't—the title provides power and prestige. I think it's those things more than just the family's wealth that he is envious of." His tone held all the hurt and disdain he felt for letting something so unimportant destroy their relationship. "I think that is why he has fallen in with such terrible people... because he wants to feel powerful and they have spun a fine tale to make him believe he could be."

"Is it possible that they have some involvement in the attempt on my life? If they are as terrible as you believe, and if they are determined that Elsworth should inherit... could we be painting him as a greater villain than he is?" Lilly asked.

"I don't know," Val answered honestly and hope flared for just a moment in his eyes. "Right now, it's too great a risk to eliminate anyone as a suspect. And even if he isn't responsible for the attempt to shoot you, his behavior toward you is unforgivable regardless."

"The thing of it is... he slings words like arrows," Lilly said haltingly. "But I find it difficult to believe that he has the nerve to do anything more than that. Even with his veiled threats, I think he only wanted to intimidate me."

"You could be wrong. But the timing of it is suspect," Val said, moving toward the other chair and sitting across from her. "If I marry, he loses any hope of inheriting substantial wealth. And the morning after we announced our intent to wed, you are nearly killed. I owe you an apology, Lillian. If you want to call a halt to this, I won't stop you. I acted rashly and impulsively and, in so doing, I have placed you in danger."

"But you don't know that for certain. We are still thoroughly in the dark here. It's only a guess that it was Elsworth... but who else could it have been?"

"I've been considering that. I've been considering every possibility, in fact. There is the matter of your bequest," he answered. "What happens if you do not meet the terms?"

She wasn't entirely certain. It wasn't a question that it had occurred to her to ask because she'd had no intention of letting it get away from her. "There are other relatives of my mother's to whom it would be passed, I assume. But I don't even know them."

"You don't have to know them," he said bluntly. "If the solicitor disclosed your name, your direction would not be difficult to obtain, would it? Either way, your relative or mine, someone tried to kill you yesterday. And if it was Elsworth, the timeline of our impending nuptials could very well prompt him to take more immediate action. That is why I lied to grandmother about the wedding, and why I continue to let her believe we will be waiting for the banns to be read and getting married in a more respectable manner. The truth, that we will be going to the church tomorrow, creates more risk in this situation."

"Oh," she said. "I see. How will we find out who was responsible?"

"I'm working on that. Trust me to see to it," he said. "After we've married tomorrow, we'll go and see this solicitor who contacted you and get all the particulars related to other potential heirs."

Lilly nodded. "I shouldn't have bothered you with this tonight."

He frowned at that before replying, "I'm not bothered... but it was a reckless thing to come here. For a multitude of reasons."

There was something in his tone that seemed to highlight the intimacy of their current situation. She was in his bedchamber wearing only her nightclothes. He'd shed his coat and waistcoat along with his neckcloth and stood before her clad only in very form-fitting breeches and his shirt. It was open at the neck revealing strong, corded muscles and just a hint of dark, curling hair. Curiosity overwhelmed her. It wasn't as if she'd never seen a man without a shirt before. Admittedly, there had never been one she'd been quite so curious about though. If she were to be entirely honest, she'd traversed the corridor to his chamber hoping that something improper would occur.

"Am I in danger then?" she asked. The words came out in a tone that was both challenging and unintentionally provocative. It wasn't what she meant to do. Certainly, she understood that they were in a potentially scandalous situation, but they were supposed to be married the very next morning. *So it was only improper by a matter of hours, really.* That she was attempting to reason with her own conscience was proof enough that she clearly knew better!

He rose abruptly and walked away from her, putting nearly the whole expanse of the room between him. When he turned back to her, his jaw had tightened, the muscle working there as he placed his hands on his hips. Eventually, he tipped his head back on a heavy sigh as if asking for some sort of celestial guidance. "I won't hurt you. I would never hurt you... but there is more than one kind of danger."

"Such as being ravished like a heroine in a gothic novel?" she asked. "Is that the kind of danger you mean, Val?"

The muscle in his jaw ticked faster and he raised his head to look at her once more. His eyes seemed to burn with an inner fire, *a passion*, she had not yet seen from him as he stared at her intently. "That is one sort. What do you know about ravishment, Lilly?"

"Only what you've shown me thus far. Which is not nearly as much as I'd like," she answered breathlessly. "But you could always enlighten me further."

"Do not play games with me. I'm not some young pup to be led around by his nose... or anything else," he replied.

That sounded vaguely naughty to her though she didn't precisely understand it. "In the drawing room, you said that a man liked to purchase pretty things for the women in his life."

"I did. And it's true enough," he said. "That velvet is rather fetching on you."

"And how many women are you currently providing fripperies and frivolities for?" she asked. The moment the question escaped her, she hated herself for asking it. It was weak and desperate. Needy. It was all the things she'd vowed never to be and that she despised.

"Are you asking if I have a mistress, Lillian?"

"It's a pertinent question on the eve of our marriage, don't you think? I know you said you would not have them after, but you were gone all day... and, well, I wondered if perhaps you were making your goodbyes."

He shook his head, his lips turning upward in a tight smile. "As to my whereabouts today, I was looking into some of Elsworth's business contacts and, sadly, came up short of any truly useful information. In regards to your other question, about my mistresses or the lack thereof... now is certainly a better time to ask than after the wedding, I suppose. To answer your question, I do not currently have a mistress. I did have one until recently but we had parted ways before I made your acquaintance. And I've no plans to take another."

"Until we decide we no longer desire one another's company and embark upon our separate lives? Or just until you're bored enough with me to look elsewhere?"

"I could promise you fidelity. I have already, in fact. But you've no faith in men, and your lack of it, based on your experience, is well-founded. The truth is, Lillian, I never imagined myself getting married... not for quite some time at any rate. My grandmother has effectively tied my hands on that score."

"I understand that marriage to me is not a choice—"

"I never said that," he interrupted her. "I had until the end of the year. I could easily have taken myself off to Almack's, picked out some meek and overly-bred society miss who'd never challenge me, who would never break a rule, and proceed to have exactly the kind of marriage every other member of society has. But I never wanted a wife I would simply tolerate. Or who would tolerate me."

"I rather think the point is that you didn't want a wife, at all," she retorted.

"You're wrong," he said. "I wanted a wife, Lillian. I just didn't want *any* wife. And I knew from the moment I saw you in the park, your bare toes in the grass when it was far too cold for such a thing, that you were different... that no matter how far I go or how much I look, there will never be another you."

Her heart fluttered in her chest and her breath rushed from her lungs at those words. It wasn't love. He hadn't offered her love. And the truth is they didn't know one another well enough for love. But it seemed they certainly knew one another well enough for like... and perhaps for a bit of lust. "Do you think perhaps you could ravish me just a little bit? I am here, after all, and we were interrupted in the park yesterday morning, and in the garden yesterday evening, I might have panicked a little bit. But I think I rather liked what you were doing then."

Chapter Thirteen

S HE'D DONE HIM in. Completely. Entirely. She'd robbed him of sense, of speech, and of will. Because there was nothing he wanted more in life than to give her precisely what she asked for. "I think I might be able to manage that."

She blinked at him in surprise, as if his answer had been unexpected. "Oh, well, that was… how does one typically begin the whole ravishment process? Should I move to the bed?"

Christ above. If he went any harder, his breeches would do him permanent injury. "Not if the goal is only a little bit of ravishment."

"What then?"

Val closed the distance between them until he was standing next to her chair, looking down at her lovely, upturned face and the thick braid of dark hair that cascaded over her shoulder to rest against the velvet of her wrapper. God above, she was beautiful, he thought. Perfect, even.

"Give me your hand," he said.

When she reached out, he took her hand in his. Her skin was soft and delicate, the bones of her hands felt fragile in his much larger and stronger one. But there was a strength in her, a boldness, that left him awed by her. Closing his hand about hers, he pulled her up to standing. She fell against him, the softness of her breasts crushed against his.

Val lowered his head, claiming her lips. Somehow, he held himself in check and didn't just consume her as his own desires demanded. He savored the kiss, noting her response. Every hitch of her breath, every sigh, when her hands clenched on his shoulders, or her fingers twisted in the fabric of his shirt—all of it was catalogued and stored for future reference.

Turning them slightly, he settled onto the chair and pulled her down so that she was draped across his lap. Then he reached for the ties of her wrapper, tugging them until the garment gaped wide and he could slip his hand inside. Only the sheerest linen remained between his palm and her naked flesh. He settled his hand at the curve of her waist, feeling the gentle flare of her hip below. Then, as he pulled his lips from hers and began to kiss the delicate line of her jaw, the soft skin of her neck just below her ear, his hand drifted upward. He felt her breath catch as he skimmed it over her ribs and then she let out a shuddering sigh as he cupped the fullness of her breast in his palm.

The feel of her burned him like a brand—the softness of that perfect mound in sharp contrast to the taut peak that he yearned to taste. With that goal uppermost in his mind, he pushed her wrapper off her shoulders entirely. The sheer linen of her nightrail laid over the lush curves of her body like a veil. While he could not see her fully, just enough was revealed to torment him.

Unable to resist the sweet temptation any longer, he dipped his head and pressed a kiss to one linen-draped nipple. Then he closed his lips over it and laved the turgid bud with his tongue.

A soft gasp escaped her and her head dropped back even as her fingers slid into his hair and held him close. *As if he had any intention of going anywhere.* Never in all his life had anything tasted as sweet.

With her back bowed over the arm of the chair, her head back and the lushness of her breasts on perfect display, it was still not enough. So he reached for the hem of her gown and slid his hand beneath it, skating over the soft skin of her thigh, then moving inward. When he brushed the dark curls at the apex of her thighs, she gasped again.

"Part your thighs for me, Lillian," he said. "If you truly want to know what ravishment feels like."

She did, just enough that he could slips his hand between them. But as he caressed her, touching her with gentleness that was hard won, she opened to him completely. Only then did he part the soft folds of her sex and gently stroke that small bud that would bring her pleasure.

"Tell me, Lillian, have you touched yourself this way?"

The gasp that escaped her was both shock and pleasure. "I can't... why would you ask me that?"

He grinned, then dipped his head to press a kiss to her other breast, neglected for too long. When he felt it had been suitably compensated, he replied, "It's all right if you have... every woman is different. Some like a light and gentle touch, the barest hint of pressure. Other women like a firmer touch. Fast, slow, firm or soft... I only ask so that you can tell me what it is that you like."

"I don't know," she said. "I've never... I didn't even know I could feel this way," she admitted breathlessly.

God, but he ached for her. "Then we'll discover what you like together."

Val took her lips once more, claiming them as much from his own desire as the need to muffle any sound she made as he explored her intimately. He learned soon enough the touches that made her squirm, the ones that made her tense, and the ones that made her shudder. And even though it caused him an agony of need, he refused to hurry. Until she was clinging to him, gasping for breath, and her whole body trembling in his arms, only then did he push her over the edge.

HER BODY WAS on fire. She was burning up from the inside out. And she was his entirely. She wanted to plead with him, to beg for something she couldn't name. Regardless, she was straining toward something, some ephemeral thing that hovered just out of her reach. And then his touch became more insistent. His fingers moved over her flesh in a way that heightened the impossible tension inside her.

"Let go, my sweet Lillian," he whispered against her ear, and then his teeth scraped along the side of her neck just below her ear.

She broke, shattering into a million pieces as a feeling unlike anything she'd ever known consumed her. Wave after wave, she shuddered in his arms, clinging to him as he stroked her with a gentleness that made her want to weep. All the while, he pressed soft kisses to her cheek, her neck.

"Is that enough ravishment for you?" he asked with a wicked grin.

"Is there more?" she asked.

His grin faded, replaced by a look of hunger that might have frightened her before. But now she only yearned to know where else he could take her.

"Are you trying to kill me, Lillian? Because if you keep saying such things, I will die of the agony of wanting you."

"I don't want that," she said, pulling herself up until they were face to face. His hand was still between her thighs, still tracing delicate circles on her skin that made her shiver.

"You are remarkable," he said.

"Wanton and reckless. Wicked, I think you said earlier," she replied.

"I was wrong. Magical, yes. Wicked, I think not."

"Wanton then," she said.

"God, I hope so."

She kissed him, pressing her lips to his and nipping at the fullness of his lower one just as he had done to her. His answering groan told her precisely how much he'd liked it.

"Do you think I could ravish you just a little?" she asked in a teasing and coquettish tone that was rather a surprise to them both.

He dropped his forehead to hers and let out a shaking breath. "You don't know what you ask."

"No," she admitted. "I don't. But I clearly want to."

He shook his head. "I can't. I want to, but I only have so much control, Lilly. And we have tested it sorely. If I let you touch me..."

"I know the particulars of what is to happen on our wedding night... in the vague sense, at least. I know that our bodies will be joined. But the thing you did just now, bringing me such pleasure with only the touch of your hand—can't I do that for you?"

She heard the breath rush out of him, felt the shudder that racked him. Then he closed his hand over her wrist and pulled her hand lower, sliding it between them until she could feel a hard ridge beneath her palm. He pressed her hand there, closing it around him. Then he groaned, a primal and animalistic sound that made her feel powerful. Just as abruptly, he pulled her hand away and somehow, even with her seated on his lap, managed to create distance between them. He was obviously torn between what he wanted to do and what he thought he should do.

"Show me how to touch you," she urged. "How to make you feel what I did."

"I don't think either one of us is quite ready for that," he said, his expression taking on a pained appearance. "It's time for you, Lillian, to go back to your room while I still have the strength to let you."

"But I want—"

"Tomorrow," he said, and pressed a kiss to her lips. "Tomorrow."

"You're certain?" she asked. "There's nothing I can say to persuade you?"

A strangled laugh escaped him. "I'm sure there is. And God help me when you discover it."

She wasn't quite sure how it happened but, suddenly, her wrapper was back on her and he was tying it with an efficiency that set her mind to wondering about his familiarity with women's clothing. Then he lifted her to her feet, pressed her walking stick into her hand and unceremoniously shoved her out the door. But as she stood there in the hallway, she heard the strangest sound and could feel the reverberation through the door. "Are you hitting your head?"

"Yes," came his muffled reply. "I am. If I'm lucky, I'll render myself unconscious. And while I'm doing so, I'm cursing both you and my own nobility with every strike. Go to bed, Lillian. Heaven help us both if you do not."

Even with her disappointment at having their very intriguing and scandalous exchange halted, she couldn't help but smile. He truly wanted her, just as she wanted him. They might be marrying in haste, but perhaps they wouldn't have cause to regret it.

Walking away from Val's chamber, she headed in the direction of her newly-appointed accommodations. As she paused in front of the door, a shiver raced through her. It was not of the pleasant variety. Glancing back down the corridor, she saw Elsworth emerge from the shadows near Val's room. He gave her a mocking bow and began to move toward her.

Lilly didn't hesitate any longer. She opened the door, all but threw herself inside and then turned the key in the lock. For added measure, she pulled a chair over and placed it beneath the door knob. It was a good thing as she heard the metallic snick of the key being inserted into the lock on the other side. Where had he gotten a key to her room? From the butler? From somewhere else in the house? Had he stolen it from his grandmother or the housekeeper? She didn't know. But as the door knob rattled, she vowed not to be some helpless victim. Should he get inside, she'd give him the fight of his life.

She lifted the walking stick high and brandished it like a club. The elaborate silver handle turned in her palm and with a sharp click, the handle separated from the shaft to reveal the gleaming metal of a blade.

"And he doesn't wish to be called a spy," she muttered, freeing the blade completely. It was, to her mind, a far better weapon as it was one she certainly knew how to use. Effie had insisted that the lot of them have fencing lessons and she was never more grateful to her forward-thinking friend and mentor.

The door pushed inward but only by an inch or so. The chair did its job, halting its progress. If he attempted to force it open, the resulting destruction and ruckus would bring everyone in the house running.

"Aren't you a smart little mouse?" he whispered through the crack. His words were slurred and he was obviously deep in his cups.

"What is it you want?" she demanded.

"Only to sample whatever delights it is that have blinded my cousin to your grasping, social climbing ways. Tell me, Lillian, did you learn those tricks from your whore of a mother? Or is that something else that your Miss Darrow provides instruction in?"

Approaching the door cautiously, Lilly kept the blade out of his sight. But as she neared it, she could see him peering in at her. It wasn't just that he had overimbibed. His eyes were red-rimmed and bloodshot. There was also a sallowness to his complexion and deep hollows beneath his eyes. He was clearly foxed. Completely and utterly foxed, but not just foxed. She'd seen enough people on the streets of London who'd succumbed to opium to know that he'd been sampling that deadly flower. Even through that narrow crack in the door, she could smell the brandy and smoke on him. He shoved at the door again and, without hesitation, she slipped the blade through the opening, slicing his forearm.

With a cry, he stumbled backward, clutching the wound with his hand. "Bitch!"

Lilly stepped forward, pressing her face to that small opening and peering out at him. "Return to your chamber, Mr. Somers, and I won't have to tell anyone about your unwelcome visit."

He looked up at her then, pure hatred and venom in his gaze. "Tell anyone about this, and the whole world will know you were servicing my cousin on the eve of your wedding."

With that, he rose and stumbled away, still clutching his forearm and cursing her under his breath.

Lilly closed the door again, locking it firmly, as if that did any good. And the chair was once more placed securely beneath the knob to prevent anyone else from entering. Warily, she backed away from it and climbed onto her bed. The blade from the walking stick was placed carefully on the table beside her. But she didn't recline. Instead, she sat there and watched the door, her heart racing. Every creak and groan of the house made her jump. She wouldn't be caught unawares. Not by him.

Chapter Fourteen

L ILLY ENTERED THE church on Val's arm at five minutes to nine o'clock, the first hour in which any wedding ceremony could be legally performed. She was tired. Her sleep, limited as it was, had been fitful the night before after the encounter with Elsworth. It was something she'd have to share with Val, she knew, but it didn't seem quite the time.

As she looked toward the altar, a smile spread across her face. He'd said he would take care of the witnesses and when she saw Effie standing there, next to a man with dark good looks and questionable fashion sense, she couldn't help but smile.

"Thank you for thinking to invite Effie," she whispered. "With Willa in the country, it's nice to have someone here that I consider family."

He nodded but seemed uncomfortable with the praise. "You're very welcome."

"Who is that with her?"

"He's a friend," Val replied. "Lord Highcliff. He issued the invitation to her on our behalf."

"Why would he do that?" Lilly asked, eyeing him with curiosity.

"I believe that he and Miss Darrow are well acquainted with another," Val answered.

He wasn't lying. But he wasn't telling her the entire truth. Lilly was certain of that. If he was as easy to read at the card tables as he was with her, it was a wonder he'd ever managed to fleece anyone. "I don't know whatever made you think you could be a spy! You're a terrible liar. Say what you mean, Valentine."

"I think they have an affection for one another… but one they are both clearly in denial of at present," he admitted. It was still carefully worded and very cagey, but his meaning was abundantly clear.

Lilly looked at them, once more, her gaze traveling back and forth between them. Surely not. The man was barely respectable from what she had heard. He was not dressed in the standard of the day. He'd eschewed Beau Brummell's more minimalist and masculine style in favor of something that harkened back to an earlier time—so much so that he appeared rather foppish. The morning coat he wore was not the gray, blue, black or even deep green favored by so many. It was a shocking shade of chartreuse that clashed with his blindingly yellow waistcoat. If that wasn't enough, his breeches had been tailored so closely to his body that it was surely a wonder they had permitted him in the church.

As they neared the pulpit, the bishop emerged from a doorway to their left. He was dressed in a red cassock and looked terribly important. *And terribly disapproving.* "This is the couple, Lord Highcliff?"

"Yes, your grace," Highcliff replied. "Lord Valentine Augustus Somers, Viscount Seaburn and Miss Lillian—forgive me, my dear, but I do not know your middle name?"

"It's Avon, my lord."

"Like the river?" he asked.

"Yes." The name had been a final insult from her father given the manner in which he claimed her mother had died. She should only be thankful he hadn't named her after the Thames.

"Shall we get started?" Effie asked cheerfully, clearly knowing that it was a sore subject.

"Yes," the bishop agreed. "You have the license?"

Highcliff produced it from inside his coat pocket, revealing that the lining was a shade of pink she had never seen before. The effect of so many colors was dizzying.

The bishop reviewed the license. He made a sound that could have been assent or denial. Then he immediately opened the small, ornate tome on the altar table and began to read from the *Book of Common Prayer*.

At first, Lilly wasn't entirely certain what was happening. Then as she realized that her wedding ceremony had begun so, well, unceremoniously, she had to stifle a giggle. Perhaps it was her degree of exhaustion or the turmoil that had led them to that point, but it all seemed rather ridiculous to her. Or it did until she looked up and met Val's gaze. He didn't appear amused. In fact, he looked serious and intense, as if what was being said was of life or death importance. In that regard, Lilly supposed he was correct. It sobered her giddiness immediately.

In all, it was quick and efficient and alarmingly anticlimactic. Val slid a ring on her finger, they signed their names in a book, as did Effie and Lord Highcliff, then they were all shuffled out of the church and were standing in the middle of the crowded street before she could even appreciate all that had occurred.

"That was..." She trailed off, uncertain what to say about the very brief ceremony.

"I believe the word you are looking for is perfunctory, my dear Lady Seaburn," Highcliff offered, ever helpful. "I'm afraid a special license on a Tuesday only gets you perfunctory. Pomp and circumstance are reserved for those who have a planned wedding with the posted banns and orange blossoms. It does not accompany a hastily called in favor, sadly."

"Well, I suppose it's efficient, at least," she said.

"Thank you, Highcliff, for your assistance," Val said.

"You are more than welcome, my friend. I've arranged a carriage for you which is waiting just down the street. It will take you to my house in Richmond… out of the city and away from your grandmother and Elsworth. It's hardly a wedding trip, but it will at least offer a bit of privacy. I'll send a note around to the dowager duchess when I've returned home," Highcliff said, his manner breezy and indolent. "The last thing anyone wants is a search party to interrupt their wedding night!"

As Lilly watched him, she noted that the movements were not truly natural. It was almost choreographed, like a person executing dance steps with a kind of studied precision. An act. All of it. His clothes, his manner, even the affectation of breathlessness in his speech. It was all an act.

"You and my husband aren't simply friends, are you, Lord Highcliff?" she asked.

"My dear, what else would we be?" Highcliff asked, staring at her with something akin to shock.

"I think I would classify you as comrades-in-arms. But it isn't cards for you, is it? It's something else altogether," Lilly observed and allowed her gaze to land pointedly on the hideous waistcoat. "You've created quite the illusion, my lord. I hope it serves you well."

Highcliff grinned. It was the first honest expression he'd worn the entire time. It vanished as quickly as it had come. "I think you are a dangerous woman, Lady Seaburn. And my dear friend should be very cautious with you, indeed. Off with you both," he said dismissively. "Now, Miss Darrow, may I see you home?"

"Thank you, Lord Highcliff. I would be delighted," Effie said, and placed her hand on his arm as they walked away.

"What's he really like in private?" Lilly asked.

"Intense, terrifying, impatient, unwilling to tolerate any foolishness or cowardice, and loyal to the very depths of his soul," Val replied. "Shall we go?"

Lilly glanced down at her hand and the very large emerald that winked on her finger. It was all really happening, she thought. "I suppose we should. It was rather nice of Lord Highcliff to arrange everything just so."

Val laughed at that. "Highcliff has been called many things, Lilly. I doubt nice has ever been one of them, but I will be certain to tell him so. He will enjoy that tremendously."

⫸⫷

THE CARRIAGE RUMBLED through the streets of London, its pace often slowed and sometimes even halted by the congestion that was a plague on the city. Highcliff was draped across one seat with practiced indolence and an expression of disaffected ennui. Effie sat on the opposite bench facing him, prim, proper and all the things a lady should be. He watched her for a moment and noted that she watched him, as well. Some things would never change it seemed. No matter how different they were and no matter the past that lay between them.

"The curtains are closed," she said, after a long and silent moment. "You need not put on such an act in here for me... not when we both know the truth."

His lips quirked even as he sat up and assumed what was a more normal posture for him. There were times when the act of addlepated dandy exhausted him. But it had been worth its weight in gold with the information to which he had become privy to as a result. After all, people were willing to say just about anything in front of a person they thought to be both stupid and disinterested.

"All of your charges are getting married off—and to titled gentlemen to boot. Soon, you'll have a line of matchmaking mamas at your door demanding entry for their desperate daughters," he observed.

"My charges have no mothers and they have, at best, disinterested fathers. I'm not interested in taking on pupils who have parents to see to their futures," she replied sharply.

"Always the savior, Effie," he murmured softly. "Who saves you?"

"I do not need saving," she replied. "You know that better than anyone."

Recalling the night they'd met, the terrible moment when she'd been forced to defend herself against something no woman should ever have to endure, his fists clenched. No, he hadn't saved her. She'd saved herself, leaving the man who would have assaulted her writhing on the ground in agony as she'd dusted off her torn and dusty skirts. It had been a darkened highway in the countryside. Two drunken louts who'd fancied themselves highwaymen had stopped her carriage. One had decided to take more than just her purse. As he'd ridden up onto the scene, one man had fled, leaving the other in the middle of his attempted assault which she had soundly thwarted with a well-aimed warming pan.

"I suppose I do," he agreed.

"When will you give it all up?" she asked, changing the subject abruptly.

"When there are no more traitors amongst us or when I have drawn my last breath," he answered honestly. Ferreting out those who profited at the expense of their own countrymen was the only skill he possessed that was of use to anyone. He'd made it his life's work. But it had taken much more from him than simply time. His entire life was a lie and his soul grew blacker and more bitter from it by the day.

"And at what cost to you? You live a constant charade, Nicholas, hiding behind a mask!" She reached across the distance of the carriage and grasped his hand in hers.

It was a gesture meant to comfort. He knew that. But it burned him like a brand, nonetheless.

She continued imploringly. "If you do not cease this, there will be nothing left of you to save. You lose yourself to it a little more every day."

Deliberately, he pried her hand from his. "Be careful the filth of me does not rub off on you. I would not have you stain yourself on my account. I'll not add that to the black marks that already darken my conscience."

She pulled back, almost as if he'd struck her. "We were friends once."

They had never been friends. Or rather he had not. He had loved her from the first and, even then, he'd known that he was unworthy of her. But he'd played the part of boon companion for as long as he could because it had given him the chance to bask in her presence. "Friends? Is that what we were? It was a lark, Effie... two young people enjoying the summer in the countryside before the harsh realities of the world intruded."

Pain flared in the depths of her warm, green eyes. Just as quickly it was gone, masked by her uncanny ability to use etiquette as armor. "Regardless of the circumstances in which our friendship ended, my affection for you was genuine, then as now. You will always have it, whether you wish to or not."

"Why did you refuse Sutton's offer, Effie? Surely it wasn't out of affection for me?" He was twisting the knife, being cruel to be kind. He wanted to stamp out any lingering softness she held in her heart for him.

"I refused Sutton because I did not wish to marry Sutton. Contrary to your overblown sense of self-worth, people do make decisions in this world that have absolutely nothing to do with you," she chided.

He grinned, but it was a cold expression, one that hinted at the darkness that had become a part of him over the years. "So my half-brother, then the heir apparent before his unfortunate duel, deigned to offer the role of lady wife to the bastard daughter of a neighbor. The daughter who happened to be the only friend of his own bastard half-brother born of their mother's infidelity... a girl, I might add, that he'd never even before looked at. Yet, it had nothing to do with me? If you believe his offer was based on anything more than his hatred of me and his desire to take something he thought was mine... well, you are fooling yourself about him as much as you ever have about me."

"I cannot attest to his motives in making the offer, only to my own in my refusal. I didn't wish to be his wife," she said simply.

"And did you ever wish to be mine?" He wanted to call the words back, to have never spoken that secret desire to her. It left him naked and vulnerable in a way that he had never been with another soul in his life.

"No," she said firmly. "I adored you, Nicholas. I enjoyed your company, your wit... but I knew even then that you were not a man meant to be my husband. Nor any woman's for that matter. It wasn't simply that you found yourself in danger, but that you courted it with a recklessness and abandon that told me the truth of it from the outset. You wanted to die. I knew that you'd never make yourself into a husband whether you wed or not, but whatever poor woman was foolish enough to try being a wife to you would quickly be made into a widow."

He wanted to deny it. He wanted to tell her she was wrong. But he'd never lied to her even if he'd had to lie to others in her presence. She always knew the truth of him, it seemed. "And since you couldn't save the bastard son who loved you, you saved the bastard daughters of the world that made him."

"I saved those who reminded me of where I might have been had my father been a different man."

A man like yours. She didn't utter those words. They didn't have to be spoken. But they hung between them just the same. Everything about him that she now detested and feared had been forged as much by the cruelty of the man the world knew as his father as by the violence he'd witnessed and dealt during the war. That boy she'd known, the one who loved her and saw her as so far above him, that boy was no more. He'd been stamped out and eradicated years before.

The carriage halted in front of the elegant Georgian townhouse that functioned as the Darrow School for Girls. It was a reprieve, but not truly a welcome one. "You are home," he said. "I would help you down, but it's best by all accounts that we are not seen together."

She rose and moved toward the door of the carriage. At the last moment, she turned and looked back at him. "I still have your chess board. You are welcome to come for a game anytime. You know where my study is."

"I do," he said. But he didn't offer any commitment to the invitation. They both knew he would accept it however. He couldn't do anything else. Being in her presence cut him like a dull blade every time—jagged, painful and deep. Despite that, the pain of being forever absent from her life was more than he could bear. So he would accept her olive branch and return some night to play chess with her while he quietly railed against the fact that nothing else could ever exist between them.

Chapter Fifteen

T HEY DID NOT go immediately to Highcliff's Richmond home, but instructed the driver to take them instead to the small office in Cheapside that housed the offices of the solicitor Lilly's great-aunt had retained. They needed answers about the bequest and who would benefit if Lilly failed to meet the terms set forth.

As they neared the address, Val surveyed her in the pretty amethyst-colored day dress she wore. His ring winked on her finger and the posy she'd carried during the ceremony was still clutched in her hand. "It isn't exactly how one envisions spending their wedding day, is it?" he asked.

"I'd never envisioned having a wedding day," she admitted. "As a rule, governesses and companions simply fade slowly into spinsterhood. Marriage and weddings are not supposed to be for us, only for the girls we help to raise."

"But you don't like rules," he said with a smile. "And so you've broken another one, shattering expectations of you left and right, as it were."

She laughed softly at that. "I suppose I have."

The carriage door opened and the driver lowered the steps. Val climbed out first and then reached back for her, taking her hand. "Let's go see what we can find out about who may have tried to murder you, shall we?"

She shivered at that, but nodded in agreement.

Together, they entered the building and climbed the stairs to the small office on the second floor. It was dark and dingy, smelling of mold and something else he could not quite name. Knocking softly on the aged wood with its cracked and peeling paint, the door slowly swung inward. The hair on his neck lifted, standing on end as his skin prickled with the sense of looming danger.

"Wait here," he said.

"In the hall? For anyone to come by? I think not. I may be a bit reckless and dislike rules, but there is one rule that I will not break today. There is safety in numbers," she said firmly.

It was logic he couldn't fault. "Stay close to me."

"Closer than your own shadow," she said.

Entering the offices slowly, they paused in the small antechamber. There was a deserted desk there and a handful of chairs. Another door opened off the room and it was ajar. The smell from the hall grew stronger the deeper they moved into that space and he knew instantly what it was. *Death.*

"Nothing good will be found behind that door, Lilly. You don't have to look," he said.

"You don't know what the solicitor looked like, Val. I do. If it is Mr. Littleton... we'll go together," she insisted.

He hated that she was correct. But there was nothing to be done for it. Using the toe of his boot, he pushed the door open further and stepped inside. The terrible smell pervaded everything. Whoever had killed him, Val would bet, had done so right after the poor man's initial meeting with Lilly. It was a wonder she hadn't been murdered while sitting in the man's office.

They found him slumped on the floor behind his desk. There was a puddle of blood, long since congealed, beneath his head that spread out in a rivulet over the carpet and the uneven floorboards. Next to the body lay the discarded weapon, a wicked-looking tool used to stoke the fire in the brazier that occupied one corner of the room.

"We need to summon the watch," Lilly whispered, her voice strained. "That is Mr. Littleton. Oh, Val, you don't think this happened because of me, do you? This poor man—"

"This didn't happen because of you," he said. "This happened because of someone else's greed. You are not at all responsible even if this is in some way tied to the bequest from your great-aunt. The killer alone bears sole responsibility for this man's death and likely for the attempt on your life. Though, on that score, we still cannot discount Elsworth."

"He's had to be dead for days now! Possibly since the same day I met with him!" Lilly said in dismay. "With everything that Elsworth has done, I was certain it would be him, but now—well, I'm just not sure anymore."

"I do think he likely died just after you left this office. Which begs the question of why you made it home unaccosted save for a crow stealing your bonnet," he said. "They would have followed you, Lilly, and they would have eliminated you before eliminating him."

"Eliminated." She said the word as if it left a sour taste in her mouth. "What a terrible way to put it! What if... Val, what if they were following? What if my encounter with you in the park was the only thing that prevented them from... I was too distracted by everything to consider it. I can't say I was being followed, but I can't say I wasn't either!"

"Lilly, this is too upsetting for you—"

"Yes, it is," she agreed. "But I'm not upset with you or even your choice of words. Because it's accurate. Eliminated. Like a problem or a nuisance. An inconvenience. That's what I've always been in life... to my mother, to my father and now, apparently, to whoever else stands to gain from my great-aunt's generosity."

He had no answer for that. His own father had been distant and uninvolved, but Val had known that he had his father's love even if it was absent at the best of times. And his mother had loved him the best she could when he was very young, before he'd lost her to her own melancholy long before he'd lost her to the permanency of death. Even his grandmother, managing and cantankerous as she could be, was only interested in what was best for him. Other than Miss Euphemia Darrow and her half-sister, Lilly had no one to put her needs and safety first. Certainly, the people who should have seen to those things had failed her terribly.

"We need to summon the watch," he said.

"We need to find the documents pertaining to the bequest... if they're not here, then we know that whoever killed him took them, and we can be absolutely certain that the bequest was the cause of his death."

Val wanted to protest. Remaining there was dangerous and damning. But she wasn't wrong. "Five minutes," he said. "If we don't find it in five minutes, then we give up. Agreed?"

"Agreed," she said.

"I'll take the desk. There's less chance of my clothing disturbing the scene or being... stained," he finished.

She swallowed convulsively then nodded. "Right. I'll check the cabinets over here," she said and swept her hand toward a large barrister case in the corner and another piece of darkly-finished furniture next to it.

Stepping around the body carefully, Val began combing through the documents on top of the desk. "What was your great-aunt's name?"

"Margaret Hazleton, Lady Marchebanks," she answered.

Val stopped in his tracks. "You can't be serious!"

"Well, of course, I'm serious. I'd hardly joke about something at a time like this. Why does that matter?"

"Because her nephew, or rather her husband's nephew, is one of the men with whom Elsworth is in business. All of these mysteries are connected, Lilly, and we get deeper into the middle of it every time we turn around."

"Find the bequest and let's get out of here," she said with a shiver. "I'm starting to have a terrible feeling about all of this."

He went back to searching the desk as she searched the barrister case. Finally, in the bottom drawer, he found a lock box. Taking it out of the drawer, he placed it on the desk. "Give me two of your hair pins," he said.

Immediately, she withdrew two pins from the mass of dark curls and walked over to press them into his hand. It didn't take Val long to pick the lock. Inside, he found the will and the additional instructions left. Tucking both into his pocket, he returned the pins to her just as a floorboard creaked in the antechamber.

"What was that?" she whispered.

"Someone's here," he replied just as quietly. "Come on."

They crept toward the door to the outer office. Val peered out but saw no one. Hoping that the noise had just been someone passing by in the hall, he motioned for Lilly to follow him quietly as they moved through the small antechamber. As they neared the door, another noise, the scrape of furniture moving on a wooden floor, sounded behind them. He looked back just in time to see the heavy desk being shoved toward them, pushing them back toward the wall as a man darted past them. Val didn't have the opportunity to see much more than a shock of blond hair that looked strikingly similar to his cousin.

"Damn and blast. Are you hurt?" he asked her.

She had her hand pressed to her chest, over her heart. "Only startled. No. Not startled! Frightened half to death. We have to go... if he comes back with others, I cannot imagine what danger we will face."

He could. And it was the same fate that had met the unfortunate Mr. Littleton. "Let's get the bloody hell out of here."

THEY WERE NEARING Lord Highcliff's home in Richmond and Lilly was marginally calmer. Not that she'd ever been hysterical, but finding a corpse was certainly an uncommon occurrence for her. During the journey, Val had been perusing the documents pertaining to the bequest.

"This is the strangest thing I've ever seen," he finally said.

"What is it?"

"There's no mention in here of the funds being released upon your great-aunt's death. Everything states that the funds will come to you when you marry. So... you're certain that he stated she was frail and ill?"

Lilly considered it carefully. "Well, he said she was ill... and that my seeing her was an impossibility. That I'd never get to her in time. But he didn't say time for what. Death was implied but never stated specifically."

"Lady Marchebanks, to my knowledge, is neither old and infirmed nor particularly frail... she is, in fact, quite healthy. Which begs the question why? Why the secrecy?"

Lilly shrugged. "It is a scandal. The very public seduction of my mother, my illegitimate birth, her suicide... those are all very valid reasons for not wanting to publicly acknowledge our kinship."

He returned the sheaf of papers to her. "I'm not certain that's it, but I can't fathom why they would reach out, offer you this very generous marriage portion and never want any contact. There's a mystery there and I mean to solve it!"

"We've more than one mystery," she stated. "Who was the blond man in the office? Was it Elsworth? And was he responsible for Mr. Littleton's death?"

"I don't know. It may have been, but that person was very physical. I can't imagine Elsworth shoving a desk. To my knowledge, he's never worked that hard in his life."

Lilly didn't comment. She could imagine it. After all, he'd been prepared to force his way into her chamber. "And if it was Elsworth? What then? Mr. Littleton deserves justice. No one is so important or above the law that they can commit such heinous crimes with impunity."

"No, there can be no impunity for that," he agreed. "If it was Elsworth, I will be certain that he is punished for his crimes. I'm trying to protect the family name and, to a degree, that means protecting him... but it doesn't mean he won't face consequences in a more discreet manner."

Which was all well and good for them, but what of Mr. Littleton? "Are you certain someone will discover Mr. Littleton's body? I don't know if he has a wife or children, if someone is even worrying about him!" she said. "I hate to think of him just lying there."

"An anonymous note was sent around to Bow Street along with the necessary sum to spur them to action. His death will be discovered and investigated," Val promised her. "Now, let's try to put it out of our minds. It's hardly an auspicious event for our wedding day, now is it?"

She smiled sadly. "No, but then it seems we've done nothing in the regular order or way of things."

Val laughed. "That is very true. Will you regret that?"

She cocked her head and considered her answer. "No. I don't think I shall... I think, if what occurred in your room last night is any indication, I should have very few regrets about our marriage."

At that less than subtle reminder, his eyes flashed with desire. "Behave, minx. Breakfast first, and then we'll see to our other needs."

Lilly grinned and looked away. But her grin faded quickly. There were other events from the previous night that bore discussion. "I should tell you something, but you must promise me that you won't lose your temper."

He gave a weary sigh. "How can I promise you that when I've no notion of what you're about to tell me?"

"Well, it is upsetting, but I handled it. I took care of things and I do not need you to avenge me or anything else so silly—"

He'd leaned forward and grasped her hand in his. "Lilly... tell me."

Her breath rushed out in a huff. "When I left your chamber last night, Elsworth was in the corridor and he followed me to my room. I ran and got there before him, locked the door... and thankfully had the presence of mind to put a chair beneath the door knob. Because he'd had the presence of mind to bring a key."

Val's eyes narrowed. "That isn't presence of mind. That's premeditation and they are very, very different things. I'll kill him."

"He didn't gain entry!"

"But he tried," Val insisted. "He came to your room with a key, intending to let himself in. And what do you think his intentions were, Lilly? To have a spot of tea and discuss the latest novels you've read?"

Lilly drew back and glared at him. "I don't think I like your tone. It isn't as if I invited him! And if you must know, I can take care of myself very well! If you don't believe me, ask him about the cut on his forearm when next you see him!"

Her husband's eyebrows arched upward. "You cut him?"

"Yes. It was very helpful of you to provide me with that clever walking stick and its concealed blade. It would have been more helpful if you'd told me there was a concealed blade. Luckily, I discovered it by accident just in the nick of time."

He blinked at her. "You got it open?"

"Well, yes. It's a simple latch really, once you know to look for it," Lilly answered. "Don't tell me that you haven't mastered it?"

"I found it to be a bit tricky, honestly," he admitted, clearly embarrassed.

She smiled at him. "It's your hands... they're too large. That walking stick might be intended for a person of your stature, but the handle and the mechanism are more suited to the slighter dimensions of a woman."

133

"Huh," he said. "Then perhaps I should get you fencing lessons."

"My dearest husband, perhaps I could give you fencing lessons. I'm rather an expert," she pointed out with no small amount of glee.

He shook his head ruefully. "Of course, you are. Remind me to thank Miss Darrow when next we meet. I owe her a debt for her somewhat irregular thoughts on the education of women."

"I'll be certain to mention your approval," Lilly retorted dryly.

"We're off topic… you distract me so that I cannot think clearly," he admitted. "Tell me what it was that Elsworth said to you?"

"That my mother was a whore. That I was a whore. That Effie was likely a whore. He was drunk, Val, and I think under the influence of opium. He was hardly sensible. Just angry and resentful. Jealous and hungry for power he does not have, just as you suggested."

Val shrugged. "None of that matters at this point. This… what he did… what he *intended* to do… it cannot go unanswered, Lilly. I will call him out."

"You cannot," Lilly replied. "With what I've gathered from things you've said thus far, Elsworth is really just a pawn in a game being played by others. He's committing treason, yes, but he's not the mastermind of it all. If you challenge him now, Val, you'll never find out who is truly behind all of this."

He rose and shoved his fingers into his hair in frustration. "Damn it! I don't care. You are my wife. Even if you were not my wife, his behavior is beyond anything that could be overlooked."

"It is. It absolutely is. But in this instance, I defended myself, and no permanent injury was done to me. He cannot say the same. When he reached into the room, I may have nicked him just a bit."

"Just a bit?"

"It was only his forearm," Lilly stated. "We cannot afford to be hotheaded and allow our tempers and our prides to sway us! You've worked too hard and sacrificed too much to ferret out just these sorts of plots to allow what was truly a minor incident to destroy everything now. For lack of a better way to put it, given enough rope, Elsworth will hang himself, as we both know."

He halted his pacing and looked at her. "You're right. I know you are. But when I think of it, I want to thrash him."

She smiled. "I am your wife, as you said. If you didn't want to thrash him for that, it would be cause for concern. But I don't want to talk about Elsworth anymore. We are here in this beautiful house, about to partake of this lovely feast, and we're shouting at one another because you're angry at your cousin for something he *almost* did. Let it go... for now. Until we have what we need from him, at least."

His eyes narrowed and he fixed her with a sharp gaze. "We? You're saying that quite a bit. I wasn't aware that my 'spying', as you put it, had become a joint endeavor."

"Well, yes," Lilly said. "I think, in all fairness, that I'll be much better at this spying business than you are. Now, tell me precisely what your garishly-dressed friend is doing with this charmingly elegant house that looks not at all like his tastes."

He was silent for a moment, surveying her critically. Lilly feared that he might not be willing to let the matter go. But finally, he let out a heavy and resigned sigh before saying, "This is far more understated and traditional than I would have pegged Highcliff for. He does have a flair for the dramatic."

Recalling the other man's outrageous clothing, Lilly made a face. But her husband was correct. The house wasn't overly large. Built in the Palladian style, it faced the river and offered stunning views. The staff was also limited, only the butler, the housekeeper, the cook and a pair of maids lived in. There weren't even any footmen. A stable hand had come forward to carry their bags inside as they were shown to the dining room where an elegant breakfast, including a divine cake that Lilly thought too pretty to eat, had been laid for them. She wanted nothing to do with food. The very idea of any celebration at such a time made her feel slightly ill. But such care had been taken, it seemed wrong to disappoint the servants by not even pretending to partake and enjoy it all. Despite everything, she could still acknowledge that the scene had been set perfectly and every last detail had been taken care of.

"This is all rather unexpected," she said. "For a man who is report-ed to be a confirmed bachelor, Highcliff seems to understand a great deal about what is customary following a wedding service."

Val's only response was a noncommittal grunt as he began filling a plate with food. "You seem very interested in Highcliff," he finally commented as he took his seat.

"He's intriguing," Lilly said. "I rather suspect that there are few people in this world who know who he really is."

"That's true enough," Val said. While he knew the man better than most, even he was not fully in the loop.

"How does he know Effie? In all the years I've known her, even after we had ceased being pupil and master, she never mentioned him to me."

Val gestured toward her empty plate. "Why are you not eating?"

"I'm not hungry," she said, recalling the events of the morning, and sat back. "Are they lovers?"

He choked on the bite of potatoes he'd just eaten. "I don't know," he answered between coughs. "Is it our business if they are?"

"Well, of course, it is," Lilly answered. "Effie is my friend. In truth, she's almost like my mother, certainly the only one I've ever known. Willa and I were very young when she found as at that horrid school and brought us back to London with her. I cannot even imagine what would have become of us at the other school. She raised us, she taught us. I like to think, though other girls came after, that we are more like family to her because we were the first. She often said there wouldn't be a Darrow School at all if she hadn't stumbled upon us when she did."

"That still doesn't give you the right to pry into her personal life,"

Val said reasonably. "She is a woman grown and if she chooses to have a lover—"

"He could break her heart," Lilly interrupted him. "And I wouldn't like him very much if he did that."

Val set his fork down and shoved his plate away, as if the conversation had robbed him of his appetite. "I cannot attest to what is occurring between them, but I do not believe he would toy with her affections. Whatever is said of him, he is an honorable man. Let us worry after our own hearts and allow Miss Darrow and Lord Highcliff to worry after theirs."

Not for the first time, she was struck by how handsome he was. Beautiful, in fact, with his dark hair and flashing eyes. And memories of the previous night and the pleasure he'd shown her, as well as the pleasure he'd denied himself, assailed her. "There are a lot of things I'd like to put from my mind," she said, "if I were to be provided with an appropriate distraction."

"There is nothing appropriate about the distraction that you have in mind, minx," he replied, but his lingering and heated gaze revealed that he did not mind the suggestion at all.

"Aren't you the least bit eager?" she asked.

"You know that I am... are you certain, after the events at Mr. Littleton's office—"

"The things that occurred in Mr. Littleton's office are precisely the things I want to be distracted from, Husband," she said. "Take me upstairs."

He rose and held out his hand to her. "We're going to scandalize the servants."

"Oh, Valentine," she said, rising to her feet and placing her hand in his, "I think you're rather missing the larger picture. Our marriage will scandalize all of society. The servants in this house are the least of our concerns."

Chapter Sixteen

A
S THEY NEARED the bedchamber that had been prepared for them, Val was in for an even greater surprise. For a man who eschewed romantic entanglements, Highcliff had certainly made quite an effort to set the scene for seduction. Roses and candles were everywhere even as champagne chilled on a table.

"Well, I will say this for Lord Highcliff, he continues to surprise me," Lilly commented dryly.

"No truer words were ever spoken. It is rather unexpected but not unwelcome, however," he said. "You should have a bit of romance and seduction."

"I don't need those things, you know? I have made it clear that I am already entirely seduced and completely eager to undertake the duties of the marriage bed, have I not?"

"That you refer to it as a duty and the marriage bed proves to me that you do, indeed, require romance and seduction," he said with a soft laugh. "Now, turn around and let me unlace your gown. I know you're eager to be shed of it."

She shuddered, whether with anticipation or with a reminder of why they both wanted to be rid of the clothing they wore. Regardless, she turned and he began to free the lacing of her gown until the fabric sagged from her shoulders and then simply slithered down her arms to rest on her hips. With a gentle tug, it fell the rest of the way to the floor and puddled at her feet. Next, he freed her stays and her petticoat until she wore only the amethyst-colored slippers and lovely embroidered stockings and garters and a delicate chemise. She stepped away from him then and moved toward the bed.

It wasn't shyness or hesitation on her part, because she seated herself on the bed, facing him expectantly. "If I'm going to reveal all, I certainly think it's only fair if you do as well," she challenged.

Val felt a smile tugging at the corners of his mouth. He'd done more of that since meeting her than he had in a very long time, he thought. Laughing, smiling, genuinely enjoying himself. Was it an indication of things to come? He didn't know, but he certainly hoped so. "As the lady wishes," he said, and promptly shed his coat. His waistcoat followed, along with his cravat. Then he seated himself to remove his boots.

With that task done, he pulled his shirt over his head and tossed it aside. "The breeches stay on… for now. I can't trust myself and I certainly can't trust you and your curious hands."

She leaned back on the bed, resting on her elbows. The pose was unintentionally provocative, thrusting her breasts forward and highlighting just how translucent her chemise was. "Do you really mind so very much?"

Val didn't answer. He simply rose from the settee and crossed to the bed. Without preamble or warning, he leaned down and claimed her lips in a searing kiss. His fingers delved into her dark hair, sending pins scattering as the mass of it tumbled down over her shoulders. It felt like spun silk in his hands and, without conscious thought, his fingers tightened in the mass of it, tipping her head back further, allowing him to deepen the kiss. It was more ravenous than romantic and, heaven help him, she responded in kind. And then, bolder than he'd ever imagined, she laid herself back on the bed and held out her arms to him, and he was powerless to resist such an invitation.

Climbing fully onto the bed, he held himself above her, resting his weight on his forearms as he kissed her lips, the curve of her cheek, the firm line of her jaw, and then down her neck until he could reach the delicate ribbon that tied her chemise. Tugging it free, he spread the fabric wide, baring her gorgeous breasts. The sunlight streaming through the windows painted her skin with a golden glow that made him think she might actually be the goddess she appeared to be.

"I hate telling you that you're beautiful," he whispered. "It seems like such a weak description of all that you are. Like some trite thing you've heard hundreds of times before."

She smiled up at him. "But it didn't matter when anyone else said it. Only when you do."

"Then you are without a doubt the most beautiful woman I've ever seen... inside and out."

Her hands came up, coasting over his chest, touching him with curiosity, her expression one of wonder. His jaw clenched and he submitted to her exploration, though he was already struggling to control his urges. Their prelude to lovemaking the night before had left him as primed as an untried youth. Shifting slightly, he came down beside her, allowing himself to do some exploring of his own. He touched her everywhere he could reach, and then tugged her chemise lower. As if she'd read his intent, she lifted her hips and he coaxed the garment over them until he could skim it over her legs and toss it aside entirely.

Only when she was laid out before him did he lean forward and place a tender kiss upon her breast. Immediately, her hand slid into his hair, urging him on, and he gave her what she wordlessly requested. He lavished attention on that tender flesh, with his hands, his mouth, his teeth—he didn't stop until she was gasping with pleasure and writhing with need. Even then, he only shifted his attention to her other breast, offering it equally attentive ministrations. But then he slid his hand along the softness of her inner thigh, just as he had the night before. There was no need to coax for she knew precisely what awaited her. She parted her legs eagerly for him, welcoming his touch, straining toward it.

Stroking the soft, silken heat of her, finding her wet and eager for him, was nearly his undoing. But he was determined that he would bring her pleasure before seeking his own. With that thought in mind, he moved lower, pressing soft kisses over her ribs and the soft curve of her belly, until he could kneel between her parted thighs.

"What are you doing?" she asked. Her voice was tight with a mixture of curiosity and trepidation.

"Something you will like very much, I think. Trust me, Lilly?"

"I do," she said.

Val dipped his head and pressed a kiss to the dark curls that shielded her sex. She made a sound, part shock and part pleasure. Then he parted those tender folds and tasted the sweetness of her. Her body tensed, her head fell back and she arched toward him. And then he devoured her. He was relentless as he teased her, tasted her and drove her toward the edge of pleasure, only to halt and ease her gently back from the precipice.

"Are you trying to kill me?" she asked.

He smiled against her skin and then nipped at her thigh. "Pleasure is even sweeter when you've had to wait for it."

"I've waited, Valentine. Who's the virgin here?"

He laughed at that. "I may not be virginal, Lillian, but this is different for me, too."

"Why?" she asked with puzzlement.

"Because it's you… and because it matters so much more."

She gripped his arms then, tugging him upward. Against his better judgment, he allowed it. "Then make me your wife… in every way. I want to know how it feels."

It was impossible to resist that sweet plea. Val left her only long enough to shed his breeches and then rejoined her on the bed. She welcomed him eagerly, wrapping her arms about him and parting her thighs so that he settled easily between them. He could feel the heat of her. Closing his hand around the base of his shaft, he guided himself to her entrance and then slowly pressed into the softness of her body. He was attuned to her every sound. Each soft sigh, every startled gasp, and breathless moan were a map to the thing he sought most—to bring her release before finding his own. Pressing deeper, he breached the fragile barrier of her innocence, and then he stilled completely.

Jaw clenched, every part of him tensed, he struggled to go slow, to fight the instinct that urged him to simply claim her. But he could not fight her, and when she gripped his hips and arched upward, taking him deeper, he was lost.

IN ALL THE whispered exchanges between the girls at school, when they'd all discussed in the vaguest terms that represented the sum total of their knowledge what that moment would actually be like, nothing could have prepared her. The slight stinging pain had been only momentary. And with the overwhelming sensations of him pressing deeper inside her, it was easily forgotten. Nothing had ever felt so wondrous or so right. Had she been able to think clearly at all, it might have frightened her how much she needed him in that moment, how much she craved his touch. The intimacy of it transported her to some other plane it seemed, where nothing existed but the two of them and the glorious points of contact between them.

As he began to move, setting a gentle rhythm, it robbed her of even the hint of thought. She was reduced to pure sensation. He'd given her pleasure, but the intensity of what she felt in those moments was incomparable to anything that had come before. It consumed her and she could do nothing but cling to him, wrap herself about him and hold him close as he took them both to the edge.

The gentle pace quickened and she could feel his muscles clenching beneath her hands as she touched him, smoothing her palms over the hard planes of his back and along his sides. The heat of him, the rawness of him in that moment, drew her like a moth to a flame. She moved with him then, matching the rhythm he'd set and arching upward to meet him stroke for stroke. His head dropped forward, his forehead resting against her shoulder and her name escaped his lips on a ragged breath.

Then the tension that he'd built so perfectly inside her simply shattered. She cried out with it, unable to stop herself. And then she felt him shudder against her, felt the rush and heat of him as he stilled against her completely. Then he kissed her. Not the drugging, heated kisses that had brought them to that point, but the sweet brush of his lips, featherlight and achingly tender. In a matter of days, not even the course of an entire week, she'd done the one foolish thing she'd thought herself above throughout her life—she'd fallen in love. But he had not. It was a terrifying prospect to know that her heart was engaged and the state of his was yet unknown to her.

Chapter Seventeen

"WHERE ARE YOU?"

The question, asked softly and with gentle amusement, pulled Lilly from her thoughts. At some point, Val had moved to her side and they lay together in a tangle of limbs and discarded clothing. "I'm right here." She'd been replaying the moments in her mind. Down to the second, she could pinpoint when she had lost all control and had all but begged him to make love to her. Not verbally, but she'd certainly communicated her desires clearly enough. She'd been wanton enough that even she was shocked at her behavior. And yet through all of it, he'd appeared to be in complete control. That left her wondering if perhaps her desire, because of her newly-discovered feelings for him, if in fact they were real and not simply a product of her own imagination and lust, somehow surpassed his. Did he want her as much as she wanted him? Or would he soon grow bored with her and move on?

He touched one finger to her forehead, smoothing the worry lines that formed there. "Only partly. If you can be so lost in thought at such a moment, I have clearly failed in my duties of seduction."

"I didn't think it was supposed a duty," she replied with a laugh, striving for a bit of levity and failing.

"If it is, I'll sign up for it every day," he offered and rolled to his back. "What troubles you, Lilly? I didn't hurt you, did I?"

"No," she said honestly. "Not at all. It was… it was perfect. So much more than I ever imagined it could be."

She sat up and looked at him over her shoulder. It was easier than meeting his gaze directly. There were things she would admit, and others that she was not yet ready to. Perhaps it wasn't even love, after all. Perhaps she was simply so consumed with lust and the glorious pleasures he'd shown her that she wasn't able to think clearly. "I didn't know I would lose myself to the moment so completely. I was a bit caught off guard by that, I think. Is it always like that?"

He didn't answer immediately, but took his time, obviously considering his words carefully. Yet, the entire time, he touched her. His hands stroked over her back or traced delicate patterns along the crest of her hips. Finally, he said, "It's different every time, I think. The mechanics of it might be the same, but the feelings, the sensation, the significance of it—that varies."

"And with the partner, I presume. That would have some effect."

His hand stilled, resting on the curve of her hip in a manner that felt possessive. "Are you asking if it's different because we're married or because it's you?"

She cocked her head to one side, and considered her answer. "Both, I think. I am not experienced the way your other lovers have been… and while I was thoroughly lost to the moment, you were not. You maintained control to the very end."

He rose up and rested his weight on his elbow, then twined his free hand in her hair, urging her back to him. "Is that what you're worrying about?"

"Not worried. Curious," she answered.

"Then let me ease your curiosity. There is nowhere and no one I would rather be with than you. From the moment I saw you, I smiled," he said. "And I don't do that really. In two days, I've laughed more, smiled more and been happier, even with all that has occurred, than in the last decade of my life. Sometimes, Lilly, you just meet people and they change you... or they guide you to rediscover the parts of yourself you thought lost. You reminded me of who I was before I went to war. Before I came home and began all my clandestine activities."

"Spying, you mean?"

He grinned. "You just like to say that word, I think. I didn't spy. I listened."

"Which is rather what spies do. They observe, without letting on they are observing, and then they report back to people in authority. That is what you do, isn't it?"

"What I did," he corrected. "I'm done with that now. Highcliff knows I'm out."

"Are you certain you want to give it up?"

"I'm certain I never wanted to start it to begin with," he said. "But I'm good at cards. Better than good. I have a knack for knowing what has been played, what hasn't and for predicting, with a high degree of accuracy, what cards others are holding. I can't explain how I do it, only that I do, and that it's impossible to cheat me or anyone else at a table I'm playing at. But I don't like it. I never have."

"So you're happy with me... and that's why I lost all touch with reality and you were still thinking to the very end?" The doubt in her tone was quite clear.

He huffed out a breath, half-laugh and half-groan. "I wanted it to be good for you. No. I needed it to be perfect for you. There is only one first time, Lilly. And bad or good, it sets the tone for our relationship moving forward... add to that the fact that it was your first time ever and not just with me, it was even more important. When the two of us are on more even footing in terms of knowledge and experience, I promise you, you may drive me as mad with lust as you wish."

Could it be that simple? She certainly hoped so. "I rather like the sound of that," she said.

He eyed her for a moment, seeing far more than she wished for him to, she was sure.

"What's really bothering you? Do you regret our marriage? I know it was hasty and I know that we likely both went into it for the entirely wrong reasons. But that doesn't mean we can't make it work, that we can't make it something extraordinary for both of us," he said.

Hating her own neediness and craving for reassurance, Lilly lay down next to him. Immediately, he pulled her close and held her against his chest. "I am afraid to expect anything," she admitted.

"Because you think I'll disappoint you?"

"Perhaps. Or perhaps I will disappoint you," she admitted. "I know nothing of marriage. I've lived my whole life in a house full of unmarried women. The men of my acquaintance, including my father, do not inspire faith in your sex, I'm afraid."

"But I'm not them," he said.

"No," she said. "You're not. You're very different from them. But that gives you a power over me that they've never had. You can hurt me, Valentine, and they cannot."

"That is the last thing I want to do," he said gruffly.

"Then don't."

VAL HOPED IT would be that simple, hoped that they would be able to avoid the fate so many did not. The last thing he wanted was the cold and loveless marriage his parents had, or his grandparents for that matter. In truth, the Somers' track record was less than stellar. He couldn't name a single happy union in the whole of his family, extended or otherwise.

"I think I'm hungry now," she said.

He laughed at that. "Of course, you are. Get your lovely and rather perfectly-formed arse out of bed and into something resembling clothing and we'll go below stairs and try to cajole Highcliff's cook into feeding us something."

He lay there for a moment longer, watching her get up and cross the room. She'd managed to restore some semblance of order to her chemise, but her hair, a mass of dark and unruly waves, was beyond all hope. She looked like a woman well and thoroughly ravished and he was more than happy with his handiwork. And as soon as they'd gotten some food into the both of them, he fully intended to have an encore.

Lilly opened the armoire where the servants had indicated that items had been placed for her. As their own bags still sat unpacked by the door, he didn't know what was in there. But he heard her gasp as she opened the doors.

"Oh, I really do like your friend, Highcliff," she said.

A spurt of jealousy hit him squarely, prodding his temper to life, but he quickly squashed it. "What sort of silk or velvet has he lured your affections with?"

She laughed delightedly and pulled out a lovely confection of silk that would simply skim over her figure and reveal far more than it concealed. There was a wrapper of the same shade lined with velvet. It was an extravagant purchase. The only thing preventing Val from calling him out was the knowledge that Highcliff had likely sent around a note to the very same dressmaker he himself had obtained for Lilly and instructed her to send something "suitable for romance".

"If I thought for a moment he picked that out himself, I'd blacken both of his eyes," Val said without rancor.

"Well, I'm sure he didn't. That would be scandalous, indeed. Actually, it's still scandalous, isn't it? But it's so pretty," she cooed. "I don't even care."

Val watched her stroke the velvet in a way that made him reconsider the notion of letting her out of the bed, much less out of the room. "Stop that. If you want food... if you want anything other than to be back in this bed, you'll put that wrapper on and find yourself some slippers."

"Slippers? Even my feet need to be covered?"

"The floors are cold," he said, and reached for his own breeches. He pulled them on quickly, then his shirt. "Food. And then back to bed."

"Fine," she said and reached back into the wardrobe for a pair of slippers.

When they were both at least somewhat decent, they went downstairs and found the house all but empty. Even the live-in servants were out. Only a note had been left for them, along with a hamper of food. It stated that per Lord Highcliff's instructions, the two of them were to be granted run of the house and complete privacy for the duration of their stay.

"What were you saying about blackening both of his eyes?" Lilly challenged.

"I stand corrected. He is a god amongst men. If there's a bit of ham and some fresh bread in that basket, along with some good wine, I may very well kiss him myself the next time I see him."

"No doubt, that would go over well at your club," she said.

"Hardly that. The members of Brooks' will not turn a hair if you gamble away your fortune, place bets on a lady's honor or even duel over it, but there are some things even they will not turn a blind eye to," Val said.

"And is that your club? With your remarkable skill at gambling? Brooks'?" she asked, dishing things up from the hamper.

"I'm a member at Brooks'. I'm also conditionally permitted in White's and Boodle's, so long as I'm accompanied by a member. Generally, the play I was involved in happened in less reputable establishments," he admitted ruefully.

"Brothels," she surmised.

"Is that ham? It smells divine," he said.

She laughed at his blatant attempt to change the subject. "Don't think I don't know. The Darrow School is in a very fashionable section of Mayfair... and there are quite a few houses on our block that are... well, not simply residential. I've seen you and your carriage coming and going from Number Thirty-seven Cavendish Place. I shall simply knock on their door and inquire as to what sort of establishment it is."

Val choked on the grape he'd just eaten. Coughing, sputtering, eyes watering as he wheezed for breath, he had a moment of truly wondering if he might die before the object was finally dislodged. "Do... not... ever... knock... on... that... door," he said gasping.

"Good lord, you act like they'd haul me in and put me to work!"

"They might. I gamble there, because that's where the sharps congregate and where they fleece the unsuspecting. But it's run by very unscrupulous people, Lilly. Do not ever go there. Dear God, do not even walk on that side of the street if you can avoid it."

"Surely it cannot be so terrible if you've frequented the place without incident?"

"I never said it was without incident. In fact, your association with me could potentially make it a greater danger to your... have you ever heard of the Hound of Whitehall?" he demanded.

"No. What a strange name! Should I have?"

No, he supposed, she should not have. A sheltered young woman living in a school of other young women and none of them associating with foolish men who played foolish games, why would she have? "Well, you do not wish to know more about him. That I can promise you. Just stay away from there!"

She eyed him while considering the order for a moment. "I will agree on one condition. You must stay away, as well."

He had no wish to go there again unless absolutely necessarily. The Hound was ruthless and his people were quick and sometimes too eager with their dirtiest work. Not to mention that he was already in deep with him for the favor he'd asked earlier. "I will not go there unless I absolutely must... and if I do, I will not do so without telling you. That is the best I can offer."

"Then I will avoid it on the same terms," she said. "And we will not argue about it."

Then he would simply break his word and never tell her, because the thought of what might happen to her in such a place terrified him. The very idea of her facing off against a man as ruthless as the Hound left him feeling weak in the knees and in the gut. "Fine. Let us eat and then let us return to our newly-wedded bliss upstairs. After all, tomorrow we go back to the dragon."

She laughed. "You shouldn't call her that. She loves you very much, you know. Even if she does try to manage you."

"She didn't try. She succeeded. You do realize that the two of us being here is entirely at her hand, don't you? She put us together and somehow knew exactly what I would do!"

Lilly smiled again. "Then perhaps you know where your uncanny ability with cards came from, after all."

Chapter Eighteen

T HEY RETURNED TO the family's townhouse the following day and were met with disapproving glares and stony silence. Stepping into the drawing room, wearing a sprigged muslin morning dress that had mysteriously appeared by courier just before breakfast, another gift from Lord Highcliff who seemed to have thought of everything, Lilly prepared to face her former employer. She had the feeling it would require a dramatic mea culpa and profuse apologies to even begin to set things right.

"Your grace, I understand you must be so very disappointed," Lilly began.

"I am not disappointed," the older woman snapped. "I am heartbroken and deeply affronted. My own grandson and I am not even permitted to attend his wedding!" Her complaints were accompanied by a theatrical sniff as she touched a handkerchief to her curiously dry eyes. "A wedding, I might add, that would never have occurred if not for my beneficence."

"It wasn't that we didn't desire your presence, but that, in light of events that had occurred and Val's concern for my safety, he felt we should proceed cautiously," Lilly explained, looking to Val for help. He simply shrugged and crossed to one of the chairs that flanked the fireplace where he promptly sat and waited for her to sort out the issue.

"Because he thinks his cousin is a murderer," the dowager duchess snapped. "I know what he thinks. It's utter foolishness. Elsworth isn't capable of such a thing!"

Lilly had her doubts. More so than even before after seeing a man that could easily have been Elsworth fleeing from Mr. Littleton's office. Not to mention his threats toward her, both overt and subtle. "I know you want to believe the best of him—"

The dowager duchess cut her off with a laugh. In fact the old woman laughed so long and hard she collapsed into a coughing fit. Finally, wheezing a bit, she managed, "Believe the best of him? My dear girl, it isn't that I think him too good to commit such atrocities! I simply question his intelligence in carrying out such a plan... as well has his nerve! He is weak. He always has been weak. I love him because he is my grandson but I am not blind to his faults. Nor am I blind to Valentine's!"

Lilly sat back, stunned by the admission. "Oh, well... we didn't really think he was doing it on his own," she explained. "At least not the planning portion of it."

The dowager duchess' eyes narrowed. "And who do you think is planning it, then? Me?"

"Of course not!" Val finally interjected. "We both know if you wanted to do us harm, you'd simply skewer us with your vicious wit. But as to who may be planning it all and having poor, dupable Elsworth carry out their dastardly deeds, I'd rather not say until we have more information."

The deceptively frail-appearing woman made a harrumphing sound. Then, in a tone dripping with bitterness, she added, "Fine. You will do as you wish regardless. I'm just your poor, old grandmother... too old, too weak, too feeble-minded to be of any use to anyone. I might as well go ahead and rattle off to my grave."

"Please! If you died tomorrow, you'd only haunt us until we did your bidding," Val replied sarcastically. "Not even death could prevent you from getting your way."

Called on her bluff, the dowager duchess sat up a bit straighter. "I will haunt you. Every day of your wretched life, you rotten boy! And there will be a wedding... an actual one. With all the trimmings and all the fuss. You'll not deny me that. I'll see you married in St. Paul's under the mournful gaze of every marriage-minded mama whose efforts were foiled by my own excellent matchmaking. It will serve them right for salivating and chasing after you the way they have. No dignity whatsoever!"

"But we did get mar—" Lilly began and was abruptly cut off by Val making a panicked gesture.

"Whatever you say, Grandmother. Your wish is our command."

Apparently telling the dowager duchess that they'd already been married in St. Paul's would not be in their best interests.

"We wouldn't have it any other way, your grace," Lilly added, before glaring at Val. The last thing she wanted was a society wedding. They would be the subject of so much gossip anyway it only seemed to be adding fuel to the fire to her mind. "And we'll have to wait until my half-sister returns from the country, of course."

The dowager duchess nodded. "Yes, having your half-sister there, along with her husband, that reprobate Lord Deveril, will help to combat any whispers regarding your suitability. Your father is a gentleman, after all. Your half-sister is married to a lord, no less. And with Valentine's expectations of a sizable inheritance and a duke-dom... well, who would dare gainsay his choice, regardless?"

Everyone would. But Lilly didn't say that, instead she just smiled and tried to will away the sick feeling that had settled like a brick in the pit of her stomach. "Naturally you are correct, as always, your grace."

"You should call me Grandmother, dear. We are family now, after all."

"Grandmother," Lilly said, the word feeling positively unnatural on her tongue.

"Now, you must go upstairs and have your maid get rid of every terrible thing I made you wear for the last few months. It was all part of the plan, you know?"

"I'm beginning to see that," Lilly said.

"Good girl. Get rid of all of it and then we will go shopping. I know my dear grandson provided some things for you, but aside from marrying you, my girl, his taste is rather questionable, as well. He knows how to dress women, but not how to dress ladies. And we need for all of society to look at you with envy!"

That was the last thing in the world she wanted. Looking at Val with pleading eyes, she silently begged for his assistance.

"Grandmother, I understand that Lilly's wardrobe will certainly need to be updated beyond the few things we've purchased, but it is our honeymoon. The shopping expedition can wait a day or two, can it not?" he asked.

"Very well. We'll need those scratches on her cheek to be fully healed before we are seen too much by those who would gossip about it, at any rate," the dowager duchess agreed. "And do try to not let anyone else shoot at her, Valentine. It's most disconcerting!"

It was obvious that he was fighting back a grin as he replied, "Certainly, Grandmother. That is precisely what my dear bride said about nearly having her head blown off... it was quite disconcerting. If you'll excuse us now?"

"Go on then. Rotten, irascible boy," the dowager duchess groused.

As they rose and left the drawing room, Lilly was fuming at him. "Your grandmother is right. You are rotten and irascible. And incorrigible!"

"But I'm not a boy," he replied. "I'm very much a man... or do I need to prove that to you again?"

She blushed to the very roots of her hair. "We will not indulge in such activities in the middle of the day in a residence we are sharing with your grandmother," she hissed.

155

"Oh, but we shall," he said. "She wanted us married, she can live with the scandalous consequences of it."

That sobered Lilly quickly. Any hint of amusement and teasing fled. "I don't want to be in society, Val. I don't. They are vicious and terrible and they'll eat me alive. It'll be whispers and the cut direct and all manner of terrible, humiliating things!"

He stopped then and faced her squarely. "You know that will not happen? That woman in there—that tiny, fragile-looking and yet made of forged steel woman—she chose you. She decided from the moment she laid eyes on you that you and I should be together and then she engineered us both right to the altar. And I personally couldn't be more grateful to her for it. But if she wants society to bow and kiss your slippers, they will bloody well bow and kiss them. Because she never fails to get what she wants."

"But my whole life—"

He kissed her then. Just a quick press of his lips to hers, a gesture of affection and quite possibly even exasperation. "Trust me, Lilly... and trust her. I promise that you can."

She so desperately wanted to believe that. In her whole life, there had only ever been two people she could trust—Effie and Willa. Not even the other girls at school had been confidantes for her. She'd always been cautious, aware that anything she said might later be used against her. It was a hard lesson learned at her father's hand. "I do trust you both, but only so far. I can't help that. But I'm trying."

"Even after all we've shared?" he asked her.

"Yes," she replied. "I can trust you with my body. It's easy enough to see you are not the sort of man who would ever hurt a woman physically. But that doesn't mean you won't break my heart... and your grandmother—well, she'll be kind to me so long as it serves her purposes to do so."

"You are wrong about her. She admires you, Lilly. She sees something in you that made her draw you into the fold of our family," he said.

"Wrong about her, but not about you." His election not to address her statement about him being the potential cause of her heartbreak had not gone unnoticed. "You can't even say that you won't break my heart, can you?"

"I can say that I do not wish to… and that I will do everything in my power to prevent it. Is that enough?"

It would have to be. "I don't want to think anymore. Can you make the incessant whir of thoughts simply stop?"

His eyes darkened with sensual promise. "I can. And I intend to, as soon as you climb those stairs… or should we scandalize everyone and I can carry you up?"

Part of her wanted that, but she decided that discretion was not without its merits. "Wait five minutes and follow me," she instructed.

"Only if you promise to be naked when I arrive," he bargained.

"Then we have a bargain, Husband."

Chapter Nineteen

IT WAS LATE afternoon, inching toward dusk, when Val managed to rouse himself from their bed. All of Lilly's things had been moved into his chambers at his request. He didn't much care if it sent shockwaves through the entire house. Being apart from her was not something he was willing to do. For her safety and his own peace of mind, he wanted her close. But that wasn't his only reason. Living in a house full of servants, as well as his impossibly nosy grandmother, he was reluctant to let everyone know if and when he was visiting his wife's chamber. The only way to avoid that was to avoid traipsing down the corridor every time he wished to have a word with her, or anything else for that matter.

She slumbered on, clearly exhausted. But then he'd noted even the morning before as they'd walked into the church how tired she looked. She'd had far too much to deal with of late. Threats and attempts on her life, Elsworth lurking in the shadows at every turn. Relatives turning up out of the blue to leave her a fortune assuming she'd dance to their tune. He couldn't eliminate the threats and he couldn't change the nature of her relationship with her relatives, but he could put a halt to Elsworth's skulking.

Thinking of the way all of his interactions with Elsworth went, Val steeled himself and his temper. He intended to have a conversation with Elsworth and nothing would stop him. No sniping at one another, no veiled insults, or they'd never get anywhere. He would tell his cousin what he knew and he would find out just how deeply he was into the mess. With that in mind, Val began to dress, pulling on his discarded breeches and shirt. He donned his waistcoat but left off with his cravat and coat. It was hardly a formal occasion, after all, accusing one's cousin of treason.

After donning his boots on the off chance that Elsworth might make a run for it and he'd be forced to give chase, he left the room. He spared one more glance at his wife's sleeping form before closing the door gently behind him so as not to wake her. He headed down the stairs and to the small billiard room off the library. It had always been Elsworth's preferred space though he had no skill for the game. It was the seclusion of the space that had always appealed to him, Val thought. Even when they'd been younger, long before the bitterness and begrudging behavior had developed between them, Elsworth had often preferred his own company and the questionable pleasure of solitude.

As he entered the room, his cousin looked up from his seat before the window. Immediately, Elsworth crumpled the note he held in his hand and tried to hide it. A guilty flush crept over the man's face and it was quite apparent that whatever had been in his note, he'd not wanted anyone to see.

"Bad news?" Val asked.

"Not at all. Insignificant," Elsworth answered, but his words and his expression were incongruous. "I see you've managed to tear yourself away from the considerable charms of your new bride. She might be common, but she is rather pretty."

"Damned by such faint praise. What bothers you so much about her, Cousin? That she is secure enough in herself that she doesn't require your approval or that our grandmother clearly sees a kind of strength and intelligence in her that has earned the dragon's respect?" Val asked.

"Do you really think that? Our grandmother holds her in no particular esteem," Elsworth said with a dismissive laugh. "You underestimate the old woman still. She understood that you, with your rebellion and your need to court scandal, would only ever marry a woman who was unsuitable. She simply placed the least objectionable version of that before you!"

There was some element of truth to that, but it was an oversimplification. As in so many situations, his cousin was incapable of seeing beyond his own very black and white vision of the world. But addressing that would only undermine his purpose in speaking to his cousin. "I didn't come here to fight with you, Elsworth."

"We can do nothing else. You should go back to her and begin trying to produce the requisite heir. It would certainly be a better use of your time," Elsworth said dismissively.

"I know about Marchebanks," Val said abruptly, not even acknowledging Elsworth's crass suggestions. "I know about the offer you had to invest in the munitions shipments... what I don't know, Elsworth, is whether or not you realized those munitions would never reach British troops. Did you have any idea?"

Elsworth rose then, his temper flaring. "Contrary to what you think, Valentine, I am not a fool. The return would have seen me set up for life!"

"The only return you'll get from this is the hangman's noose!" Val shouted back at him. "How, Elsworth? How can you betray your own country?"

"It's easy enough... I detest England. I detest this miserable system of class where I must bow and scrape at your feet for even the smallest bit of coin! I should have been the viscount. I should have the promise of a dukedom lying ahead of me! Heaven knows I'm more suited to it than you with your common whore of a wife!"

Val didn't take the bait. He would not allow Elsworth to stoke his temper, even though he longed to slap the whelp for uttering such an insult. "Tell me where the ambush is to take place, Elsworth! If you do, I might be able to keep your name out of it, to make it appear as if you were duped by these individuals rather than being a knowing participant!"

"Why would you?" Elsworth challenged.

"Because it will kill our grandmother... and while you may detest me, I know you care for her," Val offered.

"Do you? You're wrong. You think I don't know how she detests me? That even after all you've done, that you are still her favorite? No, Cousin. I care not a whit for anyone in this family," Elsworth denied hotly.

"Then do it to save yourself," Val urged. He didn't believe Elsworth. He knew the man was simply speaking from wounded pride and not a sincere lack of feeling. He could see it in his cousin's gaze. "If you tell me... if you give me what I need to stop it, I might be able to keep you from swinging at the end of a bloody rope!"

Elsworth looked at him for the longest moment. "It's too late for that."

"It's not. It is not! Tell me, damn you!" Val insisted. "Let me help you for once in your blasted life!"

"Why?"

Val shook his head. "Because you are family... because once upon a time we did not hate one another. Do you not recall our childhood? We laughed and played together. We did not have this viciousness between us then. For the sake of the boys we once were, let me help you."

His cousin looked away, a muscle working in his jaw and his eyes glistening curiously. After a moment, he turned back to Val. "The ship sails in two days, but it will never make it to India. They'll be set upon near the Channel Islands, Lihou to be specific, and the lot of the cargo stolen," Elsworth said.

"Who? Who are they going to?"

"There are a few stalwarts in France yet who think that they can pick up where Bonaparte left off. They're wrong. They can't. We both know it. Selling them guns is like selling coal to the devil—useless. You must see that!"

"I see that you could be starting another war… and we've lost too much already. Do you not understand how precarious our position is? The cost of war is great to our nation, but profitable to many. Who are the owners of these munitions factories? Do you even know? Who in parliament is awarding contracts to them? I know that Marchebanks likely has his hand in it!"

Elsworth turned away. "You see plots where plots do not exist, Cousin. These French fools are naught but dreamers… like the Jacobites who followed Prince Charlie. They have no leader, they have no one to rally behind. So their efforts will fail and putting guns in their hands will make no matter in the end."

"Says the man who has never been to the front lines and watched the blood of his countrymen being spilled," Val snapped. "It isn't just the French! It's the poorly-supplied soldiers in India who are dying because they haven't the necessary tools to battle our enemies there!"

"Spare me the dramatics, Cousin. Just because you're haunted by your experiences on the Continent doesn't mean we're on the verge of another war! And those primitive villagers in India are hardly a real threat! You're a fool to think otherwise!"

Elsworth would never see the truth, because it was completely removed from his sheltered existence. Trying a different tactic, Val admitted, "I am haunted by it. But I'm not a fool, Elsworth. You think I play cards because I enjoy it, because I long to feel the thrill of winning… but you're wrong. I play because it's at those tables that deals such as the one you've made with Marchebanks are brokered. I know what you agreed to, and I know you haven't a clue what sort of catastrophe you are about to bring raining down on you. If you allow me, I can help you. There is a way through it, Cousin."

Elsworth looked away then, his slightly weak chin trembling for a moment before he managed to clench his features tightly and rein in that telltale sign of emotion. "I betray these men, I die. I betray my country, I still die. There is no way through it. And you, Cousin, may go to the devil!"

Elsworth rose then and strode from the room. A moment later, Val heard the front door slam and knew that his cousin was gone. Not just from the house, though. Any hint of the boy Elsworth had once been was gone, as well. All that remained was a bitter, jealous shell of a man. Resentment had ruined him. Envy, the insidious poison of a covetous heart, would see their family ripped asunder in a way they could not recover from. All that was left was to tell the powers that be and allow them to take him into custody with Marchebanks. Perhaps then one of them would talk and spill the remainder of the information needed to prevent disaster.

Chapter Twenty

HOURS LATER, WEARING a coat and hat hastily borrowed from one of the footmen, Val huddled outside a crumbling warehouse near the docks. With the hat pulled low, his face was concealed from any passersby. There was enough mud and muck splashed on his boots to hide their quality and he was rendered all but invisible. To any passerby, he appeared just another drunk in the rookery, lounging against the side of a building and tippling from a bottle of cheap gin. He'd allowed Elsworth to get a head start, but only by a few minutes. He'd followed his cousin from the shadows, staying on him until he'd reached his destination. The very same warehouse Val now huddled outside of.

It was a dangerous place. The warehouse was situated on the docks and getting there through the rookeries, he'd risked life, limb and purse. Somehow, he'd made it through without being robbed or killed just for the buttons on his waistcoat. Sadly, men had been killed for less. That Elsworth could walk through those neighborhoods unaccosted meant that he was a familiar sight there. *Or a protected one.* Was there some other shady underworld figure who wielded power comparable to the Hound? Or was the Hound himself not to be trusted?

Val dismissed that notion almost instantly. The Hound of Whitehall was guilty of many things, including a bit of smuggling and thumbing his nose at the Crown. But he'd proven time and time again that he supported the soldiers. Many nefarious plots and schemes that would have compromised national security had come to their attention through him. He'd gone so far as to summon Val to his tables when he knew key players in such intrigues would be present.

Cursing under his breath, Val waited. The temperatures were dropping. It was growing colder by the minute. But he couldn't leave until he had something more to work with. He might not be close enough to hear what was being said inside, but he was near enough that he could watch the comings and goings. He'd seen Marchebanks enter. To pass the time and to blend more with his surroundings while convincingly passing for a just a random drunkard, he stood with his arms folded over his chest, softly whistling a rather dirty tune he'd picked up from a gaming hell years before.

As another carriage rolled up, he pulled his hat lower, making certain his face was concealed, and watched the vehicle closely. The door opened and, to his dismay, it wasn't a man who climbed out but a woman. Her face was concealed within the hood of a velvet cloak, but the sweep of her scarlet skirts over the filthy street was oddly familiar to him. Where had he seen her? She moved with an uncommon grace that tugged at his memory. He'd seen her before, whether at one of the hells or in a Mayfair ballroom, he couldn't say. Focusing his attention on the man accompanying her, Val noted that he, too, kept his face hidden behind a heavy cloak, but he was massive. The man stood a head and a half taller than the woman did with broad shoulders and a rough build that hinted at manual labor or perhaps the streets.

As they vanished into the warehouse, Val left his post and slipped down the alley. Carefully, he stacked crates until he could reach a small ledge that ran along the outside of the building. Praying it would support his weight, he reached for it and pulled, testing its sturdiness. When it didn't simply snap off in his hand, he pulled himself up and managed to perch atop it. Inching to his right, toward a window, he peered into the building. It was dimly lit and, through the grime, he could just make out the trio of players and the lady's massive guard standing in the center of the large and utterly empty space.

She had not lowered her hood, which meant she was either very cautious about being seen or that even her compatriots didn't know her identity. Val was leaning toward the latter. He shifted slightly, trying to get a better view. The ledge creaked ominously under him and all those inside turned in the direction of the sound. With the darkness outside and the light in, not to mention the filth of the window, he didn't worry that they'd seen him. But he did worry they might send the behemoth to investigate. Dropping back down onto the boxes, he left quickly, exiting the alley from the other end and emerging into a dirty street pocked with ruts and dotted with piles of excrement whose origins were best left unidentified. He shuffled away, singing softly under his breath and altering his gait as to appear old and stooped. A few minutes later, the behemoth moved past him, scanning the street ahead. Val just kept up his pretense, head down, swaying from side to side, appearing to be a drunken sot for all the world.

Stumbling toward one of the many prostitutes working that stretch of road, he pressed a coin to her hand. "Be a love and try to distract that big fellow, would you?"

"Lud, I don't want a brute like that," she said in shockingly genteel tones.

"I don't wish for you to actually entertain him," Val said, shocked to find the prostitute in question sounded more like a society matron. "I just need to slip past him."

"Before he realizes you're a young lord and not a drunkard from the streets?" she asked.

"Just so," he said.

She glanced down at the coin. "It'll take more than one of these. I'll not entangle myself in your intrigues for so little."

Val grinned. "Be at the corner of Jermyn Street and Duke Street tomorrow morning at ten. You'll get more than a coin. You'll get a job."

An expression of distrust crossed her face. "What sort of employment might that be, my lord? Whatever you think of my current circumstances, I assure you that you have thoroughly misread the situation."

Perhaps he had, Val thought. She was dressed in a manner that was far more circumspect than any woman of the streets he'd ever seen. But that raised other questions. Why was she out there? Was she involved in something nefarious? Was it perhaps the same nefarious dealings that had brought him out into the rookery at night? "Being a companion... my grandmother needs one," he offered.

"Why doesn't she have one already?"

"Because I married the last one," he answered. "And I'd like to return to my lovely new bride without that brute running me through."

After a moment's hesitation, the woman gave a curt nod. She slipped the coin into a hidden pocket in her skirt and then sauntered past him toward the larger man. In a rougher and more cockney tone, she said, "My, but you're a big one. Looking for a tumble, are you, 'ansome?"

"No," the man replied.

Val slipped into another alley and made his way to the next street over. Deeper and deeper into the rookeries he went until, over the tops of the buildings, he could finally see the spires of Whitehall in the distance. He let them guide him home.

LILLY WAS HAVING dinner with the dowager duchess. Neither Elsworth nor Val had shown their faces since the afternoon. It was worrisome to say the least. Where one was, the other had likely followed and that could only lead to danger.

"I have never known more inconsiderate men in my life, Lillian," the dowager duchess said. "Except perhaps for Valentine's father… and my late husband. All the Somers men are bad. It's in their blood."

"Val never speaks of his father," Lilly said, hoping to direct the conversation.

"I should say not," the dowager duchess replied. "He hardly knows him. I daresay that is true for all of us. Richard, my son, decided to live a life of adventure!" This was uttered with the gravest of contempt, as if it were a deeply personal affront to her and all that she valued. But then again, perhaps it was. "He fancies himself some sort of scholar! Living in huts and tents and cavorting with natives like some sort of buffoon!"

"Well, that is fascinating! Where has he traveled to?" Lilly asked. It wasn't fascinating, not at all. But if it kept the woman from speculating on what Val and Elsworth might be doing and why they might both be absent at the same time, it was well worth it.

"Oh, it is not! It's rude and inconsiderate. As for where he's gone, I honestly couldn't say. It's not here or anywhere civilized and that's all that matters!"

"I'm certain there is a great deal to be learned from other cultures," Lilly offered placatingly.

"Certainly, there is! But did he have to be the one to learn it? No. Of course not! It was one thing for you to have a position, my dear, when you had no one else to see to your future and your needs. But Richard is a duke! He has responsibilities. He should be seeing to his estates and leaving it to someone else to unearth dusty relics from ancient civilizations. Honestly, I find it difficult to picture him digging in the dirt. He's likely paid someone to do so and is overseeing them. If he can do that in India or China, or wherever it is he's gallivanted off to this time, he can do it in Somerset and see to planting some wheat or other crops on our estates."

While Lilly would never dream of saying so, the dowager duchess was really terribly practical. Almost to the point of appearing bourgeois. It would not endear her to anyone for her to say so. "It is very frustrating to deal with impractical people," Lilly commiserated mildly.

"It is!" the dowager duchess agreed and sipped her wine. "It is my hope, my dear, that your experience and your own practical nature will have a stabilizing influence on Valentine."

Her practical nature was debatable. Mercenary perhaps, with her love of jewels and rich fabrics. Lilly's gaze dropped to the heavy ring on her left hand. She was still adjusting to the weight of it. The band was etched with a design of intertwining vines and was topped with a large emerald flanked by pearls and diamonds. It was beautiful but the significance of the ring and what it represented in terms of her status was far more staggering than its monetary value.

"Do you have regrets, my dear?"

Lilly looked up to see the dowager duchess eyeing her with concern. "No, of course not. Why would you think that?"

The older woman looked away. "I did rather manage the both of you into this debacle. There is something I have to confess…"

"And what is that?" Lilly asked, wondering if she truly wanted the answer.

"The bequest that came from your great-aunt… well, it didn't really originate with her. It was genuine and would have been yours regardless of whom you married. But I needed you to be in a position where you would feel compelled to say yes when my grandson asked you."

Lilly placed her wine glass carefully on the table. "I see. And you were certain that he would ask me?"

The dowager duchess shrugged. "Well, it's no secret that you are stunning. I had only to take one look at you and know he would be smitten."

"I thought—" Lilly broke off, not certain how to express her thoughts or even if she should.

"Do not be missish. If you have something to say to me, you should say it," the dowager duchess stated.

Anger bubbled inside her. "I have lived my whole life believing that no one cared for me at all... except for my half-sister and Effie. This bequest from my great-aunt made it appear otherwise. That perhaps my mother's family had just been unable to locate me. And that had they been able to, they might have actually wanted to form a bond with me. But that was all a lie. You've managed us all into the positions you wanted us to be in. And I'm right back to where I started, with no one to care for me at all except my half-sister and Effie. You gave me a family and then you took it away."

"It was only money, my dear," the dowager duchess said.

"No, it wasn't. It was an overture of goodwill from people who truly don't care if I live or die and never have. It was a lie cemented with contracts and conditions so that I'd do what you wanted," Lilly replied. "I fear I've lost my appetite. If you'll excuse me, I'm going upstairs."

As she rose and fled the room, she could hear the dowager duchess calling her name. But she didn't turn around. She couldn't. After all those years of being alone, she'd thought she had, if not a relationship with her family, then at least some sense of connection to them. And it had been nothing but a whim, a fabrication from an old woman with more money than heart, it seemed.

Chapter Twenty-One

V AL ENTERED THE house and found it abnormally quiet. It was the dinner hour and he could see light spilling from the dining room, but there was no sound at all. Approaching the room cautiously, he opened the door and found his grandmother seated alone at the table. The usual bevy of footmen were stationed there, all of them to serve one lone, old woman as she stared at her dessert as if it might bite her.

"Where is Lillian?" he asked, stepping into the room.

"You are not dressed for dinner," his grandmother admonished immediately.

"As I am not having dinner it hardly signifies. Where is my wife?" he demanded. The unshakable feeling that something dreadful had occurred would not leave him. He could see it in the defeated set of his grandmother's shoulders, in the way that she would not quite meet his gaze.

"A better question might be where have you been, out carousing when you've been married less than a handful days!" his grandmother retorted. "She was not hungry and retired early."

"I was out. I had business to tend to. I want to know what happened here," Val insisted. He could tell from the pallor of his grandmother's face, from the slight trembling of her hand that she was upset about something.

"Gaming," she said, and her expression was disapproving, but there was a slight tremor in her lip that gave away her emotional state.

Val knew he'd have to tell her something. He couldn't simply let Elsworth's crimes blindside her. Glancing up at the servants, he said, "Leave us. All of you. You may clear everything away later."

When they had all gone, his grandmother turned to him. "Was that really necessary? Surely letting them witness my scolding at your hands would only add to my punishment," she snapped.

"I'm not punishing you," he said. The oddity of that statement struck him then. "Wait… why would I punish you?"

The Dowager Duchess of Templeton did something he had never seen her do before in all of his life. Her lower lip trembled again, more violently than before, and then a single tear rolled down her cheek.

"I'm afraid my managing and plotting, all my manipulations have caught up with me. She hates me now. And with every right. She'll take you away and I'll never see my great-grandchildren… assuming I survive until they are born."

Val sat and leaned back in his chair. Whatever had occurred had been between his grandmother and Lillian, not between Lillian and Elsworth. That, at least, offered some relief. Hurt feelings could be mended. He wasn't certain that his cousin's ultimate aims were so benign. "She doesn't hate you. I'm certain it's only a misunderstanding."

"It isn't. It's so much worse than that. I told her what I did… I didn't realize it would hurt her so terribly. It was foolish of me to do it and even more foolish of me to confess it!" she cried, wringing her hands in clear distress.

Now he was beginning to worry. "Let's just clear some things up first. What is it that you did?"

"I did some research after I hired the girl… I discovered the name of Lillian's mother and then I contacted her great-aunt, a woman who I had been acquainted with in the past. They're terrible people, really. Cold, crass, calculating! But under the circumstances, I required their, well, assistance."

"Go on," Val said, a sinking feeling settling into his gut.

"I explained the situation and stated that I wished to arrange a small marriage portion for her, as sort of a bequest from the living, but that she would likely not accept it from me and asked if I could so under her name as she was the girl's great-aunt after all. They had suffered a reversal of fortune and were struggling. So, in exchange, I also gave them a bit of money to ease the way so to speak and it secured her agreement. So I set up a meeting with her solicitor and we covered all the particulars." By the end, all of the words were tumbling out at once, and his grandmother was openly weeping. She'd not done so even at the death of his grandfather.

Val recalled the conversation with Lilly from the park. That bequest had been more than simply money to her, more than the promise of financial security. For her, it had been an overture of acceptance, an acknowledgement of her as a member of their family. "The solicitor told Lillian that her great-aunt was sick and likely would not even survive for her to go and visit. Is that true?"

"No," his grandmother said. "She was quite hale and hearty, actually. That bit of fiction was created by Mr. Littleton, I suppose, or perhaps at her great-aunt's request to prevent scandal and to prevent their actually having to meet as—well, they would never have agreed to any sort of acknowledgement of her had it not been for the money. They really are terrible!"

"Well, for heaven's sake, don't confess that to her, as well. She's been hurt enough by those people... and by your meddling," Val stated.

"I know it was terrible... I only wanted to ensure that she would have appropriate inducement to accept the offer I knew you would make. From the very moment that girl stepped into my drawing room, I knew that you would suit. And I knew that you would not be able to resist her. You're quite transparent, you know!" she said accusingly.

"There are only two people in the world who would say so… you and my wife," he said. As upset as she was, he had to wonder if it could get any worse. Regardless, he didn't have the luxury of waiting. Events with Elsworth were coming to a head and she would have to be warned. "But as today is the day for confessions, I fear I must tell you about your other grandson and the enormous mess he has made for us all."

"Oh, what now?" she wailed.

"He knew about the changes in your will—"

"Potential changes!" She paused long enough to dry her eyes, before continuing, "Nothing was set in stone, yet. In truth, I'm not even sure I would have been able to go through with it."

Val sighed. "Yes, potential changes… but he was less certain of my response to your managing than you were. He did not believe that I would capitulate to your wishes and wed, either a woman of your choosing, your meddling or one chosen on my own. To that end, he has been engaging in business on speculation of his soon to be changed circumstances."

"Has he lost our fortune when it wasn't even his to gamble with?" she asked with a gasp. "I can't be poor, Valentine. Not again. Not at my age!"

There was nothing for it but to speak quickly and put it all on the table. It would break her heart, but doing so slowly would not make it less painful. "His business endeavors are profitable… but illegal and immoral. He has thrown in with traitors who are selling shipments of munitions to the British government, stealing them back en route to their destination and then selling them to those in France who would stir rebellion and war once more."

Her face paled and she clutched at her chest alarmingly. "Oh, God. Oh, dear lord in heaven!"

Val poured more wine into her glass and pressed it into her hand.

"Sip that. And do not dare to have been an audacious woman for all of your life and succumb to apoplexy now that I need you to be made of sterner stuff!"

She gave a startled laugh. "You're certainly right, of course. Apoplexy is only for weak-minded fools or those who have the theatrical skills to use it well and judiciously. You're certain of his misdeeds, then?"

"Yes. And what's more, the nephew-by-marriage of this great-aunt of Lillian's whom you've embroiled yourself with is also part of the scheme... quite possibly the mastermind. In fact, I'm not entirely certain, knowing what I do now of your plots and schemes, that you didn't first put them on to Elsworth."

More hand wringing and then she drained her wine glass before promptly holding it out for him to refill. "What will we do, Valentine? This could destroy us!"

"It will not. I'm doing what I can to put a stop to it. And I know you dismissed concerns for Lilly, but our marriage puts her in the way of far more than just his inheritance. If he is no longer in line to inherit the funds these people are counting on for their future endeavors, he will be of no use to them and they will not let him walk away with what he knows. He knows that as well as I do. Any man can be driven to commit atrocities if he feels his own life is at stake."

"You really think he tried to kill her?"

"I really do," Val said. "I don't think he wants to, and I don't even think it was his idea. Mr. Littleton has also been murdered. I suspect that Marchebanks, who is the nephew to the woman you bribed to provide this bequest to her, is attempting to claim those funds for himself. Eliminating Lilly eases his path to getting those funds immediately and the future influx from the easily led and managed Elsworth. In short, we've both put her in danger, albeit unwillingly, and now we will both have to get her out of it."

The old woman nodded. "You should go to your wife. When he

returns home, I will deal with Elsworth."

"How do you mean to do that?" he asked.

"There is a plantation in Jamaica that needs to be managed. I think it will do him good to get away from England and see to business on the family's behalf," she said firmly. "He'll be leaving immediately, even if I have to charter a ship for him myself. Discreetly, of course. One doesn't make a production when one is attempting to flee the country."

It was a solid plan, hopefully one that would get Elsworth out of the line of fire and keep him from getting into even more trouble later. Val rose. "I'll see you in the morning, Grandmother."

"Tell her I'm sorry. I never intended for my actions to hurt her or cause her harm... I just didn't realize—well, it doesn't matter what I didn't know. It only matters what I've done and that she has been hurt by it."

"I will tell her," he promised.

"I like her, you know?" his grandmother admitted. "From the very start, even before I decided upon this course for you. I liked her as a person. She was polite and well mannered, terribly intelligent, and I could see that hint of rebellion in her eyes that told me just how she struggled to maintain that always poised and polished image."

"I know that you did. And tomorrow, you will tell her so yourself," Val said.

"I will. If she is amenable to speaking with me. You will smooth the way, of course?"

He nodded and then turned to leave the room.

LILLY SWIPED ANGRILY at her eyes and the moisture gathering there. She had not actually let her tears fall, but they kept forming and she kept dashing them away. It shouldn't have hurt so badly. But then again, she shouldn't have put so much stock in that false overture of familial concern. It had represented the thing she had longed for her entire life—acceptance. And now, faced with the prospect that it was all a lie, she felt unsettled, angry, hurt, and as if she had somehow been reduced to being a small child again, longing for things that were truly never to be.

The door opened and she felt his presence as he entered the room. She didn't know where Val had gone or what he'd been doing, but she was fairly certain it had something to do with his cousin. Regardless, she kept her face averted. The last thing she wanted to do was let him see her in such a state.

"We need to talk, Lilly," he said softly.

"Can it wait until morning?" she asked. "I'm quite tired and I'd just like to sleep."

"I don't think it can, actually. Grandmother just told me what happened at dinner... but there are other equally pressing matters to address," he replied.

Lilly took a deep and fortifying breath before turning to face him. "I feel like such a fool. I should have known that it wasn't truly a gesture of goodwill from my mother's family. I can't believe I was so gullible!"

"It was never her intent to hurt you or even to deceive you. She simply wanted us to be together and did whatever she thought might be necessary to make it so," he offered.

"Well, it does hurt. I'm as alone as I ever was," she said.

He took on a mock wounded expression. "Surely not! Do I mean so little to you then?"

Lilly smiled in spite of everything. "You know what I mean!"

He moved forward and sat down beside her. "I do know. I know that it pains you to think that you've no family, that you've no one to care for you... but you do have people who care for you, Lilly. If you let her, my grandmother would be your greatest ally. She did choose you, after all."

"Why did she?" Lilly asked. "I can't imagine that there are any young women out there more unsuited to being a future duchess than I am. Are you certain she likes you?"

He laughed then, and when he spoke, his tone was very gentle. "Quite certain. She's unorthodox in her thinking and more than a little rebellious in her own way. You, Lillian Burkhart Somers, Viscountess Seaburn, are not the only woman who dislikes having to obey the rules."

"I dislike being lied to, regardless of her lack of ill intent," Lilly stated. "Though I daresay I shall forgive her in short order. She will command it and I will have no option but to obey."

"She's an old woman and one who is used to getting her own way," he said. "And in most cases, not that I will ever admit it to her, her way has been the best one. I am sorry you were hurt by her managing and manipulation in this instance. But she did reveal to me that she was acquainted with your great-aunt, who is quite healthy, and that she agreed to the scheme only because they were desperate for money. Which means that Marchebanks was likely doing whatever he had to do in order to get his hands on the money to be settled on you as well as anything that Elsworth might inherit in the future."

"So the money was real, but my family having any concern for me whatsoever was complete and utter fiction," she surmised. "Was the dowager duchess going to have Mr. Littleton send me a false notification of my great-aunt's death or would the funds simply have appeared as if by magic?"

"It would have come to you regardless, and still will. The bequest is very real. My grandmother intended to honor that regardless of whom you chose to marry. She is inordinately fond of you, whatever you may think."

Lilly felt very small in that moment, as if she were sinking in upon herself. "I think it only hurts so much because it's what I used to dream about as a child... that one day someone would tell me I'd always been wanted."

He pulled her close, holding her. It wasn't in his power to take her pain away. Nothing was ever so hurtful as disillusionment. "You are wanted... perhaps not by your mother's family or even your father's, but by Effie, by Willa, by my grandmother... and very much by me."

Lilly didn't wish to talk about it anymore. Whatever had been done by the dowager duchess, she would make her peace with it eventually. But for now, she very much needed to move on to other things.

"What did you discover today?"

"My valet might be a daily trial to me, but he does have his uses... he managed to discover from Elsworth's valet that my cousin required several stitches for a mysterious cut on his arm. Your handiwork, I can only presume."

Lilly nodded. "Very likely. I didn't question him to see just how serious an injury I had dealt him."

Val nodded. "I also discovered that at the time of our visit to Mr. Littleton's office, Elsworth was meeting with his tailor... and the valet was present for the meeting. He's deeply disappointed in my cousin's fashion sense."

"So Elsworth couldn't have been in Mr. Littleton's office!"

Val let out a sigh. "Initially, I thought so, too. But then I discovered the direction of this tailor... he's only a street removed from Mr. Littleton's office. And with the numerous alleyways connecting the two, it would have been possible for Elsworth to slip out the back unnoticed."

"Fenton hardly strikes me as the sort one confides in, so how did he convince Elsworth's valet to simply tell him everything?" Lilly mused.

"Port. He bribed him with port."

"Your valet steals spirits and you're perfectly fine with that?" she asked with a laugh.

"It wasn't actually purloined… I gave it to him for the express purpose of bribing his brother-in-arms for information."

"Your cousin is many things, and he's certainly made threats, but is he a murderer?"

"I can't answer that… not yet at any rate. And until I can, you will do whatever is necessary to avoid him. Now, go to sleep. I should have some answers by morning about this bequest my grandmother conned your family into making to you. Then we'll know more where we stand."

Lilly laid down on the bed, and pulled the covers over her. "Thank you, Valentine."

"For what?"

"For being a better man than anyone believes you to be," she said.

If he replied, she didn't hear him. She'd already drifted off to sleep.

Chapter Twenty-Two

THEY WERE STROLLING arm-in-arm down Jermyn Street toward Duke Street and the endless parade of people using that route to reach Piccadilly and all the shopping beyond. Beside him, Lilly was in a far better frame of mind than she had been the night before. While breakfast had been a slightly tense affair, it appeared that she and his grandmother had reached an uneasy truce.

"Where are we going?" she demanded.

"We have to meet someone," he said.

"Who?"

"Your replacement," he answered.

She paused, her steps slightly out of rhythm with his for a moment. "I presume you mean as a companion and not a wife!"

He laughed. "Certainly. I happened to encounter this particular woman in Whitechapel, while coming back from the same seedy warehouse where I'd observed my cousin and his compatriots. She offered invaluable assistance in providing the much-needed distraction I required in order to get away without being caught!"

"If you encountered a woman on the streets of Whitechapel in the evening, then she is... well, suffice it to say, improper!" Lillian replied in a heated whisper.

"In most cases that answer would be yes and I believe the term you are looking for is prostitute," he replied, seemingly careless of the fact that several people around him gasped and one woman placed her hands firmly over the ears of the child walking next to her.

"Really, Valentine! You enjoy being shocking!" she accused.

He couldn't bite back a grin at her scandalized tone. "Where's my rule breaker now? Don't go all buttoned up and straight-laced on me, Lilly. I couldn't bear it!"

"Well, your grandmother will not bear this! Have you considered what she will do when she finds out what this woman's background is? And what of this poor woman? It's terribly cruel to pull her out of such an environment only to toss her back into it in a matter of days or hours simply because the notion of your grandmother employing such a woman amuses you," Lilly pointed out.

"Trust me," he implored. "She's not in the common way, at least. She speaks very genteelly and whatever circumstances may have led her to Whitechapel, I'm convinced that she is not a fallen woman! I think this could be a good solution for everyone."

Val turned away just in time to see the woman in question. She was standing across the street from Fortnum and Mason, watching all the fashionably-dressed people going into and out of the store. "There she is," he said, pointing her out to Lilly.

He heard his wife's gasp and surveyed the woman's appearance once more to see what might have been so shocking. She stood on the corner, waiting to cross the street, with her hands clasped in front of her and her shoulders straight. Her pelisse was a bit shabby and worn, but not so much that anyone looking at it would have thought her out of place on those streets. Indeed, she might have been a governess or a servant dressed as she was. Even her bearing and posture was that of a lady. Which meant Lilly's gasp was one of recognition and not surprise. "Do you know her?"

"I do, indeed," Lillian replied. "She worked at Millstead Abbey School when I was there so many years ago. What are the odds, Val, of her being the woman you ran into last night and being a past acquaintance of mine?"

He frowned. "Limited. The odds are extraordinarily limited. I'd daresay impossible, even. And I think we need to find out precisely what she's about."

As they approached the woman, her gaze was drawn to Lilly. In fact, she watched Lilly with a depth of emotion playing over her features that left Val utterly puzzled.

"Who are you, Madam?" he demanded.

She looked to Valentine and then back to Lillian and it was to his wife that she spoke. "When I was at the Millstead Abbey School, you knew me by the name of Anna Hartnett."

"I remember you," Lilly said. "You were very kind to me... the only kind person in that whole wretched place. But then one day you were simply gone."

"Not one day," the woman answered. "It was the day your father came to Millstead Abbey and dropped off your half-sister. That was the very day I was banished from there, sent off without a recommendation."

"What has my father to do with all of this?" Lilly asked.

Val was watching the two women. It hadn't been immediately obvious to him, but now, staring from one to the other, it could not have been more clear. There was a marked resemblance, one that left him all but speechless. Surely, it was not what he thought. But then the woman who had called herself Anna Hartnett looked at him and it was such a knowing, measuring gaze, that he knew instantly he was correct.

"Let us go in and have some tea," he said. "There's a coffee shop just around the corner that should have a private parlor available."

The woman glanced down at her shabby pelisse, but then simply lifted her head high again. "Certainly. I think there is much to discuss, my lord."

>>><<<

LILLY RECALLED A dozen instances where Miss Anna Hartnett had been all that was kind and loving to her. She'd tended scrapes and bruises, snuck her extra treats from the kitchen, and soothed her when she'd been ill. In retrospect, the amount of attention the woman had lavished on her while still managing to do her work at the school was nothing short of miraculous. It hadn't lasted very long, less than a year. Had it not been for the presence of Willa and the bond that had formed between them almost instantly, no doubt the loss of Miss Hartnett would have left her utterly despondent as a child.

Despite that, she found the woman's presence under their current circumstances to be highly suspect. The sheer number of coincidences required for her to encounter Valentine while he was out engaging in his clandestine activities as an agent of the Crown, even if an unofficial one, was impossible to fathom. It was even more impossible to accept. There was clearly a connection somewhere and she wouldn't be satisfied until she knew precisely what it was.

Lillian stood apart from Miss Hartnett as Val engaged the private parlor for them and ordered refreshment. After a moment, they were shown into the small room and the door closed behind them. It was a cozy space, filled with well upholstered chairs and a small table, though it was certainly cramped.

"Why are you here?" Lillian asked, as soon as the three of them were alone in the room.

Miss Hartnett smiled. "You are certainly as direct as ever, Miss Burkhart."

"Lady Somers, Viscountess Seaburn," Val corrected the woman. "Lillian and I were married only two days ago."

Miss Hartnett frowned. "If you were married two days ago, what on earth were you doing traipsing through Whitechapel?"

"I think we're entitled to ask the questions here more than you are,

Madam," Lillian interjected. "The confluence of fate and coincidence that would have to occur together to bring us back into one another's circles of acquaintance are too impossible and too improbable to be borne! Who are you really?"

Miss Hartnett raised her eyebrows. "That is a very pointed question, my lady. Think long and hard about whether or not you truly wish to have it answered."

"I don't think we have a choice," Val said. "We're in a bit a situation ourselves and I have to think perhaps they overlap. You weren't just a simple streetwalker as I originally thought. Nor are you simply a gently-bred woman fallen on hard times. I think you were there, in that precise location, for a reason. Why were you lingering near that particular warehouse last night?"

Miss Hartnett inclined her head in acknowledgement of his assertion. "No, my lord, I am not now nor have I ever been a woman of ill repute... only a woman of poor judgment. As to my identity, the name that I abandoned years ago, at the same time I was forced to abandon my daughter whom I loved so dearly, was Elizabeth Ann Burkhart. And I do believe that I am now your mother-in-law."

Lillian stood so quickly that the chair she'd occupied rocked back and would have tumbled over had Val not righted it. Her breath was coming in pants and her palms were sweating. Her heart raced in her chest and she blinked rapidly as her vision began to darken around the edges. She would not faint. She had never fainted in her life. "You are not my mother. My mother is dead. She left me on my worthless father's doorstep and drowned herself in the Thames!"

She was still shaking when Val took her hand.

"Whatever you decide to do when we leave here today, I will support you in it entirely. But for now, we must hear her out because there are things that have brought us all here together that we cannot ignore. Marchebanks is your cousin, and therefore he is her cousin... and he is the man who is responsible for the schemes Elsworth has fallen in with."

"But it's lies... it's all lies!" she insisted. It had to be lies. If not, everything she'd believed about her entire life was false. Still, she sat, sinking down into the chair and staring at the woman across from her with a fury that ran so deep she couldn't even fathom where it had come from. Had it been trapped inside her all along?

"You have every right to be angry," the woman said. "I must start the story from the very beginning. It should offer a certain amount of illumination about Alfred Hazleton who is now Lord Marchebanks."

There was a knock on the door and a serving girl entered with a tea tray and sandwiches. She paused after taking only two steps into the room, the tension clearly palpable.

"You may leave it on the table and we will serve ourselves," Val instructed.

The girl nodded, deposited the tray, and left hurriedly.

"Go on, Miss... what should we call you?"

"You may call me Miss Hartnett. That is the name I have used most frequently and I believe it is the one that your wife will be most comfortable with," she said with a sad turn of her lips.

Val poured tea for everyone. When he placed the cup in front of her, Lilly stared at it as if it were something foreign that she had no notion what to do with. Even as he added cream and sugar to it, just as she liked, it sat there untouched.

"Go on, Miss Hartnett," Lillian said. "Tell your story."

"I met William Satterly during my first season... but I thought him arrogant and he thought me beneath his notice. It was only later, in my second season, that he began to turn his attentions toward me. He was actually charming, and I found myself questioning if perhaps I had been hasty in my judgment. I didn't know then that it was all a bet. That he had wagered my cousin that he could seduce me and my cousin, because he was always a terrible person and utterly without conscience, took that wager. Suffice it to say, I made several errors in judgment. Falling for him, trusting him, and allowing myself to be alone with him. He is not a man who takes no for an answer, regardless of how forcefully it is uttered."

Lilly flinched, recalling the very similar situation she'd found herself in with the son of the family she'd first worked for. But he'd been small and thin, a boy she could fairly easily get away from with the training that Effie had seen to for all of them. Miss Hartnett had likely had no such training.

"When I discovered I was with child, I told my mother and she was stricken with apoplexy and took to her bed. My father was ashamed of me. He disowned me and tossed me into the street. Not knowing what else to do, I went to the rooms that I knew William kept near his club and I knocked on the door and pleaded to speak with him. The doorman never let me in, but William did come out, and my cousin, Alfred, was there with him. The two of them came out together laughing uproariously and right in front of me, Alfred handed William a sovereign and called the wager his."

The woman paused, sipped her tea, and then continued. "My aunt, Margaret Hazleton, Lady Marchebanks, took me in, but it was made clear to me that I was there on her charity and her charity alone. I was a virtual prisoner in their home, hidden away in an attic room that wasn't even fit for servants. When I gave birth to you—"

"Not to me," Lilly insisted. "You are not my mother. I have no mother."

Miss Hartnett nodded her head. "Very well. When I gave birth to my daughter, I did so alone, with only a housekeeper to attend me. And less than a week afterward, I was kicked out of their house and told to make my own way in the world. It was foolish, but I went back to William. I thought, despite everything he had done, that when he saw our daughter, he would have some of the feelings for her that I did. Because I had loved her instantly. More than I could have ever imagined loving anyone or anything. But while I lurked about his rooms, I heard him approach and he wasn't alone. Alfred was with him and they were arguing about Alfred's scheme to get a manufacturer to sell goods to the army and then steal them back. William might be a terrible man, but he is at least a patriot. They argued so fiercely that I was afraid to let my presence be known. So I left. I found a group of women in a hovel in Whitechapel. All of us had children, small infants, and all of us needed to earn a living. I slept on the floor with my daughter in my arms, and another woman cared for her in the day while I worked as a seamstress in a shop where I had once purchased my very own ballgowns."

Lilly listened to all of it and felt as if her entire world were shattering—as if she were shattering. But she couldn't think about her mother, she couldn't think about why she had done what she had or how she might have suffered. "What goods was Marchebanks selling and stealing back?"

"It was general supplies then I believe. He's moved on now and managed to get a few arms manufacturers in his pocket," Miss Hartnett replied. "That is why you were following him, wasn't it, my lord?"

"I wasn't following him," Val admitted. "I was following my own troublesome cousin, Elsworth Somers. He did not have William Satterly's patriotism to steer him clear of such schemes, it would seem."

"I don't want to hear any more," Lilly said. "I want to go home."

"I would say one thing more before you leave," Miss Hartnett implored. "I did not abandon you on your father's doorstep by choice. Alfred discovered that I had overheard their conversation because I, emboldened by desperation and the foolish belief that he would not do violence against his own kin, attempted to blackmail him into providing a place for me to live with you—with my daughter. I barely escaped with my life. And I knew the only person who might protect my daughter from him was William Satterly, but only if he was left with no other choice. I loitered outside their home for hours. I watched William enter and still I waited. It was only when I saw his mother's carriage turn up the street that I knew what I had to do. I left my child, and a note, on their doorstep and I fled... not because I did not want her. Or because the burden of her was too much for me. I did so only because I knew I had to leave her behind in order for us both to live."

Lilly rose to her feet again. "I'll wait for you at the doors. I can't hear anything more."

"It's the truth," Miss Hartnett said.

Lilly looked at her. "I believe that it is. But I can't hear anything further now. I simply can't." With that, she turned and fled the small room.

Chapter Twenty-Three

V AL STARED AT the woman before him and was torn. They both needed comfort and he was at a loss in terms of how to provide it to either of them. Rising to his feet, he reached into the pocket of his waistcoat and retrieved a card that belonged to his man of affairs. He pressed it into her hand along with some coins. "Go to him first thing in the morning. I'll have made arrangements by then for you to have a place to stay and adequate funds to see to your needs."

Miss Hartnett—no, Miss Elizabeth Burkhart—gave him a baleful stare. "I am not here for charity."

"I know that you are not. I don't think you knew who I was last night and I certainly don't think you knew who would be with me today."

The woman looked down at the card in her hand. "I thought she was dead. I lingered in Millstead, eking out a meager existence there as a maid of all work. But a fever swept through the area and the school. I went there in the days after and I begged the headmaster to let me see her. He told me she was among those who had perished. I didn't know until two months ago, when the marriage of Wilhelmina Marks, her half-sister, was reported in the papers that my daughter yet lived. When she's ready to hear that, will you tell her?"

"When she is ready to hear it, you will be able to tell her," Val offered kindly. "She is hurt and she is shocked to the very core of her being at this moment. But she longs for a family more than anything else in this world, I think. Given time to absorb this information, she will come around."

"I hope you are right. In the meantime, watch her carefully. Alfred is a devil, and I imagine your cousin is, as well."

Val nodded. "Do as I said. You cannot mend your relationship with her if she will have no notion where to find you." With that, he walked out, leaving his wife's mother behind in the small parlor.

He found Lilly sitting at a table near the doors. She was staring out into the street as the rain trickled down. When he approached her, she looked up at him. "There's a man outside watching us."

Val looked up and across the street. Standing in a doorway was Stavers, the brawler turned butler. "Wait here."

"I will not stay in this establishment with her," Lilly said. "And I'm not angry and I'm not even hurt. I just can't. I can't take it all in."

Val sighed. "Come on then. We'll get you into a cab and you can wait there while I see to this other business."

"You know him?" Lilly asked.

"I wouldn't say know is precisely the right term... there is a man of somewhat questionable morals and ethics whose assistance I enlisted in finding out who had made an attempt on your life—whether it was Elsworth, someone hired by Elsworth or if Elsworth was even involved. That man is a representative, if you will."

Val watched her look through the window at the burly and dour-faced man and then back at him.

"I don't think I like you doing business with these sorts of people," she said.

"This is the last job I am to do," he said. *Until the Hound called in his favor.* "Once all of this is behind us, you and I will retreat to the countryside, if you wish, and we will become the most boring people in all the world."

She heaved a heavy sigh of relief. "That sounds like heaven. I don't think I can bear any more dead relatives who aren't and dying relatives who aren't."

Val grinned as he led her outside and hailed a hansom cab. Seeing her into the back of it, he pulled yet another coin from his pocket. "I have to talk to someone just across the way. You will wait here with my wife until I return. Is that understood?"

The driver accepted the coin, lifted it to his mouth and tested the metal of it with the few teeth that remained in his skull. When it proved to be real, he offered up a gap-toothed grin. "Aye, m'lord. 'Appy to wait, I am!"

Val dashed across the street, dodging carts, pedestrians and horses alike. As he neared the doorway where Stavers lurked, the man stepped back and opened the door that he'd been guarding. So he was to meet with the Hound himself rather than just the lackey. He glanced over his shoulder at the still waiting cab, and then followed the butler inside.

The building itself was under construction. White cloth draped most of the surfaces, and plasterers had scattered in the middle of their shift. Their work was only half-completed, leaving intricately carved panels interspersed with exposed brick and wood. In the center of the room, impeccably dressed and sitting on a crate as if it were a throne at the palace was the Hound.

"Hardly your typically luxurious surroundings," Val remarked.

"You came to me about attempted murder and I find myself in the midst of a treasonous plot," the Hound said.

Val arched one eyebrow. "Your diction has improved."

"My mastery of diction and the English language is unchanged. What has changed is my willingness to let you see something beyond the underworld thug most people believe me to be," the Hound said in a supercilious fashion that sounded far more like a duke than Val himself would ever be capable of.

"I see. Go on. You have my attention."

The Hound's lips quirked in amusement. "Careful, puppy. I've paved the bed of the Thames with bodies for less. Elsworth Somers did not carry out the attempt himself, but he did pay someone to do so. A man by the name of Foster. Not to worry. He won't be completing that job or any other. As to your cousin's involvement in this other scheme, he's in well over his head. But I think you know that, don't you?"

"I'm aware. What I don't know is the name of the ship they mean to transport the weapons and who'll be in on the attack. I don't suppose this is something you'd consider handling, would you?"

The Hound drummed his fingers on his thigh for a moment. "I could be persuaded to see this thing through for you... for a cost naturally."

"Not simply out of the goodness of your patriotic heart?" Val asked with a grin.

"I'd help for that, but I wouldn't spearhead the operation. You, Viscount Seaburn, are interfering with my ability to retain my anonymity and my low social profile. Why should I do this for you?"

Val considered. "Well, I'd owe you two favors instead of one."

"No, you wouldn't. I don't need favors to end traitorous plots. That's a matter of duty for any Englishman, no matter his profession or standing. I'm not even certain you owe me the first favor as it all seems to be part and parcel of the same plot. Lillian Burkhart, I beg your pardon, Lillian Somers, is a by-blow of Alfred Hazleton's cousin... the one that died all those years ago. Isn't she?"

The status of Elizabeth Burkhart as being very much amongst the living was not his secret to tell, so Val simply concurred, "She is."

"And Hazleton, who recently got the Marchebanks title and all the Marchebanks debt, is front and center in this plot. Did you know his mother was French? Oddly enough, they escaped France with a great deal of their wealth intact. Her skirts were so laden with jewels it was a wonder the bloody ship didn't sink," the Hound said. "Unfortunately, they had less success keeping their wealth. Spendthrifts and gamblers."

"You really should consider going to work as an agent," Val offered. "You'd be very good at it."

"Contract basis only. I'm not good at working for other people outside of a limited capacity," he answered. "I'll get you the name of the ship. Then I'm out of it. Who you choose to pass it on to is at your discretion."

"Send word when you have it. It'll be dealt with. Now, I need to get my wife home. It's been a difficult morning," Val stated.

"Delicate, is she? Hardly seems like one of Miss Darrow's girls!"

Val laughed. "No. I wouldn't call her delicate. But since you know so much about Marchebanks, you ought to know this, too. I'd considered not bringing it up, but I think it has bearing. My wife's mother is very much alive and has been living under an assumed name for all these years because Lord Marchebanks wanted her dead. His treasonous plots go back quite a ways, it would seem."

The Hound sighed. "Now you're just goading me. You want me to hate him so badly that I will agree to take it all off your hands."

"Did it work?"

"Yes, damn you, it did."

Val smiled. "Any information can be sent directly to Lord Highcliff."

The Hound's expression of ennui transformed into one of shock. "That popinjay?"

Val grinned as he turned to head for the door. "You're not the only one who knows how to disguise his true nature, my good man!"

Leaving the building, Val had just stepped outside when the driver of the hansom cab across the street, the very one that housed Lilly, fell off the box and landed with a thud on the pavement. Another man jumped up and grabbed the reins. Val didn't have to ask for Stavers' assistance. The unlikely butler had already broken into a run, heading for the end of the block. Val cut across the street, and managed to reach the cab first. Traffic was too heavy and the street too congested for the driver to make a hasty getaway. But rather than be caught, the man simply abandoned his post, jumping down from the box and rolling away from the clashing hooves.

The coach lurched and swayed alarmingly, the horses now given their heads with no one on the box to control them. Trying to balance on a moving coach, climbing up toward the now vacant box, Val lost his balance and slipped, saving himself at the last moment by grabbing the railing along the top of the coach. By some miracle, he managed to avoid getting his legs crushed under the wheels. The second time, when he reached for the box to hoist himself onto it, he made it. But the reins were lost beneath the carriage itself and he'd have to grab hold of the bridle itself to slow the horses down. The only way to achieve that would involve climbing out onto the back of one of the beasts who likely would not take kindly to it.

His heart was pounding the entire time. If he failed, it wasn't just his neck on the line. A runaway carriage in London's busy streets was no laughing matter and it was just as likely that Lilly would be killed along with him and whatever poor, hapless bystanders were in their path. It was that thought which spurred him on, which allowed him to leap from the box and onto the horse's back.

He had to grab the breast collar, pulling it tight, until the horse finally began to slow. The carriage finally halted near the intersection ahead of them. It was a busy one, and had they not managed to stop in that spot, it was likely that one or all of them would have been injured or killed. His heart was still racing as he climbed down. From the street behind them, he could see the hansom driver limping toward them. Stavers was still in pursuit of the man who'd carried out the abduction attempt. And he could see the back of the Hound's elegantly tailored coat as he disappeared into the throng of London's well-to-do shoppers.

When the driver reached them and took over the calming of the horses and there was no threat of the cab once more running away with them, Val opened the door and found Lilly sitting on the banquette, ashen faced, and her long-lost mother laid out on the seat beside her, her head bleeding and completely unconscious.

"What happened?"

Lilly shook her head. "There was a commotion outside and she jumped into the carriage. Then it took off and I heard the driver shouting and then saw him fall. You know better than I did what occurred."

Val grimaced. "It appears that someone attempted to abduct you and that your mother, forgive me, Miss Hartnett, was attempting to save you or at the very least assist you."

"Pardon me, guv'nah, but there's a hackney here for you," came the call of the hansom driver.

Val turned around and found a large hackney carriage pulling up near them. He eyed the driver suspiciously. The man tipped his hat.

"The Hound sent me to carry you home, m'lord," the driver offered. "You and the lady."

"Ladies. And one is injured," Val said.

The driver nodded. "I'll be quick and careful in seeing you back to your house, m'lord."

It was good enough for Val. He helped Lilly down and then lifted Miss Hartnett into his arms, just as Stavers rounded the corner.

"He got away, my lord," the butler said. "I'll be sending some fellows I know around to keep watch for you. My employer would be most displeased if anything else were to happen to the ladies."

Val would happily take all the help he could get. "Are they as inconspicuous as you?"

For the first time in their acquaintance, the butler cracked an actual smile. It revealed enough missing teeth that Val was certain his earlier estimation of Stavers as a pugilist was likely correct.

"More so, my lord. More so," the man said, still grinning as he walked away.

Gently lifting Miss Hartnett into the carriage, he climbed in after her and settled down on the seat opposite. Lilly was glaring at him.

"What is it?" he asked.

"The Hound... The Hound of Whitehall, the very man you warned me against, and yet you are familiar enough with him that he is arranging transportation for us?" she demanded.

He sighed. "Let us get home, get Miss Hartnett settled in and the physician summoned, then we will discuss it."

"Yes, we most assuredly will," she agreed, her tone chilling.

Chapter Twenty-Four

LILLIAN HAD NEVER been more furious in her life. He had lied to her. He'd told her that he would not have any dealings with that man and she would avoid him as well. Now there she was, with the woman claiming to be her mother ensconced in a guest suite down the hall, and everything was spinning out of control. Pacing the small sitting room that connected to their bedchamber, she was trying to control her temper. But it was not a good day. There had been too many upsets, too many unknowns, and too many lies from everyone around her.

A knock on the door prompted her to bark an order for the person to enter. As the door swung inward and she saw the Dowager Duchess of Templeton standing there, her brow arched in the same imperious manner that was so often on her grandson's face, Lilly felt slightly ashamed of herself. "Forgive me for being short. It's been a trying day, your grace."

"So it has," the dowager duchess said, and let herself into the room. She closed the door behind her with a quiet snick and then moved to the small settee. "I'd have a word with you, if I may, Lillian?"

"Certainly," she agreed. They both knew that however it had been phrased, it had not been a request.

"Sit, my dear. It makes my neck ache to look up at you," the older woman said.

Capitulating, Lilly moved to the chair opposite the settee and faced her former employer. "What did you wish to discuss, Madam?"

"Are you well?" the dowager duchess asked. "You have been through quite a bit in the last few days and I imagine that the shock of last night, accompanied by the shock and scare you had this morning is quite trying to you."

"I am quite well." It was a lie. She wasn't well at all. Her insides were roiling and it felt as if the ground were pitching beneath her feet. The whole world was upside down for her in that moment.

"Well, I am certainly happy to hear it. What I have come to say to you is not something I've said to anyone else in all of my years. So you must take it for all that it is worth and to me that is a great deal," the woman said. "I am sorry, Lillian, for the lies I told and the manner in which I meddled in your life. Mind you, I do not apologize for putting you in a position where marrying my grandson seemed a favorable thing to you, only for the way in which I went about it. I didn't think of how it might hurt you. I was careless with your feelings and, for that, I truly apologize."

Lilly blinked at her for several seconds, the silence growing between them. The very idea of the Dowager Duchess of Templeton apologizing to anyone was beyond her ken. Yet it had just happened. To say that it would take some getting used to was putting it mildly.

"Well, say something, girl," the dowager duchess finally snapped.

Shaking off her stunned stupor, Lilly nodded. "I thank you for your apology and I accept it."

"But we are not as we once were," the dowager duchess surmised.

"It is not an easy thing to learn your trust has been violated, your grace. I think, in time, we will be as we once were. But not today, or even tomorrow."

The dowager duchess nodded. "I see. Will you be taking him away then?"

"Taking who away?"

The old woman sniffed. "My grandson, of course. I did all of this to see him settled with a wife before I pass on from this world. No doubt, you will want to be well rid of me. If you prefer the house here in London, I suppose I can take myself back to the country... where I will die, alone, rattling about in that big old house like some sort of phantom creature."

Lillian rolled her eyes. "You really don't know how to stop manip- ulating people, do you? No, I'm not taking him away. We're not going to the country, at least not yet, and neither are you. For heaven's sake, this house is quite large enough for all of us!"

"No, it isn't," the dowager duchess answered. "Not if every time you leave it, you come back with another long-lost relative!"

"That wasn't my doing," Lilly answered sullenly. "I should not have brought her back here regardless. We could just as easily have obtained some other lodging for her and tried someone to see to her care!"

The dowager duchess fixed her with a piercing stare. "And is that really what you want to do?"

"No," Lilly replied. "I don't know what I want to do. I want to not have all this turmoil and danger at every blasted turn!"

"Watch your language, dear. It has been difficult, but that's no reason to be common," the dowager duchess said. "Avoiding one's problems and one's turmoil does not make them go away. Sometimes, my dear, there is no way over and no way around. Sometimes the only way is simply to go through. I very much think that is where you are now. You must confront your feelings and you must, when she is well enough, confront your mother. And I think the two of you, and Valentine, when the time is right, should confront the entirety of your family. This clandestine business has to stop and there's only one way to manage that... drag it all into the open."

Lilly gaped at her. "The scandal would be disastrous for the family!"

"Pish posh. If the family name has survived all that Valentine has done to it over the years, it can survive this. We will not live in fear and we will not be cowed by traitors. Elsworth will be facing the music, as well. I had thought to send him to Jamaica but I have reconsidered. He must, no matter how it pains me, pay the price for his actions," the dowager duchess insisted. "It is something we must all do."

Lilly eyed the old woman speculatively then, noting the tremor in her hand, the slight quivering of her lip. Rising from her chair, she moved to the settee next to her and took her hand. "You love him."

"He is my grandson, foolish as he may be. Of course, I love him. But that doesn't mean I can't also be furious with him and even ashamed of him. He let himself be blinded by envy and greed and, in so doing, turned his back on those who cared for him. Even Valentine, in his own way, cares for Elsworth. They might snipe at one another, but when they were boys they were closer than brothers, I thought."

Lilly thought back to the story Val had told her of the local girl he'd fancied. "Did Elsworth run with Marchebanks even then? When they were boys together?"

"Yes, he did," the dowager duchess answered. "I never liked him, you know? Always thought he was a bit too puffed up for someone we knew even then hadn't a sovereign to his name. And, of course, back then, there was still a possibility that he might not become Marchebanks. You mother's aunt is actually only a year or two older than her. Born from the father's second marriage, you see. Then, it was still possible she'd present the old lord with an heir."

Lillian filed that information away. She wasn't certain why, but it seemed as if it might be important.

"WHY DO YOU keep summoning me to this house for injured females?" the physician demanded. "Viscount Seaburn, this borders on unseemly."

"How is she, Doctor?" Val asked, ignoring the man's comment.

"She'll heal. I'd recommend getting some food into her, though. She's far thinner than she ought to be and I daresay a good, healthy diet will help put her to rights. A few days rest and she'll be right as rain."

Val looked at Miss Hartnett—Miss Burkhart—who looked shockingly like Lillian and nodded. "Very well, I'll see you out."

"No need. I know the way," the doctor replied. "Why, I'm beginning to feel at home here."

Val grinned in spite of himself as the doctor made his way out. His grin faded as Elizabeth Burkhart stirred. She opened her eyes and searched her surroundings. When her gaze settled on him, she let out a sharp gasp.

"Is she hurt? Was Lillian hurt?" she demanded immediately.

Val shook his head and took a seat in the chair by her bed. "She's fine. Shaken but otherwise unharmed entirely. She's with my grandmother. Why did you jump in the carriage?"

She settled back against the pillows. "I recognized the man who leapt onto the box and struck the driver. He works for Alfred. I've seen him frequently over the last few weeks since I returned to London. I thought, between the two of us, we'd be able to overpower him. Or at the very least, I could help Lillian free herself."

"What have you seen while observing him?" Val demanded. "Any information at all that will nail his coffin shut, so to speak, will be of assistance."

"I've seen him with a blonde man," she said. "The same one you've been following from time to time."

"That would be my cousin, Elsworth Somers." Val offered. "He's fallen in with Marchebanks more out of stupidity than immorality. But there will likely be a cost regardless. Do you know the identity of the woman they were meeting with the other night?"

"Don't you know?" she asked, clearly surprised at his ignorance on the matter.

"No. Why would I?" he demanded.

Her shocked stare might have been comical if they weren't discussing such serious matters. "You truly have no idea what you're dealing with, my lord. There is no one more evil than the woman you saw. In fact, I'd go so far as to suggest that she was the guiding hand behind Alfred's fall."

"Then tell me who it is, Miss Burkhart, so that I may put this all to rest."

"You'll never put it to rest... not in its entirety. You see, it's none other than my aunt. Margaret Hazleton, the widow of Alfred's late uncle and the woman who has been his lover for decades," she answered. "Since long before his uncle died, to be sure!"

And suddenly the tiles all clicked into place, every puzzle piece fitting together. "My meddling grandmother arranging the bequest to prompt Lilly to agree to my suit, and doing so through none other than Margaret Hazleton, literally put a price on my bride's head."

Miss Burkhart nodded. "I have no idea what that means. She's detested me from the moment I entered this world. I could never prove it, but I long suspected that my ruin at the hands of William Satterly had been orchestrated by her. The plot was entirely too sophisticated for Alfred to have come up with on his own. I can assure you that if Margaret had anything to gain either financially or socially by seeing my daughter harmed, she would not stop until the task was complete."

"Just as she won't stop until you are dead."

The voice from the doorway belonged to Lillian. Val rose immediately and turned to face her. She looked calmer and certainly more amenable to a conversation with the injured woman before him than she had earlier in the day.

"Are you well?" he asked.

"Quite," she replied. "And I'd like a word alone with Miss... with my mother."

Val rose. "You should both rest. It's been a long and trying day... well, now may not be the time to mend fences."

"There is no better time," Elizabeth Burkhart replied. "We shall be fine."

Reluctantly, he left the room, feeling as if he'd just tossed a burning match into a powder keg.

Chapter Twenty-Five

LILLY LOOKED AT her mother and sighed before crossing the expanse of the room and taking the seat that her husband had just vacated. "I wasn't ready to listen to you before. But I think I am now."

Elizabeth uttered her own sigh. "I never meant to hurt you. Everything I've done has been to protect you. Sending you to your father—"

"Let's not call him that, shall we? We both know that he isn't a father. Not in any sense of the word that matters."

"You're right, of course. There was a reason I left you there when I did, when I knew that he wouldn't be able to just ship you to a workhouse and wash his hands of it all. I waited until I saw his mother's coach approaching. Whatever else can be said of her, she is dedicated to her family. All of them."

"And you came to Millstead Abbey School to be near me?"

"I did. I kept track of you all along. It was just terrible luck that your fath—that William saw me that day when he brought Wilhelmina Marks to the school. Terrible, terrible luck. I was dismissed, of course. But I didn't go far. I stayed in the village and would sometimes walk past the school hoping for a glimpse of you. It went on like that for nearly a year and then cholera struck. I was ill myself and barely survived. I went back to the school afterward and begged for word of you... but the headmaster told me you had died. That both you and your half-sister had succumbed."

Fury swept through her. "He lied, of course. It was right before then when Miss Euphemia Darrow came to visit the school and her friend, a young woman by the name of Gemma Atwood, who taught there. When she saw how we were treated—well, she wasn't pleased. She marched right up to the headmaster and said she was taking us with her. That we would be attending her school from that point forward where other students and staff alike would not be permitted to, much less encouraged to, speak in such a cruel manner to innocent children."

Elizabeth smiled. "I think I would like this Miss Darrow."

"Yes, I daresay you would. She was very kind to me, and to Wilhelmina. To everyone, in truth, until they give her a reason not to be. I haven't suffered terribly in my life. I don't wish you to think that I have. It's been rather ordinary, to be perfectly frank. Willa and I were close and we had friends at the Darrow School. As we've grown up, Effie shifted from being mentor and master to being a friend instead. But just because it wasn't terrible doesn't mean it wasn't lonely. I have felt, very acutely, the lack of connection. Of family. I think more so since Willa married because it left me wondering about my place in the world."

"Well, of course, it did. For the longest time, it's been just the two of you, hasn't it?"

Lilly smiled sadly at that. "It certainly seemed so at times. I don't mean to be cruel, but I don't need a mother anymore. I needed you years ago, when children called me names, when boys teased me and said awful things about what I'd grow up to be."

"We always need our mothers... but the way we need them changes over time," Elizabeth said. "I don't expect to simply act as if we've never parted. All I want is a chance to see you safe and happy. And perhaps, if at all possible, to get to know you and for you to come to know me, as well."

Lilly considered it for a moment. Part of her wanted to say no, to run from the room and let her anger and fear control her. But another part of her, the part of her that had learned so very much from watching Effie Darrow and the way she maneuvered through the world, demanded more of herself than that. "We can certainly try, I think. I should leave you to rest. No doubt, the doctor instructed just that."

"Of course, he did. That's all they ever say. Rest. You've lost a limb, you must rest. You've had a child, you must rest. You've eaten bad pudding, you must rest!" Elizabeth groused. "Worthless men!"

"Men or doctors?"

"Both, in most cases," she said. "Though I do think I rather like your husband. Viscount Seaburn seems to be cut from a very different cloth than most... and he is entirely taken with you."

Lilly blushed with pleasure and with the undeniable wish for it to be true. "He and I have an arrangement."

"My dear, you have much more than an arrangement. He cares for you... far more deeply than either of you realize, I think."

"I will check on you later," Lilly said and rose, heading for the door. As she reached it, she couldn't stop herself from asking, "Why do you think he cares so much?"

"It's quite obvious really. The way that he looks at you, the fact that he risked life and limb without even a thought to his own safety when he knew you to be in danger... my dear, you matter to him. Not only your safety but also your happiness."

Lilly nodded and then let herself out of the room. She was deep in thought as she made her way back to the chamber she and her husband shared. As she entered, she could hear him in the bedchamber beyond the sitting room speaking softly. It sounded very much like another person was in there weeping.

Opening the door, she entered to find Val standing shame faced before his valet who was eyeing the boots her husband had worn that morning and sobbing copiously.

"For God's sake, pull yourself together, man. It's only a pair of boots."

"No, my lord. It isn't just a pair of boots. These are Hessians made by Hoby himself... Wellington's own bootmaker, my lord," the valet said, as if he were holding a holy relic.

Oh, this was not good, Lilly realized. The man was on the verge of handing in his resignation.

"It was terribly thoughtless of him to scuff them so badly," she offered. "I know you've worked so very hard on seeing to it that he is turned out as a gentleman should be."

The little valet puffed out his chest. "Indeed, your ladyship. I have worked at it tirelessly and without complaint."

Val coughed and Lilly shot him a warning glare before she continued. "Go downstairs, have cook get you a nice spot of bracing tea... you can tell her to add a touch of brandy to it on my orders. And perhaps some of her lovely teacakes. Take yourself a nice rest and then you may see about repairing the damage. If they cannot be repaired, then we will have them replaced and see that they are properly disposed of."

The valet sniffed and gave a nod. "Thank you, my lady. You are so very, very kind."

When the man had gone, she wheeled on her husband. "Do not be unkind to him!"

"Unkind to him? The man falls to pieces at the slightest thing! If I scuff a boot, he's in tears, if I tear a shirt, he's worrying about it incessantly. He clenches his fists while I tie my cravat because he thinks the knot lacks appropriate sophistication," Val said, clearly exasperated.

"He takes pride in his work. His job, and any future employment that he might ever obtain should you decide to throw him off, is dependent upon how others see you. You don't know what it's like, Val, to be a servant. To have so little and to know how capriciously it can be taken away," she admonished softly.

⇛⇚

VAL SAID NOTHING for the longest time, just let the softly uttered scold ruminate for a moment or two. "How do you do that?"

"Do what?" she asked, as she moved to the small dressing table that had been arranged for her.

Val watched as she removed the pins from her hair, letting the abundance of dark waves down. The style had not survived the runaway carriage intact, but the tumbled appearance of it had appealed to him. Of course, so did watching her drag the silver-backed brush through the lustrous mass of it.

"Make me stop behaving like a selfish braying ass with a softly spoken word or two," he replied.

She didn't smile, but her lips did turn up ever so slightly as she tried to keep from it. "Is that what you were doing?"

"We both know it was. In truth, I'd never thought about what my appearance means to him... only what it means to me. And in the future, I shall endeavor to do better."

She let out a sigh and placed the brush back on the table. "I'm certainly glad you've seen reason. I don't think I have it in me to be at odds with anyone else today."

"And are you still at odds with my grandmother?" he asked.

"Not entirely," she answered. "We have reached a truce, however."

Val nodded and sat down on the edge of the bed. He made no effort to hide how intently he watched every move she made. In fact, he didn't think he was capable of such artifice in the face of what seemed to be his complete and utter infatuation with her.

"What?" she demanded, eyeing him in the mirror.

"I enjoy watching you," he admitted. Of course, if he were entirely honest, he would admit that he would enjoy touching her much more. "It's been a trying day. No one would question it if you were to spend the remainder of the afternoon in bed."

"I'm not so fragile that every little occurrence must send me seeking my bed to rest and recuperate," she admonished.

"I said no one would question it, Lilly. I never said you'd be resting... or that you'd be alone," he replied.

Her lips parted in surprise and he could see the blush stealing over her cheeks.

"Oh," she said.

Pressing his advantage, Val rose and walked toward her. Pushing her hair aside, he leaned down and pressed a kiss to the delicate skin of her neck. "Unless, of course, you have a better idea for how we ought to spend the afternoon?"

She let out a soft sigh. "I really can't think of one."

"Then come to bed and let me convince you properly."

"There is nothing proper about the manner in which you would do so," she replied.

"I should certainly hope not," he said, as he wound the ties of her morning dress about his fingers and tugged. When they pulled free, the dress sagged from her shoulders, dipping low to reveal the lace edged straps of her chemise and the top of her stays.

Lilly rose then, the gown falling to the floor as she turned to face him. "I don't want to think about anything else... not about your family or about my own."

Val pulled her against him, dropping his head until his lips brushed against hers. "Then I will endeavor to make you forget everything except what passes between us." With that, he swept her into his arms and carried her to the bed.

Chapter Twenty-Six

V AL DRESSED, HIS movements quiet but not furtive. It wasn't so much that he wanted to sneak away while she slept, but that he felt she needed the rest. Regardless of her protestations to the contrary and the fact that he thought her anything but fragile, she'd had more than one shock and far more turmoil than any one person should have to endure in a very short number of days. To that end, as he opened the door and stepped into the corridor, he closed the door as softly as possible and made for the stairs.

As he neared the foot of the stairs, his grandmother appeared in the doorway of the drawing room. "Where are you off to?" she demanded imperiously.

"To see someone who might be able to put an end to this business with Elsworth and Marchebanks."

She nodded. "So we'll be ruined tomorrow."

"We were ruined already, only no one else knew it."

She sighed heavily. "I would have liked to have an opportunity to introduce Lillian to society before it all went to pieces."

"You mean you wanted to set them all on their ears," he scolded. "You're as rebellious as I ever was."

"That, too... but not entirely. I would have liked to see her conquer them all. Wouldn't you?"

"She wouldn't have. And not because she lacks the poise, charm, beauty or intelligence to do so, but because some people are so blinded and so bound by their prejudice, it wouldn't matter who or what she is... only the manner of her birth," he pointed out. "Besides, she doesn't care for that sort. Nor should she. She's worth ten of any one of them."

The old woman eyed him speculatively. "Well, I see you've done it."

"Done what?" he asked.

She cackled. "Why, you've fallen head over heels in love with her, you dolt!"

A denial sprang hot and quick to his lips. But he stopped himself before uttering it aloud. It had been automatic, to deny it, to pretend he was unaffected by her, unchanged by the vows they had made. But he wasn't. So instead, he said to his grandmother, "There are worse fates than to love one's wife," he said.

"So there are," she replied. "Go and see if your worthless cousin can be saved."

"It's not too late to ship him to Jamaica, you know."

"It is," she said. "He transgressed not only against his family, but against his countrymen and his king. For that, he must pay the consequences."

Val nodded, paused briefly to press a kiss to her weathered cheek and then left the house. He made his way toward the waiting carriage at the end of the street. It was unmarked, but Highcliff was inside. He'd sent word to Val earlier, heavily coded, that relayed everything he had learned and arranging their current rendezvous point.

"You're looking shockingly pleased with yourself," Highcliff noted.

"We have the identities of all the parties involved, the Hound has found the name of the ship and will intercede there. All that's left is for the guilty parties to be apprehended," Val stated.

Highcliff laughed. "And no doubt that accounts for your very satisfied expression. You may lie to others, Seaburn, but you cannot lie to me. You are a man growing all too satisfied with his married state."

"A fact I do not deny... but it hardly warrants conversation at this point. Have you got eyes on the warehouse?"

"I do. I've got a bevy of men surrounding it, as we speak. Last word arrived half-past the hour... they're all in place."

"Then what are we waiting for?" Val demanded.

Highcliff sighed. "You're certain? If we take them into custody while Elsworth is present, there's no getting out of it for the lot of you."

"It doesn't matter," Val said. "It has to happen this way. We can't risk Marchebanks, either of them, getting away."

"Then let's get it over with," Highcliff said as he tapped on the roof of the coach and it lurched forward.

***

LILLY REACHED OUT, but her hand encountered nothing but cool sheets. Clearly, he had been up for some time. Opening her eyes, she peered about the room and found it as empty as the bed beside her. Getting up, she moved toward her dressing table and quickly dragged a brush through her hair.

"Resting. Spending the day in bed," she muttered under her breath. "And all the while, he's plotting and planning to do something reckless and dangerous, no doubt."

Fashioning her hair into a braid, she hastily pinned it up and then dressed in one of the cast-off wool dresses that the dowager duchess had previously insisted she wear. Clad in the shapeless and rather hideous garment, she retrieved an equally unflattering pelisse from the wardrobe, along with an ugly bonnet. Suitably armored, she made her way down the hall to her mother's room.

Knocking briefly, she entered even as the welcome was being called out.

The woman on the bed gaped at her. "What in heaven's name are you wearing?"

"Something that will hopefully allow me to blend into the shadows. Are you up for an outing?" Lilly asked.

Immediately, Elizabeth pushed back the covers and rose. "Help me dress... and while you're at it, tell me what sort of madness we're about to get ourselves in to."

"Val has left... and no doubt, he and Lord Highcliff are going to face off against Lord Marchebanks, your aunt, and his cousin."

"Are we stopping them or helping them?" Elizabeth asked.

Lilly considered her answer for a moment. "A bit of both, I think. Elsworth is an idiot. And a bully. And a complete snob. But what he does reflects on everyone in this house... Val, the dowager duchess."

"And your future children," Elizabeth surmised.

Lilly nodded. "He doesn't understand what it's like... to spend your life paying for the sins of those who came before you. If I can spare our children that, I would."

Elizabeth frowned. "You're not—"

"We've been married less than a week!" Lilly said, scandalized.

"And marriage is not necessarily a requirement," Elizabeth said pointedly.

Lilly blushed. "Duly noted. Regardless, he thinks he's being noble by letting Elsworth face the consequences of his actions... and while that isn't necessarily untrue, you and I both know that the consequences will be borne by every member of this family. I cannot let him do this."

Elizabeth nodded as she donned her own pelisse over her hastily-fastened gown. "Let us hope that we are in time to stop him. Luckily, I think I know where they have likely headed."

Leaving the guest chamber, they made their way downstairs and found the dowager duchess waiting for them.

"Where do you think you're going?"

"To stop Val from making a terrible mistake," Lilly said. "Please don't try to stop us."

The old woman eyed her speculatively for a moment, before turning to the butler. "Find the pistol muffs. They can't go out unarmed. I assume you know how to use them?"

"I do," Elizabeth said.

"Have the carriage readied... the older one without the crest," the dowager duchess added. "No need in announcing that reinforcements on their way, after all, is there? In these circumstances, I suppose it rather defeats the purpose to announce the presence of the Somers family. Are you certain this is for the best?"

"As certain as possible," Lilly replied and stepped away to follow the butler into the study to retrieve the guns. It was as she had stepped back into the foyer that she heard the exchange had continued between the dowager duchess and her mother.

"With all due respect, your grace," Elizabeth answered, "you don't know what it's like to live in disgrace. I'd spare all of you that if I could, and my future grandchildren."

The dowager duchess nodded again. "I defer to your judgment on the matter. Be careful. Anything happens to that girl and Val will see all of our heads roll. He loves her, you know?"

Surely she had misheard. Stepping forward, she saw the challenge in the dowager duchess' gaze. To the old woman, she said, "There are some conversations that should be left to my husband and me without your meddling."

The older woman nodded. "Well enough then. Go get him and have that conversation... as soon as it's safe to do so, of course."

"Naturally," Lilly said. With her mother beside her, they headed out toward the carriage that was just being brought around from the mews. "Where are we headed?"

"Whitechapel," Elizabeth said. "Stay close to me and keep your head down. You don't want to draw attention to yourself in a place like that."

Lilly shuddered. No. She certainly did not. "Then let's go save my husband from his too-noble self."

"You belong here," Elizabeth said as they settled into the carriage. "In Mayfair. It seems as if you were born to this world."

"That was Effie," Lilly said. "She drilled etiquette and deportment into us until there was no room left for our hoydenish tendencies... well, for my hoydenish tendencies. Willa never had those. She was always proper. Always well-behaved. I was the problem child."

"I don't think you were," Elizabeth said. "I think perhaps you were the troubled child. And it's my fault."

Lilly considered that. "I was, I suppose. But I don't think you were at fault. I think, despite my earlier behavior, that you did the best you could under the circumstances. If there was any doubt that Marchebanks was deadly... well, Mr. Littleton would have put that to rest."

"Mr. Littleton?"

"The solicitor that was handling the false bequest from the Dowager Duchess of Templeton which was supposed to have come from your aunt," Lilly replied. "They killed him. He was a kind man, or so it seemed."

Elizabeth frowned. "Mr. Littleton had been my father's solicitor before—well, before. I don't even know if he's still alive, my father."

"He is," Lilly answered. "I saw him from a distance in the park. We didn't speak, but he looked at me. Or through me. Once all this is settled, we'll get things sorted out. But you needn't speak to anyone in your family if you don't wish to. They certainly did nothing to earn your forgiveness."

"And I've done nothing to earn yours," Elizabeth replied.

Lilly sighed. "The truth helps. And you've given me that."

Elizabeth nodded. "Let's go get your husband before he destroys himself socially."

Chapter Twenty-Seven

V AL CROUCHED IN the shadows behind a stack of crates and barrels. They had not been in the warehouse on his last visit. Everything had been prepared to load the ship docked at St. Katherine's. On the one hand, they had much less time to avert disaster, on the other, it at least provided cover and allowed them to get close enough to listen to the conversation between the three key players.

"Why can't we just send the shipment on to India as planned?" Elsworth demanded.

"Because we don't have enough of the goods in question," Marchebanks snapped. "And I've already collected payment from both buyers! Don't lose your nerve on me now, Somers... or I'll find someone else to take your place!"

"If you could find someone else, you would have already," Elsworth shot back. "It's become quite clear to me, Marchebanks, that you've burned more bridges than you've built!"

A movement above him caught Val's eye. He glanced up to see a number of men moving into position from the rafters. One of them nearly slipped, catching himself in the nick of time before disappearing once more into the shadows. Still, the noise was distracting enough. As he looked on, a shower of dust drifted from those same rafters to settle on the floor near him. Cursing under his breath, he drew back, hoping no one had spotted him or the telltale signs that the warehouse was playing host to more than treasonous plots and the normal sort of dockside vermin.

From across the way, hidden in his own bower of crates and boxes, he saw Highcliff draw a weapon from the pocket of his coat. A sense of foreboding had settled over Val. It wasn't the first dangerous situation they'd found themselves in, and while he wanted it to be the last, he was hoping more for retirement than for a permanent sort of end.

"What's that?" Marchebanks said. "What have you done, Somers?"

"I've done nothing," Elsworth denied. "It's likely a damned rat. They're the size of small dogs in here."

"It had better not be that blasted cousin of yours. If he's followed you again... well, we wouldn't even have to question it if you'd managed to distract him with widowhood as we'd demanded," the woman beside them snapped.

"You think I don't know what you're about? I figured out who she is... who she is to both of you. And while I was in Mr. Littleton's office, after your minions had already been there," Elsworth snapped at her, "I found the truth of it. She's a bloody heiress!"

"That paltry sum your grandmother settled on her through my goodwill hardly signifies," the woman said.

"Paltry? Is that why you had the man killed?" Elsworth challenged.

"I had him killed," Marchebanks said, "because he knew more about our endeavors than was good for any of us! Now, there's the matter of the money you owe us, Elsworth. If you expect to profit from this endeavor, you're going to need to find some way to earn your keep as you clearly won't be getting the family fortune."

Val relaxed perceptibly. Whether Elsworth knew of his presence or not, his cousin had offered enough distraction to keep either Marchebanks or his vicious lover from investigating the disturbance.

"Well, my prospects have changed," Elsworth said. "And I find that I've developed a distaste for your business practices. You'll simply have to find someone else to buy in. I no longer want any part of it."

"You came here without the money?" the woman demanded.

"There's no money for me to give you," Elsworth told her. "You'll have to pay the captain on your own."

Val cursed again. The fool would get himself killed. Another glance at Highcliff and the other man's grim expression confirmed it. If Elsworth didn't stop talking, they'd put a pistol ball in his brain or a knife in his ribs as sure as the world.

"You forget yourself, Somers," the woman said, her tone deceptively dulcet. "You do not make the decisions here. I do. If you can't pay for your part, as promised, then we've no reason to keep you around. Especially as your loyalty has now come into question."

They were out of time. Val rose from his crouch, pistol drawn, and moved toward the trio. "Stop. He's an idiot, but he's still family. I won't let you shoot him."

The woman laughed. "And how do you mean to stop me? You're one man, with one pistol, Viscount Seaburn. We have you outnumbered."

At that moment, Highcliff rose from his own hiding place, a pistol in each hand. "I think you should count again, Lady Marchebanks."

"What is the meaning of this?" she demanded with a sneer.

"Did you get what you needed?" Elsworth asked. But the question wasn't directed at Val. It was directed to Highcliff.

"I did, Somers. Thank you for all your efforts on our behalf. I thank you, and the Crown thanks you, as well."

Val glanced at Highcliff. But if the man was putting on, he was doing so for everyone present and not just him. Had Elsworth been working for him all along? No, he most assuredly hadn't. But Highcliff was offering them all an out. By claiming Elsworth was one of his agents, undercover, then the lot of them could save face.

Highcliff sauntered toward them, at ease with the weapons he brandished and dressed far more functionally than was typical of him. Wearing black from head to toe, he looked more brigand that dandy.

"Highcliff? What is the meaning of this?" Margaret Hazleton demanded. "I'll not be waylaid by some popinjay!"

Highcliff arched one eyebrow. "It would be the first time in your life, Madam, that you declined to be laid by any man as far as I know."

A few other men drifted forward from the shadows then, runners from the looks of them. Highcliff gestured toward Lord Marchebanks and his aunt-by-marriage. "Take the two of them into custody."

"And that fellow, my lord?" one of the runners asked, gesturing toward Elsworth.

"Mr. Somers fell in with this pair under false pretenses, but once he learned of their schemes, he brought it straight to the attention of the Crown," Highcliff lied. "As his assistance in this matter has been beyond valuable, I will hardly hold him accountable for his naivete."

"Aye, my lord," the runner said and began hauling Marchebanks toward a waiting carriage.

Lady Marchebanks was having none of it, however. Rather than dropping her weapon, she lifted it higher and trained it directly on Elsworth. "You did this!"

"Drop it," Val said. "I don't want to shoot a woman, but I will."

She drew back the hammer, but before she could pull the trigger, another shot rang out. Lady Marchebanks let out a shout as she dropped to the ground, clutching her arm.

Turning in the direction the shot had come from, Val saw Elizabeth Burkhart standing at the open doorway of the building, a still-smoking pistol in her hand. Lilly stood beside her.

"I felt no such compunction to offer her mercy based on something as arbitrary as her sex," Miss Burkhart said.

"You!" Lady Marchebanks said. "You were supposed to have died years ago!"

"I did, for all intents and purposes," Elizabeth stated. "I left my daughter on the doorstep of a man I detested and I faked my own death to get away from you and your nephew—the man who has been your lover since long before your poor, stupid husband ever shuffled off the mortal coil."

Elsworth, weak-kneed after having faced what surely must have seemed certain death, sank to his knees. Highcliff approached him and squatted down. Val, still standing near enough to hear what was being said, listened intently.

"You've been given a second chance, puppy," Highcliff said. "My advice to you would be to lay low until this business is settled. And the moment it's done, you will be on the first ship bound for Jamaica and whatever property your grandmother bestows upon you to run. Whether you succeed or fail then will be entirely upon your own head."

Feeling that Highcliff had it in hand, Val closed the distance between himself and Lilly. "What the devil are you doing here?" he demanded.

"We came to stop you from letting Elsworth sink the family's name," Lilly admitted. "I should have known Highcliff would have it in hand."

"*I* had it in hand," he insisted.

"No," Lilly replied sharply. "You didn't. You were determined to be noble and let him meet his fate! But did you ever stop to think what that would do to us? To any children we might have? Do you really want to have sons that grow up knowing their name, their blood, is shared with a traitor?"

"They're connected to us either way... whether by my blood or yours," Val pointed out reasonably.

"No one knows who I am, Val. No one knows who my mother is or was."

"I'm perfectly content to be Anna Hartnett for the rest of my days," Elizabeth offered. "After all, the whole world thinks Elizabeth Burkhart died more than twenty years ago. There's no point in disabusing them of that notion."

"This is not the place to sort it out," he said. "We need to get you both home and we'll figure it out there."

He turned back to Highcliff who waved him on. Satisfied that the matter was in hand, he headed off with the two women. It was difficult to determine whether he was more proud of his wife or more angry at her in that moment. Regardless, she'd put herself in a terribly dangerous situation and that would not be ignored.

THEY RODE BACK to the house on Jermyn Street in silence. None of them uttered a word. By the time the carriage rolled to a halt, the tension inside it was palpable. As they disembarked and entered the house, Lilly let out a startled gasp as Elizabeth wrapped her in a fierce hug. Against her ear, her mother whispered, "Just let him shout. Men get all riled up over the idea that women need to be protected. None of them realize that we're far more deadly and dastardly than they will ever be."

With those parting words of wisdom, Elizabeth headed up the stairs and left them alone. But Val didn't drag her up the stairs to their chamber. No, he grasped her elbow and propelled her down the hall toward the study. Once inside, he slammed the door and glowered at her.

"Everyone in this house will hear you shouting at me whether you do it down here or in our room," Lilly pointed out logically.

His eyebrows shot upward and a second later, he was dragging his hand through his hair in obvious exasperation as he began to pace the room. "I'm certain they will. But I'm hoping that, in here, I'll be able to at least resist the urge to turn you over my knee and spank your perfectly-formed derriere!"

"Is it?" she asked, settling down into one the arm chairs that flanked the desk.

"Is what?" he snapped.

"Is my derriere perfectly-formed?"

He whirled on her then. "Do not try to distract me with flirtation and with—do you realize just how much danger you walked into tonight?"

"The same amount of danger that you did when you slipped from our bed and scuttled out of this house like a thief in the night," she replied.

"It was afternoon," he reasoned.

"But you did sneak. You skulked. You lied. You tempted me into your bed and when I was sleeping afterward, you slipped out knowing full well that I would have protested you putting yourself in such a situation!"

"I didn't sneak," he said. "I was discrete and chose not to disturb you as I was leaving."

"And that is the definition of sneaking!" She was on her feet again by this point, shouting at him and pointing her finger as if every single lesson in deportment and etiquette from Effie Darrow had been forgotten. She'd transformed into a shrill fishwife.

"It's different!" Val insisted.

"Why? Because you're a man? Men can die, too, can't they? Pistol balls end lives regardless of one's sex!" she all but snarled at him.

"No! Not because I'm a man but because I love you, damn it! I love you and I don't want to see you hurt!"

"And I love you and don't want to see you hurt!" she shouted back at him.

The room fell completely silent then except for the sound of harsh breathing. Both of them stood there, hands on hips, facing off like bare-knuckle boxers at a brawl with the admission of their feelings hanging in the air between them.

Finally, Val met her gaze and some of the heat had fled from his. "Do you?"

"Do I what?" she snapped, not quite willing to let go of the heat yet.

"Do you love me?"

Perhaps it was the uncertainty in his tone, or perhaps it was the overwhelming realization of what they'd just admitted to one another, but she dropped her arms to her sides and offered in a mildly grudging tone, "Maybe. Perhaps just a little." When he grinned in response, she added, "And did you mean it?"

"Mean what?" he parried.

"Did you mean it when you said you loved me?" she demanded, enunciating each word through clenched teeth.

"Maybe. Perhaps just a little."

With her own words thrown back in her face, the heat of the argument fled and she sank once more onto the chair. "I couldn't let you be noble to the point of your own ruin. I never intended to put myself in danger, but if there was a way to get Elsworth out of it without seeing him tried for treason, I had to at least make the attempt."

"To spare our future children shame?" he asked, dropping into the chair next to hers.

"Yes... and you, and your grandmother. Even in the short time that I've been with her, I can see that she has grown weaker. I don't know that she could have borne it really, regardless of what she says," Lilly admitted.

Val steepled his fingers in front of him. "Likely not. But I don't think Elsworth got off as lucky as anyone would imagine. He's not a man cut out for the tropics. Running a sugar plantation in Jamaica will likely be the death of him."

"Or the making," Lilly insisted. "It's hard to know what a person is capable of until they are forced to find out."

"And you, Lilly? What are you capable of?" he asked.

"Whatever I put my mind to," she said.

"Does that include forgiving your mother, my grandmother, and even me?"

She smiled. "It does. I can't say what things will be like for me and my mother going forward. We're strangers, and yet I feel connected to her in a way that I cannot explain. And it feels good to know the truth, to know that she loved me more than she hated herself. I always thought her a coward, and now I have discovered she is anything but."

Val reached for her hand, taking it in his and pulling her from her own chair until she sprawled inelegantly over his lap. His chair creaked rather ominously beneath their combined weight.

"I don't think this chair was designed for two," she pointed out.

"So long as we don't wind up sprawled on the floor, it'll be fine. I want to hold you for a while," he admitted.

"Why? I'm not going anywhere," she said with a grin of her own. "You told me you loved me and now you're stuck with me forever."

"I wouldn't have it any other way," he said, kissing her softly. "And I'm not holding you to keep you from leaving. I'm holding you because I can... because it's a way of showing you how precious you are to me."

Lilly's heart skipped a beat. "You could show me in other ways."

He gave her a look of mock outrage. "In the library, Lady Seaburn? You're positively outrageous!"

"Well, we do have a bedchamber upstairs," she pointed out.

He maneuvered them slightly in the narrow confines of the chair, until her thighs parted over his and they were face to face. "I think I'd rather see how outrageous you can be in a library. It'll be *salacious*."

"It certainly would be and you do know how much I like that word," Lilly said as she read the challenge in his gaze. "I did tell you once that I don't like rules."

"More than once. Now it's time to do more than tell me."

She reached for his cravat, pulling the simple knot free and sliding it from around his neck. "Be careful what you ask for, Viscount Seaburn. You just might get it!"

Epilogue

New Year's Eve

IT WASN'T AN overly large party. It consisted primarily of family, lacking Elsworth, of course. He'd set sail for Jamaica only three weeks earlier. There had been no trial for Lord Marchebanks, nor for his aunt-by-marriage, Margaret Hazleton, Lady Marchebanks. She'd succumbed to a fever that had far more to do with a hefty dose of laudanum than with any sort of illness. As for Lord Marchebanks, he'd suffered a worse fate. Too many men locked in prison were little more than down on their luck soldiers. A titled lord who'd chosen profit over the lives and limbs of his own countrymen had stood little chance locked behind bars with them.

"You're awfully deep in thought."

Val looked over to see that his wife had managed to sneak up on him. "You move like a cat."

"Only to a very distracted mouse," she replied with a laugh. "It's a festive gathering, Valentine. Now is not the time to be thinking such serious things."

"I was just wondering how Elsworth is faring aboard ship. He was never a very good sailor," he explained.

"I know you'll miss him. But I do not think he will miss you... not yet. You've cast a long shadow over him for too many years," Lilly said softly. "When he's had a chance to prove himself, to sink or swim on his own merits, perhaps things can be repaired between the two of you."

"I shouldn't care. He was very unkind to you."

"He was a bully to me," she answered. "Because he felt threatened by my presence and with very good reason. Our marriage was the hallmark of the end of all his expectations of a life of wealth and ease. Why would he not resent me? It would take a better man than most to swallow such a bitter pill."

Val let his gaze travel over her, taking a moment in a room filled with people to appreciate the beauty, spirit, and intelligence of the woman his grandmother had essentially handpicked for him. "If I thought she wouldn't throw it in my face for being a waste of money, I'd buy my grandmother the gaudiest diamond that Garrard's has to offer."

"Well, she would throw it back in your face... and why in heaven's name would you do such a thing?"

He grinned. "To thank her for you. Of course, if I do, neither of us will live it down."

Lilly cocked her head to one side. "Your grandmother may shun such extravagance, but I personally see nothing wrong with showing one's appreciation for someone with jewelry."

Val kissed her cheek. "And the sapphires I gave you for Christmas? Are they not an adequate demonstration of my affection and appreciation?"

Under his gaze, she lifted her hand to the sapphire and diamond necklace that sparkled about her throat. "They are lovely, aren't they?"

"They'll be lovelier when you're wearing them and nothing else."

There was a commotion from the doorway that interrupted his seduction of his wife. The butler entered, clearing his throat loudly, before announcing as if it were a grand ball and not a small family gathering, "Douglas Ashton, Lord Deveril, and Wilhelmina, Lady Deveril." The stiff and always dour man sketched a bow that was worthy of any courtier and then vanished once more, a skill all impeccable servants possessed.

But the rest of them were not so keen to observe formalities. Wilhelmina rushed across the room just as Lilly rushed toward her. The two women embraced and then giggled like school girls as they shared secrets and gossip. Effectively forgotten but hopeful it would only be temporary, Val made for his new brother-in-law.

"Congratulations are in order, I hear," Val offered.

"On my wedding?"

"On the anticipated arrival of your heir," Val answered.

"Oh, that. Hardly seems fair to be congratulated on something that seems to have damned little to do with me, doesn't it?" Devil asked. "Look at them, would you? They've gone from being perfectly sensible women to sounding like those giggling magpies at Almack's."

Val laughed. "I'd hardly express that sentiment to either one of them. They're rather like jackals, especially, I imagine, in defense of one another."

"True enough," Devil said. "I can't have any brandy. Gave it up ages ago, but I'd certainly be up for a game of billiards if you've a mind."

"Excellent," Val said and led the other man toward the billiard room.

The minute the door closed, all hints of the affable rogue faded. "Now, you'll tell me the truth," Devil said. "Is she happy? Because I promised Willa that if she wasn't, I'd run you through. I don't want to, mind you, but rogue or no, I'm a man of my word."

"She is happy," Val answered. "And if she's not, I'll find a way to rectify that. I suppose this is the point where I tell you I was entrusted just this morning with the same task. I was informed that it was my duty to threaten you with grievous injury should you break my sister-in-law's heart."

Devil grinned and selected one of carved cue sticks from the rack in the corner. "All right. We've each performed our familial duty and made appropriate threats to one another. Are we playing for money or will that get us both in trouble?"

"It will get us both in trouble," Val said. "But I like to live dangerously."

"Twenty pounds per game?"

"Seems reasonable enough," Val agreed.

"ARE YOU REALLY happy?" Willa asked.

Lilly rolled her eyes heavenward. "I'd ask you when you became such a mother hen," she admonished, placing one hand on the slightly rounded bump of her half-sister's abdomen. "But I think it's fairly obvious. And yes, for the umpteenth time, I couldn't be happier!"

Willa sighed. "I know. I'm a worrier. I can't help it. But you all married so quickly!"

"As did you!" Lilly responded. "He is very handsome though. I can certainly see why he tempted you to impropriety, my always perfectly-behaved half-sister!"

Willa grimaced. "I'm not so very proper."

"Yes, you are. And it's glorious to me to know that someone in your life means enough to you to sway you from the straight and narrow."

Willa eyed her with curiosity. "And what about your mother? How are the two of you faring?"

Lilly smiled. "Better than I anticipated. I do not think we will ever have a traditional relationship... not as parent and child. But I find myself growing closer to her daily and I cannot help but be grateful that we have found ourselves reunited through this awful mess."

With that explanation, Willa linked her arm through her half-sister's and they strolled about the room. The dowager duchess was perched with her back stiff on the settee, Elizabeth sitting beside her. Effie was in their little clutch, speaking softly to them.

"Everyone we love is under this roof, save for Marina who is tucked into the dormitory at the Darrow School and likely being spoiled shamelessly by the girls there," Lilly reflected.

"So they are," Willa agreed. "And that circle seems to grow daily. Not too bad for two girls who started out entirely alone in the world, is it?"

Lilly laughed. "No, I don't suppose it is. I am thankful every day that Effie found us. And for the longest time, that was all I had to be thankful for. Now every day brings new joys."

"I don't have resolutions for the New Year," Willa said. "There is nothing I would change about my own life. But I do have a New Year's wish."

"And what is that?"

Willa looked around the room and then her gaze landed on Effie. "I wish that everyone we love will find the same kind of happiness that you and I have."

The butler entered the room then, once more using his greatest oratory tone. "Nicholas Montford, Lord Highcliff."

Lilly watched Effie as the man entered the room. She saw the other woman's spine stiffen, saw her chin come up. It was as if tension had filled every part of her body. Then slowly, Effie's head turned, just slightly. She glanced over her shoulder in the direction of the doorway. Lilly saw such longing and such heartbreak in her friend's face that it nearly brought her to tears. To Willa, she responded, "That is the most wonderful wish and I will pray that it comes true."

The End

Author's Note

Dear Readers,

Thank you all so much for the wonderful response that I've had to the first book in the Hellion Club Series, *A Rogue to Remember*. I hope that you've found just as much enjoyment in the story of Lilly and Val as you did in that of Devil and Willa. And I know that some of you all are chomping at the bit for the story of Effie and Highcliff. It's coming. I PROMISE!!! But before Effie can have her happy ending, her charges need happy endings of their own. Effie's story will be the last one in this series, but I promise to give you little glimpses of the burgeoning love story between our fierce headmistress and her obstinate object of affection as the series unfolds. The next book in this series will be *What Happens in Piccadilly* and I will be diving into it full force. Thank you again for reading!

Chasity Bowlin

About the Author

USA Today Best Selling author and Winner of the 2019 Romance Through the Ages Award for Georgian/Regency Romance, Chasity Bowlin is the author of multiple best selling historical romance novels, both independently and with Dragonblade Publishing. She lives in central Kentucky with her husband and their menagerie of animals. She loves writing, loves traveling and enjoys incorporating tidbits of her actual vacations into her books. She is an avid Anglophile, loving all things British, but specifically all things Regency.

Growing up in Tennessee, spending as much time as possible with her doting grandparents, soap operas were a part of her daily existence, followed by back to back episodes of *Scooby Doo*. Her path to becoming a romance novelist was set when, rather than simply have her Barbie dolls cruise around in a pink convertible, they time traveled, hosted lavish dinner parties and one even had an evil twin locked in the attic.

If you'd like to know more, please sign up for Chasity's newsletter at the link below:

www.subscribepage.com/a6k1e7

Printed in Great Britain
by Amazon

28584228R00136